Naomi Wood studied for her undergraduate degree at Cambridge and has a master's and doctorate from the University of East Anglia. Her research for *Mrs. Hemingway* took her from the British Library to the Library of Congress, and to Ernest Hemingway's homes and old haunts in Chicago, Paris, Antibes, Key West, and Havana. She is also the author of *The Godless Boys*, which was published in the UK. She lives in London.

Advance Praise for *Mrs. Hemingway*

A *Harper's Bazaar* (UK) and *Stylist Magazine* (UK) Best Book of 2014

"A fascinating, astutely observed, gorgeously written account of the Hemingway wives and their charismatic, enigmatic, troubled and troublesome husband. A gem of a book."
—Therese Ann Fowler, *New York Times* bestselling author of *Z: A Novel of Zelda Fitzgerald*

"Wood's absorbing, illuminating novel offers fascinating portraits of four extraordinary women and the tortured literary genius who loved them. If you thought you knew all there was to know about Ernest Hemingway's wives, their passions, and their heartbreak, think again."
—Jennifer Chiaverini, *New York Times* bestselling author of *Mrs. Lincoln's Dressmaker* and *Mrs. Lincoln's Rival*

"It takes an unusual skill to keep someone reading a story to which they think they already know the ending. But *Mrs. Hemingway* is so beautifully written, and evocative, that I could not put it down until the last page."
—Jojo Moyes, *New York Times* bestselling author of *Me Before You*

"A wonderful book: carefully written, richly imagined, and emotionally wise. . . . Even the well-known details of Hemingway's life are made fresh, given a new significance. . . . *Mrs. Hemingway* feels truer than most of the biographies, and more real than many novels."
—*The Daily Telegraph* (UK)

"Obsessively readable, fascinating, and heartbreaking, *Mrs. Hemingway* captures a time and people in a style the legend himself would no doubt admire."   —Erika Robuck, bestselling author of *Hemingway's Girl*

NAOMI WOOD

MRS. HEMINGWAY

PENGUIN BOOKS

For Katherine

PENGUIN BOOKS
Published by the Penguin Group
Penguin Group (USA) LLC
375 Hudson Street
New York, New York 10014

USA | Canada | UK | Ireland | Australia
New Zealand | India | South Africa | China

penguin.com
A Penguin Random House Company

First published in Great Britain by Picador, an imprint of Pan Macmillan,
a division of Macmillan Publishers Limited 2014
Published in the United States by Penguin Books 2014

LIBRARY OF CONGRESS CATALOGING-IN-PUBLICATION DATA
Wood, Naomi.
Mrs. Hemingway : a novel / Naomi Wood.
pages cm
ISBN 978-0-14-312461-0 (paperback)
1. Hemingway, Ernest, 1899–1961—Marriage—Fiction. 2. Hemingway, Ernest, 1899–
1961—Relations with women—Fiction. 3. Novelists, American—20th century—
Fiction. 4. Authors' spouses—United States—Fiction. 5. Mowrer, Hadley
Hemingway, 1891–1979—Fiction. 6. Pfeiffer, Pauline—Fiction. 7. Gellhorn,
Martha, 1908–1998—Fiction. 8. Hemingway, Mary Welsh, 1908–1986—Fiction.
9. Historical fiction gsafd I. Title.
PR6123.O5273M88 2014
823'.92—dc23   2014001939

Printed in the United States of America
1   3   5   7   9   10   8   6   4   2

Set in Fairfield LT Std

This is a work of fiction based on real events.

HADLEY

1. ANTIBES, FRANCE. JUNE 1926.

Everything, now, is done *à trois*. Breakfast, then swimming; lunch, then bridge; dinner, then drinks in the evening. There are always three breakfast trays, three wet bathing suits, three sets of cards left folded on the table when the game, abruptly and without explanation, ends. Hadley and Ernest are accompanied wherever they go by a third: this woman slips between them as easily as a blade. This is Fife: this is her husband's lover.

Hadley and Ernest sleep together in the big white room of the villa, and Fife sleeps downstairs, in a room meant for one. The house is quiet and tense until one of their friends arrives with soap and provisions, idling by the fence posts, wondering whether it might be best to leave the three undisturbed.

They lounge around the house—Hadley, Ernest, and Fife—and though they know they are all miserable no one is willing to sound the first retreat; not wife, not husband, not mistress. They have been in the villa like this for weeks, like dancers in relentless motion, trying to exhaust each other into falling.

The morning is already warm and the light has turned the white cotton sheets nearly blue. Ernest is sleeping. His hair is still parted as it was during the day, and there is a warm fleshy smell to his skin that Hadley would tease him about were she in the mood. Around his eyes is a sunburst of wrinkles on the browned skin; Hadley can imagine him squinting out over the top of the boat, looking for the best place to drop anchor and fish.

In Paris, his beauty has become notorious; it is shocking what he can get away with. Even their male friends are bowled over by his looks; they outpace the barmaids in their affection for him. Others see beyond all this to his changeability: meek, at times; bullish at others—he has been known to knock the spectacles off a man's face after a snub in the Bal Musette. Even some of their close friends are nervous of him—including Scott—though they are older and more successful, it doesn't seem to matter. What contrary feelings he stirs in men. With women it's easier— they snap their heads to watch him go and they don't stop looking until he's gone. She only knows of one who isn't charmed by him.

Hadley lies looking up at the ceiling. The beams have been eaten away; she can track the worm's progress through the wood. Lampshades sway as if there is a great weight to them, though all they are is paper and dowelling. Someone else's perfume bottles glint on the dressing table. Light presses at the shutters. It will be hot again today.

Hadley really wants nothing more than to be in cold old Paris, in their apartment with the smells of pigeon roasting on the coal fire and the pissoir off the landing. She wants to be back in the narrow kitchen and the bathroom where damp spores the walls. She wants to have their usual lunch of boiled eggs at a table so small their knees knock together. It was at this table that Hadley had her suspicions of the affair confirmed. *I think Ernest and Fife are very fond of each other*, Fife's sister had said. That's all she had needed to say.

Yes, Hadley would rather be in Paris or even St. Louis right now, these cities which nurse their ash-pit skies and clouds of dead sleet—anywhere but here, in the violet light of glorious Antibes. At night, fruit falls to the grass with a soft *thunk* and in the morning she finds the oranges split and stormed by ants. The smell around the villa is ripening. And already, this early, the insects have begun.

Hadley gets up and goes over to the window. When she presses her forehead against the glass, she can see his mistress's room. Fife's blinds are closed. Their son Bumby sleeps downstairs, too, having fended off the whooping cough—the *coqueluche*—which brought them all to this villa in the first place. Sara Murphy didn't want Bumby near her children for fear the infection would spread. The Fitzgeralds were good to offer their villa for the quarantine—they didn't have to. But when Hadley walks around the rooms, touching their glamorous things, it feels awful to have her marriage end in the rented quarters of another family's house.

Tonight, however, marks the end of their quarantine. The Murphys have invited them over to Villa America and it will be the first time this vacation that the unhappy trio has been in the company of friends. To Hadley, the party feels both exciting and dreadful: something has happened in the villa that nobody else has seen, as if someone has wet the mattress and not owned up to the fast-cooling spot in the middle of the bedclothes.

Hadley climbs back into bed. The sheet is tense around Ernest; she tries to pull it back so that he'll think she hasn't yet left, but he has the cotton bunched in his fist. She kisses the top of his ear and whispers, "You've stolen the bedding."

Ernest doesn't answer but scoops her toward him. In Paris he likes to be up early and in his studio by nine. But in Antibes these embraces happen many times daily, as if Ernest and Hadley are in the first flush of romance again, even while both of them know this summer might be the end of things. Lying next to him she wonders how it is she has lost him, although perhaps that is not quite the right phrase, since she has not lost him, not yet. Rather Fife and Hadley wait and watch as if they are lining up for the last seat on a bus.

"Let's go for a swim."

"It's too early, Hash." Ernest's eyes are still closed though there is a flicker behind the lids. She wonders if he's weighing both of them up now that he is awake. Should it be wife? Or mistress? Mistress, or wife? The brain's whisper begins.

Hadley swings her legs over the side of the bed. Sunlight threatens to storm the room with a pull of the chain. She feels too big for this heat. All the baby weight seems to have thickened her at the hips; it's been so hard to shift. Her hair, too, feels heavy. "I'm sick of this place," she says, pulling her hand around her damp neck. "Don't you long for rain or gray skies? Green grass? Anything."

"Time is it?"

"Eight o'clock."

Ernest paws at her shoulders.

"No."

"Why not?"

"I just can't." Her voice catches on the last word. Hadley goes over to the dressing table and she feels Ernest following her with sorrowful eyes. In the mirror her breasts spike under the nightgown. Bone-colored light fills the room when the blinds snap. He pulls the sheet over his head and looks a tiny thing under the bedclothes. Often she doesn't know what to make of him, whether to class him as a child or a man. He's the most intelligent person she knows and yet sometimes her instinct is to treat him like her son.

The bathroom is cooler. The claw-footed tub is inviting: she'd like to get in and run herself a cold bath. She splashes the back of her neck and washes her face. Her skin is freckled from the sunshine and her hair redder. She dries herself with a towel and remembers last summer in Spain. They had seen the running of the bulls and gone splashing into the pool. Afterward Ernest had towel-dried her: going up from her ankles, between her legs, then over her breasts. Her mother would have hated such a public show. *Touching is reserved for the bedroom*, she would have said, but this, too, added to the excitement, as Ernest had gently dried each inch of his wife.

When they returned to Paris that summer, Fife was waiting for them. Nothing—Hadley was sure, or nearly sure—had happened between them until later that year. Winter. Possibly spring. Jinny had not been forthcoming on timings. If only Ernest had more sense than just to throw it all away. Hadley smiles to herself; she sounds like one of those sighing housewives in magazine stories she would never admit to Ernest she rather likes to read.

In the bedroom she throws him his bathing suit which has stiffened overnight. "Come on, Ernest." An arm emerges for the suit. "Let's go before it gets too hot."

Ernest finally gets up and wordlessly steps into the bathing suit. His ass is the only white thing left of him; it pains her to see how handsome he is. Hadley shoves towels into a beach bag with a book (an e. e. cummings novel which she is trying, but failing, to read) and her sunglasses and watches Ernest as he puts on the clothes he wore yesterday.

He takes an apple from the pantry and holds it in his palm.

Outside the villa, near the lavender in terra-cotta pots, Fife's bathing suit hangs on the line. It sways, awaiting her legs and arms and softly nodding head. The Hemingways tread past her room in their uniform of Riviera stripes, fisherman's caps, and white shorts, putting their shoes quietly on the gravel, trying not to wake her. It feels, to Mr. and Mrs. Hemingway, as if they are the ones who are having the affair.

2. PARIS, FRANCE. 1925–26.

It was a letter that finally gave them away.

From the beginning Hadley and Fife had been fast correspondents. They called each other affectionate nicknames and recounted the minor troubles of being American women in Paris. Fife would write, addressing Hadley as *mon enfant*, and talk about how overworked she was at *Vogue*, or who was a boring flirt, or how drunk she had been—and still was—as she clattered at the typewriter on the baby grand piano in her apartment on the rue Picot. Fife's letters were always gorgeously funny. Hadley sometimes had trouble working out the right way to pen a response. She'd always written just as she spoke.

The production of Fife's letters was always evident. Slugs of gin stained the page, or there was a scratch of mascara near the date, or the bruise of jammed letters where, Fife told her in the postscript, some man had seated himself on the piano keys and made her mistype the Royal typewriter. When Hadley read the letters she imagined her slim lovely friend drinking vermouth in that kimono Fife liked to wear, perfectly huge on the girl's curveless shape.

Fife had been wearing chinchilla when Hadley first met her at a party. The coat had slipped past in a rush of fur, tickling Hadley's nose, as this expensive-looking girl filled her martini glass. "Oops," she said, batting down the fur and giving Hadley a wide grin. "Sorry. It *does* get in the way like that." Fife wore chinchilla; her sister Jinny wore mink.

Evidently they were women of means, though Hadley saw from their hands that both sisters were unmarried. When they were introduced Ernest said something wicked about how he'd like to take one of the sisters out in the other sister's coat. Which animal he preferred left everyone guessing.

After the party Hadley asked her husband what he thought of this woman Pauline, whom everyone called Fife. "Well," he said, "she's no southern belle." And he was right. Black short hair, skinny and small, but it was the woman's eyes that were remarkable. Dark and lovely and quite bold, not a hint of doubt about herself. That's what she liked immediately about Fife: how assured she was, almost like a man.

Fife started to call on the Hemingways that fall after they'd seen each other at the Dôme and the Select. When they bumped into her at the club one evening, they included her in the invitation to finish the party at their apartment. After that night, Fife started coming round regularly, as if she'd picked up a taste for their bohemian poverty. Their apartment, despite its shabbiness, she said was *positively ambrosial*. Hadley wasn't quite sure what this meant, and with how much irony the woman delivered that statement.

It had been fun at first: the three of them sitting up late every night, talking about books and food and the authors whom they liked for their personalities but not for their prose. Fife would always leave early, saying, "You men need some time alone." It seemed a very modern thing to do, this referring to oneself as a boy, or a man, or a chap. Hadley disliked it.

When Fife left, the apartment always felt empty. Hadley didn't feel able to put together little witticisms about their social circle and Ernest seemed deflated. Instead of talking as they normally did, Hadley started to go to bed early. And Ernest stayed up late, working on a manuscript, drinking alone.

Then Fife stopped leaving early. One evening she stayed late ("Oh, only if you chaps don't mind having me") and then the next evening she stayed even later. The apartment rang with the woman's laughter, which had such an instant flourish that Hadley had a hard time making her own heard.

Sometimes, when it was late and they had stayed up talking, Ernest would go down and hail her a cab. She wondered what it was they talked about, Ernest and Fife, as they idled on the street corner, bundled up, their faces close against the cold, the skin of the chinchilla brushing up against his neck.

Suddenly, whenever Hadley walked into a room, Fife would be in it. Often she'd be doing something appallingly helpful: pinning clothes on the wash line, or playing with Bumby, or, to Hadley's fury, one day changing the bed linens without asking, as if their marriage bed were something she were privy to. And when Hadley came down with a cold that November, Fife was there: feeding her broths and making her compresses, keeping her warm and tucked up in bed while she entertained Ernest in the room next door.

When they went skiing that December, Fife followed. They easily accommodated her, as if there were a space in the bed already waiting. Ernest worked in the mornings, and Hadley and Fife would read by the fire or play with Bumby. In the evenings, they played three-handed bridge. Hadley always lost but she'd usually drunk too much sherry to care. When Ernest returned to Paris that January for business, before setting off for New York, she knew Fife saw him alone. Fife wrote, addressing her as *Cherishable*, saying she would stick by Ernest's side even during the dullest of his tasks. Hadley tried to keep her thoughts on skiing and the snow.

She returned to Paris when spring's blossom flowed in dusty rivers down the gutters, and the air was so full of seeds it stung her eyes. Hadley thought things would return to normal. There was, after all, no evidence: no discovered kisses, no perfume on his coat, no love letters. She hadn't even heard of any rumors. It was just a flirtation, and Fife rambled so consistently about her paramours that Hadley told herself she was nothing more than jealous.

Perhaps she should have seen more in her friend's letters. There was that rich woman's sense of entitlement: of deserving a particular object only by virtue of desiring it, whether it was a bicycle or a Schiaparelli dress or another woman's husband. How effortlessly Fife charmed others—and how charmless it made her feel. Hadley started forgetting to reply. *Hadley, mon amour*, Fife wrote that spring, asking why the letters from her quarter had dried up, and dried up quite so precipitously.

Stay away from my husband, Hadley wanted to write or even say; but she did not.

The letter that gave them away was no bigger than a memo.

Ernest had put it in one of his exercise books with the rest of his correspondence. Since the incident with the suitcase, Ernest knew Hadley wouldn't look in this drawer. At first she didn't even recognize it as her friend's hand: Fife always used the typewriter loaned from *Vogue*. But this note was big and scrawled, boldly penned. She knew instantly what it meant without even reading it: because it was addressed only to Ernest. When Fife wrote, she always wrote to Hadley or to Mr. and Mrs. Hemingway; the letters were never for him alone.

> *Cher Ernest,*
> *Didn't you think Seb looked SWELL at the club?*
> *I must admit I find him ENTIRELY agreeable.*
>
> > *Fife*

How he would have loved Fife so nakedly stoking his jealousy. He always wanted to know that he was desired. Was this evidence that they were having an affair? Or was she reading a subtext that was not there?

Ernest called out to her from the living room. "Hash?"

Her hand shook as she replaced Fife's letter back in his notebook and shut the drawer. In the living room Ernest was pooled in the light of the gas lamp, and he had that frown which meant deep concentration. He wore mittens while writing: they couldn't afford any more heating until he was paid for his articles. She sat opposite him on the only other chair they had. She could ask him. Just ask him straight if something was going on between him and Fife.

Instead, outside, evening came to Paris. Ernest worked, gazing up at her occasionally, giving her a smile, lost in his world of words. And she wondered how they had come to be like this: two unhappy parents, with the possibility of a mistress between them.

3. ANTIBES, FRANCE. JUNE 1926.

Even at nine o'clock, the sand scorches and their feet burn if left too long on the shale. They're alone: not an umbrella or a picnic or a string of pearls in sight.

Ernest and Hadley splash out into the water and make for the raft, a hundred yards or so from the shore. "Race you," he says, and when he gets there before she does, he offers her a hand from the deck. But when she reaches up he quickly retracts his arm and she drops down again into the sea. Hadley goes under with a mouthful of seawater. She kicks water up at him; he laughs and dives into the splash. Underwater, he pulls her by her ankle. As she fights against him, they are awash in bubbles. Legs jackknife against each other. Finally she uses his head as leverage, pushing him down so that she can come up for air.

Ernest surfaces, gasping for breath and smiling so much that wrinkles arc down his cheeks. She gives him her salty mouth and feels the prickles of his wet mustache against her lips. They're the same height in the water.

They swim over to the bank where the trees shadow the sea. Ernest pulls himself onto the rocks while Hadley stays kicking in the warm green water. They have perfected this dive over the past week. "Is here all right?"

"Come closer."

Hadley fixes her gaze on the horizon. Antibes is broken

in two like an egg: one half sky, the other sea. She hasn't much liked this game but she goes along with it. Ernest's preparations can be heard in the slap of his feet against the rocks. That he is nervous only makes her more so. "Ready?"

"Yes."

And he says, "Ready," too, to let her know he is about to go.

Ernest dives and she can feel his body whistling past, just over the top of her head and into the spot beside her.

"Well done!" she says, when he emerges from the sea exultant. She loves the way he looks when she praises him. There's something catlike in his pleasure—as if her words were a scratch behind the ears.

"I didn't touch you, did I?"

"No. Half an inch or so away."

"Your turn," he says mischievously.

She smiles. "You always try, don't you?"

He doesn't push her. "Back to the raft?"

She makes her way back before him and swings her legs under the pontoon so that her feet poke the barnacles under the wood. The soft parts she flattens with her toes. The sun is hotter now on her head.

The raft sinks an inch with the weight of them when they stand up on the deck dripping. He pulls her toward him in another of these Antibes embraces.

"Ernest?" He doesn't say anything.

In Paris, they were always more playful, so that Ernest could note the angles of elbows, knees, and necks for his stories. They would get it all exactly right so that he could write it up for his scenes. After a first draft they would set up their bodies again only to end up collapsing and laughing at the impossibility of what he had written: squashed arms, dead legs, a blunt foot breaking imagined lines. Sometimes it seemed to her foolish that he should go to such lengths to put it all down only to cut it all out. But this, he insists, is his method.

Ernest is not writing in Antibes; this in itself is dangerous. His imagination is not well kept when it is not focused; it tends to wander, tends to look for excitement where it should not. She wishes he could be enraptured, now, by a new novel or story, ignore Fife—ignore his wife, for God's sake—if only that writing might prove an antidote against that woman.

Hadley lies down on the raft and puts her head on the soft bit of his thigh, where the hair is worn from the roughness of his pants. On his right calf a scar bursts open like a firework: a mortar wound from the war. Ernest won't talk about the moment itself but only the time afterward: how the doctors kept a bowl next to his hospital bed and filled it with the nuts, bolts, screws, and nails removed from the leg; how he let favorite visitors take home a piece of shrapnel as a lucky charm. His biggest achievement, he said, was not getting over the nurse he'd fallen in love with, but persuading the doctors not to saw his leg off.

Sometimes it still wakes him in the night: the fear that he's about to be buried in mud, bleeding out in an Italian trench. Ernest wakes cold and sweating: frightened out of his mind. She fetches him water and when he drinks his hands shake. She hates that she cannot help him. She hates that these nights of terror sink him for days afterward.

Absentmindedly she has been tracing his scar and he moves her hand away.

"God, I was drunk last night," he says, looking away and squinting at the beach. He winds a lock of her hair around a finger.

"I'm just starting to feel it," she says. Her bathing suit has begun to dry in the heat. She feels dulled from last night's alcohol and tired from the swim.

Ernest traces a line from her brow to her chin and yawns. He is wearing the bathing suit with the double white lines across the chest; Fife may have encouraged him to buy it. Hadley thinks the suit a little flash but it's probably something approved by *Vogue*.

He pulls the straps down and rolls the suit to his waist. "Ernest!" she says, "Someone will see!"

He laughs at her and chucks her on the chin. "No one's here, kitten," he says. "You should do the same." She nudges him in the ribs but not hard; after all, she has heard of women sunning themselves half-nude on the Paris rooftops in the summer. But these are women with poetry careers, women with girlfriends, not thrifty women like her from the Midwest who keep the home accounts.

Rocking on the raft with the sun on her face, Hadley is

full of a sudden fury to have him all to herself. He is her husband; she is his wife. She curls an arm around his neck and lifts herself to his mouth. "I love you," she says force-fully. Yes, she would do anything to save her marriage: even invite her husband's mistress on vacation with them. "You know that?"

"I know it." He says it oddly, as if he is pretending to be a character in one of his stories, rather than her husband, Ernest Hemingway. The hollow reply makes her falter. She wonders then, not if she is losing him, but if he is already lost.

A pain shoots through her skull, perhaps from last night's alcohol. The raft rocks her into troubled sleep.

4. PARIS, FRANCE. APRIL 1926.

Hadley let Fife's sister into the apartment. She watched Jinny pick her way around Bumby's toys, strewn across the floor, taking a while to find somewhere to sit. Jinny looked much less at home here in these *ambrosial* surroundings than her sister. Finally, she chose the seat by the window, a Montparnasse steeple rising behind her shoulder.

Hadley was embarrassed at the gamey waft coming in from the kitchen. Often, Ernest went to the Jardin du Luxembourg and, when the gendarme turned his back, he would choose the fattest pigeon and strangle it in the park, then smuggle the bird out in Bumby's carriage. One time he had brought a bird home and it was still alive. There was a whiff of it now from the stove. She had grown tired of roast pigeon that winter.

There wasn't enough space for a sofa in this room, only for two threadbare chairs: one Ernest's, one Hadley's. There was no third chair.

The cloche hat was thrust so low that very little could be seen of Jinny's eyes save a flickering under the brim's shadow. She had on the mink coat that Ernest had commented on when he'd first met the two sisters at the party. Jinny kept on chewing her lips; she probably knew why she had been invited inside.

Fife, Jinny, and Hadley had just returned from a motoring trip to Chartres. Since the discovery of Fife's secret letter to Ernest last month, Hadley had not said a thing to anyone. Now that Jinny was here alone, she was determined to extract the truth.

"Where's Ernest?" Jinny asked. She leaned and her knees edged forward over the tops of her brogues, with her hands placed neatly on her lap.

"I imagine he's still at the studio. He'll be back in an hour or so."

The light was beginning to go and it made the apartment seem more dismal than usual. The dust from the sawmill below settled on their things like a fine layer of hair. Hadley had long since given up on keeping it from the house. "Sorry it's so cold in here; Ernest must have been scrimping on fuel." Hadley lit the stove and warmed her fingers near the flames. "We've had a lovely time getting to know you and your sister this year," she began, in a script she had rehearsed as they'd made their way from Chartres to Paris in Jinny's tin-can Citroën. "Odd to think there was ever a time when we didn't know each other. But there were years before that, when it was just Ernest and me . . . and then Bumby came along. I can't really imagine life without you two girls."

Jinny looked ready to say something but Hadley continued. "We have become good friends, your sister and I. As have Ernest and Fife."

In the window, slopes of Paris roofs went on as far as the eye could see. Pigeons—dinner—perched on the eaves. Wouldn't she prefer not to know? To go on in ignorance? But it was as if the discovery of that letter had amplified her senses. Hadley had begun to see shared looks at the market and to hear gossip behind bookshelves, people talking of the Hemingways at parties. That was the most hateful thing: feeling like she was the one person in the dark about the state of her own marriage.

Jinny hadn't yet taken off the mink. Hadley poured two cups of tea and placed them on the table. When she sat down, her knees bumped against Jinny's. "Fife was strange in the car when we left Chartres."

"How do you mean?"

"She hardly said anything."

"I suppose not." Jinny didn't take her eyes from the tea.

"She was like that for the whole trip, though. Talking and talking, then silence for hours."

"My sister has always been prone to moods."

"It wasn't moodiness."

It wasn't so much the letter but Fife's behavior at Chartres cathedral that had made Hadley determined to ask. In the church, she had caught Fife praying. Even from far away, she could see how tightly the white ball of her fingers was held above her head. Fife was desperate for something; that much was clear, since the hands didn't slacken once in the minutes she sat there. What could Fife be praying for, what did this woman lack, in any way, but a husband? What would be the words of the prayer but *Please, God, let me have him*. Then Fife's hands unfurled and she looked straight at Hadley. There was little sacred in that look.

The light outside was bright after the dark of the cathedral. Somehow, Fife had beaten them to it as she and Jinny came out from the church. Fife sat smoking by the entrance, with her shapeless man's coat and aggressively euphoric eyes.

"Look, I better go," said Jinny, standing up quickly and knocking over the tea. "Oh God, sorry. Let me get a cloth."

"It's fine."

"Please."

But when Hadley returned Jinny was already dabbing at the floor with her own browning handkerchief. "These moods of Fife's," Hadley ventured, on her hands and knees like a housemaid as she mopped up the spill. "Is Ernest in any way involved?"

Jinny's slender weight rocked back onto her heels. Her mouth gave a joyless smile. "I think they are very fond of each other, yes."

She said it slowly and quietly, as if they were once again in the cathedral.

Hadley stood and squeezed the tea from the handkerchief at the sink. She noticed her wedding ring turn greasily as she wrung the hankie out to dry. "I know this doesn't make any sense," Jinny said, joining her in the kitchen, "but Fife is very fond of you. As am I. What's happened . . ." Jinny looked around the room as if trying to find a way of making this sound less absurd. "It's accidental. She didn't mean for it to happen. I think Ernest has that effect on women. She just . . . she couldn't help herself."

Hadley was waiting with dinner ready and a bottle of muscadet when Ernest came home that evening. Over the meal he was very sweet and inquisitive about the trip and how she had enjoyed the company of the Pfeiffer sisters in Chartres. Bumby played by their feet, looking thrilled to have both *Maman* and *Papa* finally at home again. At the end, after putting Bumby to bed, she told him what she knew.

Ernest looked shamefaced and then angry that she had brought it up. She knew this would be his response; she knew he'd somehow try to pin the blame on her—as if by voicing it she had become the architect of the affair. "What would you have me do?" she asked him. "Hold my tongue?" She took the plates and rinsed them in the kitchen and came back into the room. "Fine," she said, feeling a kick in her temper—and enjoying it. "On the proviso that you will sort out this mess I will not mention it again. But you must promise to sort it out."

Ernest promised. And the silence opened up between them.

5. ANTIBES, FRANCE. JUNE 1926.

The day is reaching its hottest. The raft drifts as far as it can before the chain jerks it back to the beach. At the bank the insects are getting louder, upping their pitch as if they are being slowly squeezed. The trees' shadows pour onto the water like vinegar into oil.

Hadley is sunning herself on the pontoon and Ernest is practicing his diving when they hear a long whistle from the beach. A swimmer is approaching. Though the figure is far away enough to be faceless, Hadley knows it to be Fife. A lacework of waves follows the swimmer and her strong stroke. The Hemingways watch her steady progress.

Fife pulls herself onto the raft and smiles. She waits to catch her breath then says, with a trace of a mock English accent: "Hello, chaps. You both woke early." The woman shakes the water from her short hair. She is clear-eyed and vigorous. "The shopkeeper in Juan said it's unseasonably hot. Unseasonably, he said, *ce n'est pas de saison*. Or does that mean 'out of season'? I don't know. He said these aren't June temperatures."

Hadley was about to leave—her skin is fair and easily burns—but now she must stay as her husband's chaperone. The three of them sit on the raft with their legs dangling into the water. Her husband wears that scowl which Hadley hadn't seen before they came to Antibes. She catches his mistress steal an agonized look at Ernest's chest. He is bronzed and lovely from this dangerous summer.

"I felt a little worse for wear this morning," Fife says, returning her eyes to Hadley. Last night they drank and talked till late, gossiping about their mutual friends with an unkindness they knew was directed at each other. Zelda, Scott, Sara, Gerald; anyone was fair game.

"We all drank too much," Hadley says. "I don't know why I woke so early."

"My wife is on a mission to deprive me of my sleep."

She watches her pale feet in the sea. "Eight o'clock is hardly the break of dawn."

"I was never an early riser," says Fife, fiddling with some ribbons on the shoulders of her bathing suit. "That was always Jinny."

Light buckles on the waves that make a pleasant hollow sound as they hit the underside of the raft. Ernest removes himself and lies down at the back of the deck. Hadley watches him—within minutes she can tell he's about ready to drop off to sleep. How easily her husband takes his exit from this strange world of his own making! Though she has to admit that this jam is her own fault too. After all, she was the one who invited Fife here in the first place.

Ever the *Vogue* correspondent, Fife chatters about a pair of white leather gloves she found in Juan-les-Pins yesterday. "Well, they cost no more than a loaf of bread, so I think I shall have them. I'll telephone the shopkeeper to put them aside for me. I hate to lose anything."

The two women often gaze at Ernest for as long as they can manage, before one risks being caught by the other. It looks like you could lick the salt right off him.

Fife stands and touches her fingertips above her head—Hadley sees the curveless shadow behind her—and dives into the water. There is only a very small splash where the water breaks. "You know, I bet you could dive, Hash," she says as she pulls herself back up onto the deck. Seawater leaks distractingly down her inside leg. "You just have to try."

Fife sits close enough for Hadley to feel the *maillot* against her skin, the wool of it a little rough. Despite the warmth, Fife's skin is goosefleshed. Hadley notices that when she stoops, it's as if she's breastless. How can Ernest love her, this boy-child?

"I don't want to. I'm scared."

"Of what?"

"Of breaking something. My back. My neck."

"You won't. I promise."

The memory of her fall comes back to her. She remembers how the handyman waved up to her from the garden in St. Louis; the noise of the chair hitting the floor as she lost her footing; her hands failing to catch the window's hasp and then the terror of falling through the air and her jaw knocking shut against the brick wall, the taste of blood in her mouth. She had been six years old. Wheeled around for months in a stroller to keep her spine still, she felt as if she had been in a stroller like that all of her life. Her whole life spent in the killing blandness of St. Louis! Then Ernest had arrived, at a party one night in Chicago, unexpected, uninvited, and the world had ripped open with its riches.

"I've just never learned."

"Everyone can dive, silly."

"My back. I've always been worried about it."

"All you have to do is put your arms up, bend from the knees, aim for a spot, and go in head forward." Fife goes into the water at a perfect angle and emerges, wet and adorable. Hadley is thankful Ernest's eyes are closed. "Try it."

The one thing Hadley does not want to do is dive. She can feel how heavy her body is next to Fife's, which is as thin as a strap. She can feel the fall: her jawbone smashing, the taste of rust as her tongue split. Madly she imagines the dive breaking her back, and Ernest and Fife wheeling her around Antibes in a baby carriage.

"Go on, Hash," Ernest says, and the two women turn, thinking he had been asleep. He shades his eyes with a hand so that they cannot see his expression. "Give it a try."

More than not wanting to dive, she doesn't want to be outdone. If she's going to be outperformed at the party tonight, she might as well make a decent attempt at this. The beach shines ahead of her. Fife stands close. Hadley grips the edge of the raft with her toes. All she can think of is each stud popping from her spine like pearls coming loose from one of Sara's necklaces. The raft keeps jerking as the chain gets to the end of its reach. She's scared it'll throw her off before she's ready.

Fife holds Hadley's hands up above her head. "Arms up. Higher, Hash, yes. Now imagine yourself"—Fife's hands follow her words—"your head, your stomach, your hips, and then your legs, following the line of your arms." Her touch is gruesome and delicate and Hadley wonders how Ernest bears to have it on him. If only to flee, she jumps.

Hadley's stomach hits the water first in a perfect belly flop, but at least she hasn't broken anything. She stays a while under the sea, where it's quiet and warm, and where Ernest and Fife cease to exist. Her hair spreads around her as if it were long again, no longer cut in this unflattering flapper style, which Ernest likes and she detests. She stays unmoving for a while under the sea: suspended, outstretched, blank.

When she comes up for air, the salt smarts her eyes so that the features of the couple blur. Hadley blinks and they become clear: they're both smiling and looking down at her, brightly encouraging. The memory of the baby carriage surfaces again, and Ernest and Fife grin mawkishly like two proud parents.

Hadley climbs up onto the raft and stands dripping over Ernest. She kisses him and surprises him with her tongue. He's probably always wanted her to be a bit more reckless. "Not bad," he says.

"The dive?" she says, "or the kiss?"

"Both." He smiles, gazing up at her. In the corner of her vision she sees Fife flinch and look to the beach.

"I'm hungry," she says.

"Have you not had breakfast?" Fife asks, still facing away from them.

"Get something later," Ernest says and his hands trace Hadley's spine as if he, too, were remembering her injury. "I'll go back with you soon."

They don't speak for a while. They sit there, all three, as if waiting for something to happen. In the distance the trees on the bank seem to shrink away like dye in an old photograph. Then Fife stands and dives. Once again it's perfect. As soon as she returns to the raft, her long legs take her back to the sea.

She dives again and again, enjoying her skill, but Hadley knows the performance is misjudged. What Fife can't hear, or doesn't notice, is that Ernest lets out a louder sigh each time the raft rocks. He'll want to sleep off his hangover, she thinks, and will find this cute spectacle maddening.

Wickedly, because she knows he does not want to be left alone with Fife, Hadley says she has a headache and will swim back. Sometimes, she sees Ernest wearing a phony smile, as if he is not quite sure of his mistress, whether or not he likes being alone in her company.

"What about lunch?" Fife says, water dripping off her in a puddle around her painted toes. "Won't we get it in the village?"

"You two go on without me." She smiles at Ernest. "See you at home."

Hadley descends on the ladder and begins her swim toward the beach.

"Will you be at the party tonight?" Fife shouts from the landing.

Hadley turns, treading water, and replies, "Of course! End of quarantine! Hurrah!" She waves and gives them her best smile.

At the road she stares down at the sea: the raft is a spot of brown, unmoving. She squints, trying to make out the two figures on the deck. Perhaps they have gone swimming. Perhaps they have climbed up on the bank to make love and feel the sun's rich heat on each other's skin. Hadley can feel Fife's ache for Ernest as strongly as if it were in her own body.

When she wrote Fife, asking her to come, she was banking on the pressures of Paris transferring to Antibes. She thought this vacation would break their attachment to each other. But it has turned into a boring game of treading water. Their legs keep churning under the surface while their heads nod and smile above it. And she did not take into account how often Fife would be in a bathing suit. Oh no; she did not think of that.

6. ANTIBES, FRANCE. MAY 1926.

Hadley sent off Fife's invitation calmly one day: as if inviting his mistress to vacation with them were a matter of ordering a dress from a catalogue.

All this time alone might have turned anyone's head. Only occasionally was the quarantine broken by visits from the Villa America pack: Scott and Zelda, Gerald and Sara, when they brought eggs and butter and cakes of Provençal soap. Scott sometimes brought flowers, which always made Hadley smile, and they would talk over the fence posts about Bumby's progress.

Sara always stood at the back of the group. She had a fear of germs, and her eyes darted over Hadley as if the *coqueluche* might jump like a flea from her clothes. As soon as Sara had learned of Bumby's whooping cough, it had been no uncertain banishment from Villa America. Hadley's exile only underlined the fact that Mrs. Murphy held her, not in contempt, but with something approximating indifference. Though Sara paid the doctor's bills and had her chauffeur drop by regularly with provisions, Hadley had always thought Sara behaved toward her with a certain chilliness. If Fife had had children, Hadley was sure the treatment to her would have been different. She wouldn't have faced this banishment.

At the end of their visits the group would hand over the basket of supplies and then, like a school of fish come to observe the goings-on on the other side of the pond, they would depart back to Villa America, their silver-flecked skin and fishy scowls flashing in the hot light of midday. Scott was always the merriest, shouting joyous good-byes as he walked down the gravel path, already drunk despite it not yet hitting noon. Hadley would watch them until they were out of sight: imagining the exquisite conversations back in Villa America, where one dressed for dinner and did not always undress in one's own bed.

The gang came to relieve the quarantine every few days or so, but it wasn't like having somebody to talk to. The rest of the time, Hadley was alone. She watched Bumby while he was bedridden and burned eucalyptus for his chest. She watered the roses in the garden and waited for the Villa's next arrival. She tried hard to read the cummings novel but didn't understand it. The replies from Ernest came in slowly. He was busy writing so much in Madrid that she didn't want to disturb him. If it was going well he had to apply himself for as long as he could manage, because who knew when it would go well again? He needed to write, and they needed the money. In the days her thoughts looped around the same thing: the matter of her friend, her husband, his mistress.

Behind the invitation was a muddled reasoning. Hadley had seen, in Paris, how the trio made him feel awkward: flummoxed as to what he should do. Long April days spent in the company of wife and mistress would always make Ernest rush back to her in the evenings, as if he could finally see his wife's merits next to Fife's empty dazzle. Fife was rich and blowzy and urbane, but Ernest wanted a wife, not a showgirl. Hadley had asked him to sort this thing out after Jinny's revelation—but what it had meant was a moratorium on speaking about it, and Hadley was pretty sure things between Fife and her husband only continued.

And so she thought that she could perhaps break the affair by setting them up like this, so that the pressure of three would reduce them again to two. In Antibes, there would be none of his little exciting adventures across the Pont Neuf with Fife alone. Nor could there be the intimate walks down to the Seine with his wife to watch the barges and fishing boats. No, they would be a three again, all the time, and she had banked on Fife's presence here making the spindles of this triangle snap.

With a coldness to her thoughts that morning, a fort-night into the *coqueluche* confinement, Hadley wrote to her husband's lover and invited her to Antibes. *Wouldn't it be fun*, she wrote, *if we vacationed down in Juan this summer; all of us—un, deux, trois?*

And when she put down the pen Hadley had even felt triumphant. She wrote Fife's address on the front, and the envelope's glue was bitter on her tongue. That afternoon she gave the letter to Scott through the grill when he came, on his own this time, to deliver food and telegrams. In return she handed over the note for Fife to her fashionable Paris address. Scott gave her a strange look, over the shaker he carried of martini, as if asking her if this were a good idea.

And so Fife had come with her Riviera stripes and her fisherman's hat and her talk of *chaps* and everything being *ambrosial* or *indecent* and her kid-leather gloves. They had tried not to talk about Ernest, or Paris, or Jinny, or Chartres. Instead they sunbathed and ate well and played with Bumby, and the two women waited, as May turned to June, for Ernest to arrive.

7. ANTIBES, FRANCE. JUNE 1926.

Noon light blankets Antibes. Today is shadeless, and everything, even the walls, even the bathroom tiles, is warm to the touch. Even the grayest of the olive branches sparkle as the sun catches them.

The maid has closed the shutters and the inside of the villa is dark at the peak of day. From up in her bedroom Hadley can hear the insects whir on the roses and in the fruit trees, as if all their cogs were motoring along in constant motion.

She dumps the beach bag on the chair and pulls off her bathing suit. She has burnt out on the raft and feels stupid for having let her jealousies get in the way of her exit. She pulls on a robe, washes the suit, and wonders what it is they are doing now.

Hadley steps out into the day and hangs her suit on the line. When she comes back inside it's as if the villa has been thrown in ink. Only slowly do the forms of things emerge. She calls out to Marie, the maid, but she doesn't answer. Perhaps she and Bumby are in the backyard, or out in Juan celebrating the end of quarantine. The house is still; there is a sense that everything has been here for centuries. She calls for Marie again. Nothing.

Hadley makes her own lunch in the kitchen: a salad of leaves, tomatoes, rolled ham, and olives. The French dresser is very fine, as are the long oak counters with baskets of purple onions and papery garlic. She has always admired expensive things, but, unlike Ernest, she has never coveted them for herself. Their Paris apartment is so bare that she knows all the other expatriate women must laugh at her and yet, until this spring, she didn't much care what they thought of her. They have been very poor, but not without the promise of things getting better. That was all she had needed. In fact, she always thought herself lucky, since it was she among them who could call herself Mrs. Hemingway.

Hadley eats alone at the round table where their books sit on the shelf above. Ernest's first book of short stories, *In Our Time*, sits alongside Scott's new novel, *The Great Gatsby*. She remembers one of Ernest's stories. The images are still so cool and fresh they resurface as vividly as if they were her own memories—how the fish broke the surface of a lake and the sound of them landing was described as gunpowder hitting the water. Hadley could picture everything in that story: the boat out in the bay, the boyfriend and girlfriend trolling for trout, the old sawmill that was now a ruin. But then it came, that moment when the boyfriend tells the girlfriend how it just isn't fun any-more—none of it is fun, he tells her, desperate; none of it's going to work. She wonders how much it was about them. The story is called "The End of Something" after all.

And now Ernest has finished his debut novel, known only to their gang as *The Sun*. The novel in which all of their friends appear: everyone down to the English tourists in Pamplona and the roughnecks who sleep outside their house. Slowly, this year, Hadley has watched her name edited out of the pages—there is no room for her among the sauced sluts and the rich and the fags and the *bons viveurs*. The people in *The Sun* all talk suspiciously like Fife—always ready with a cute answer, always on hand for another glass of champagne. Did no one ever have a hang-over?

Denying her a place in the novel: it is punishment for that day, when she had packed three or four of Ernest's stories and his first novel into a small leather suitcase. She had made sure to pack the carbons on top so that he could correct those too. Ernest went loopy without something creative to work on.

At the Gare de Lyon she left her suitcases in the stateroom and stepped out for some water. Later, when forced to retell the story, she admitted she'd bought a packet of cigarettes but had only smoked one by the time she came back on board. Back in the carriage she unpinned her hair and felt the tension leave her scalp. She imagined the train gaining the platform at Lausanne, Ernest growing in perspectival haste, and then rushing from the carriage to kiss him where he stood. Already in retrospect she savored the thought of their reunion.

Not quite out of the daydream Hadley reached for the case on the luggage rack but her hands touched only air. She figured it must have slid down, but there was nothing at the end either. Hadley stood on the bed opposite so that she was level with the shelf. Only dark space. A light terror seized her. His novel. The stories. Everything Ernest had *ever* written. Surely there had been some mistake with the other passengers; the case must have been put in another room.

In the other carriages round faces looked up at her. No one offered any help. Hadley went into the adjoining staterooms. Each face was a blank coin. *Je ne l'ai pas vue.* She didn't know whether she spoke English or French. Oddly she thought how like peasants everyone looked—not the smart sophisticates of their Paris set—people who wouldn't understand the loss of a novel to someone like Ernest.

Worry knotted her stomach. The train would be leaving in five minutes or less. She spoke in English to the train guard: "My husband's work case has gone missing! It has everything in it. Please help me!"

The train guard asked the porter to check the carriages. A woman who was selling blankets and flasks of cognac came on board to help. The big station clock showed only minutes remained before the train should leave. The guard ran over to the ticket office. By now Hadley was in her carriage alone, stricken with fear, pacing back and forth.

An announcement said the train to Lausanne was about to depart and she heard the final shout, "All aboard!" The woman selling cognac was talking to another seller and pointing at Hadley's carriage. A man pushed a trolley, trailing a sickly smell of beignets. The guard came up to the window and he shook his head. "It has not been found, Madame."

Hadley sat down, winded.

"Do you want to stay?" The train's whistle sounded. "Madame, you have to decide now if you will stay or go. The train—it is about to leave."

His young blue eyes didn't move from hers.

"No. I will go," she said. The final whistle sounded. Novel. Stories. Carbons. Everything. She had made the job complete.

And there Ernest was the next morning: standing just

as she had imagined him in the cold white light, in front of the logs piled up on the platform for winter. As the train drew closer she saw Ernest scanning the carriages. She came off the train and stood still and empty-handed. When he saw her, not walking toward him, his face went pale.

She wished Ernest could have been angry. She wished he might have shouted at her. Instead he had packed his bag and caught the return train to Paris. When he returned to Lausanne without the case, he said he didn't want to talk. It was over. There was nothing to be done. Everything had been lost.

Hadley pinches a dead leaf from the vase. The roses are on the turn; the leaf powders in her hands. She finishes what's left on her plate and rinses the china in the big stone sink.

She climbs the marble stairs. The stonework is exposed in the central stairwell; it's always the coolest place in the house. The fig trees are perfectly in line with the top window: Ernest told her that butterflies get drunk off their milk in high summer and they fly around crazily, liquored up on the fruit. Not so different from the strange family that stays here.

In the bedroom Hadley pulls off her robe so that she can nap with her skin on the sheets. The thought occurs to her that perhaps Ernest's novel will not be a roaring success. Perhaps he will not find the fame and riches he hungers for. But she cannot imagine him as any less famous than Scott.

The lampshades sway above the bed in the breeze. For the first time that day when her eyes close, there is no hot glassed light pressing on her lids. It is dark in here, and quiet. She listens to her own breath as she waits for sleep.

They retire to bed when the day is at its hottest: Ernest calls it the killing time. Days ago they had fallen asleep together listening to Bumby play down in the rose garden. An hour later Hadley woke up, feeling herself observed.

The room was empty, but when she lifted her head she found Fife, not a foot away, her dark eyes observing them. She grinned, just as she had done at Chartres, and Hadley wondered if she were about to crawl into bed with them. *There were three in the bed and the little one said . . .* Seconds or minutes passed and then Fife slipped from the room.

Her feet made no sound as she went but Hadley heard the brocade curtain swing as the woman passed by it, and she tried to record this sound: to remind herself that the vision had not been a dream.

That evening neither woman mentioned anything. They ate pork with sage. Fife fussed: praising her for her culinary skills, which was just another way to insult her. "I haven't an ounce of knowledge about the kitchen," Fife said, with a flashed look toward Ernest, already nicely toasted on his third martini. "You are good at all of this, Hash," she said, gesturing with her palms toward the neatly laid table.

That night they played three-handed bridge and Hadley

lost. But when Mr. and Mrs. Hemingway made love that night, Hadley made sure to scream out as loudly as she could, and the next morning over a breakfast of sherry and toast, Ernest's mistress was quieter than usual.

8. ANTIBES, FRANCE. JUNE 1926.

Ernest wakes her an hour or so later. He's left his suit in a puddle by the bed and where he is damp he is cool. "Ernest, you smell as if you live in a shell."

"I'm a mussel come to see you."

She laughs. "A mussel is the least intelligent living thing in the universe! So that can't be you, Ernest, not with your big brain."

He is kissing her; he moves his hand to her breast.

Light pleats the shade. The sash of a kimono hangs behind the bed, glossy and green, and books pile on the side tables. A large Chinese cabinet is lacquered in dragons. Sometimes she wonders why on earth she'd want to be anywhere but here, in this bedroom, in this afternoon, far from the retinal light of the beach down below. The linen is fresh; Ernest is here.

He starts to nuzzle her neck in the place he knows is excruciating. "Stop it, Ernest. I can't . . . Please!"

"What, Hash? Kitten? What are you saying? Want me to continue, is that it?"

"Please stop!" she says, but she can't speak for how much she is laughing.

Ernest continues kissing her neck.

"Tell me about mussels and I'll stop kissing you like this," he says, "and breathing on you like this," he says, "and licking you like this."

"It's a bivalve!" she shouts. She grabs at his wrists to push him off.

"A bivalve? What does that mean? Double the potency?"

He pins her by the hands to the mattress. "You're killing me!"

"I'm a little mussel clamped to your neck. What does a bivalve mean?"

"It means it doesn't even have consciousness!"

Hadley tries to maneuver a knee to his crotch so that he will know he's in dangerous territory. But he rolls away from her. "And how does it eat?"

"It sucks up things from the water."

He makes a seal with his lips and sucks at a patch of skin. "Like this?"

She's running out of air. "It siphons it up."

"And what do they drink?"

"They don't drink."

"No champagne?"

"No champagne."

"A life without champagne!"

"They don't have enough *brain* to imagine life without champagne."

"No imagination and no champagne. I'd rather not bother without those two." Ernest rolls off her and props himself up on one arm. Funny that she's always disappointed when he does as she asks.

"Then you'd be the first suicidal bivalve the world has ever seen. You'd be studied in every lab in America for your complex character never before known in the mussel world."

"I bet being in the sea all the time would feel swell. You'd feel cool and fresh and think of nothing but water and the next meal and meeting a nice lady mollusk to suck on and that's about the sum of it."

Her breathing calms as they lie together. He looks at her face. "If I put a mirror down your nose you'd look exactly the same as you do now, Hash. Your face is exactly symmetrical. A wonder of science."

"Wide as a Polish plate, that's what my ma said."

"Your mother sounded like a bitch of the highest order."

"She wasn't winning any awards."

"That's why mothers die. So we can go on living," he says, rather cryptically, since his mother is alive and well. "But you are very, very pink," he says, moving her hair off her face.

"So would you be after being *tortured* like that."

"From the sun, I mean."

"I should've left earlier. Were you out for long?"

"Not long," he says.

"I can see your strap marks. You're a lovely color."

"So are you."

"I'm a rotten tomato. I wish I weren't fair. I wish I went tan, Nesto, like you."

"You haven't called me that in a while."

She presses a finger on her arm and watches the print go white then red. The memory comes back to her, looking up at Fife and Ernest, parental and faintly menacing as they stood watching her from the raft. The image is so vivid that in an instant her mood blackens.

Ernest rolls on top again and the breath is pressed from her. He kisses her but she can't shake the image of them at the raft. Fife, thin as a rail, going after her husband. Her husband giving in. Them kissing on the deck, or fucking by the trees, as she ate lunch alone thinking about that suitcase, and how guilty she still feels about it, the whole damn thing. No.

Hadley maneuvers herself out from under him.

"Come on, Hash." He looks not a day older than his twenty-six years.

"No, Nesto. You can't have us both."

It is as if a gunshot has blasted the room. It's the first time since their argument in Paris that this has been mentioned explicitly.

Hadley goes over to the mirror and wraps herself in her dressing gown. She brushes her hair with firm strokes. If only he weren't such a boy sometimes, if only he could see what he is doing. In the reflection, Ernest looks at her with disbelief and faint reproach: as if the charges leveled against him were both profane and wearisome. "You seem to have done nothing about this . . . this situation. I'm sorry to mention it. But I have to."

"Why?"

"Because it's impossible to go on any more like this."

"I didn't invite her here."

"Oh, don't remind me."

Several more yankings of the brush, the bristles alive on her scalp.

"I don't see why you had to bring her here. I would've—"

A door closes downstairs. Fife's voice is singsong and light as it travels up the marble stairs. "Chaps!"

Hadley sets down the brush. She can feel the left lid of her eye start its gentle pulse, then the right lid too. God, she thinks, she needs a vacation.

"Are you in?" His mistress's voice sails up the stairs.

Hadley opens the door and shouts past the curtain. "We're upstairs."

"Game of bridge?"

And without knowing why, Hadley shouts, "Down in five minutes!"

"What are you doing?" Ernest says. He looks incredulous.

"We," Hadley says as she pulls on a dress, "are going to play a game or two of bridge. We'll talk about this later."

Fife is already shuffling cards, her neat little head framed by the rose garden. A cigarette sticks from her lips; Hadley doesn't know how she bears to smoke in the heat. She wears a sailor's chemise with white shorts. This is practically a uniform in Antibes. Her lean legs are lovely and brown. The comb's journey is still visible through her hair.

"Did you have a good swim?" asks Hadley.

"It was fine. So hot though."

She wonders if this woman has just had sex with her husband.

Fife deals, placing the cards in three neat piles.

When Ernest joins them, he is wearing only shorts, and his bare chest and broad shoulders make both women smile. Despite themselves, they share a look. Fife rolls her big eyes, and Hadley shakes her head, as if his vanity is a secret shared between them.

"Hello, ladies. No need to get up."

"Did you maybe think about a shirt, Ernest?" Fife asks.

"Why deny you both the pleasure?" he says. Ernest looks at Hadley, his eyes challenging: as if to say *if you will go ahead and mention it, then so shall I.*

Bumby comes from the house, his fat little legs running over to them, followed by the maid. "*Excusez-moi, Madame 'emingway. Viens, Bumby!*"

Where he has been playing in the garden the boy's knees are dark with soil.

"*Ça va aller.*" Marie returns to the house and Bumby climbs onto his father's knee, clasping his arms around his father's neck. Ernest nuzzles his son and kisses his fat cheeks. When they'd found out she was pregnant, Ernest had been twenty-three; too young, he said, too young for kids. It had thrown him into a dark mood for weeks—where would be the time to write and go to the bicycle races and stay out all night with a baby in the house?

But now he takes a good breath of his child and turns him so that Bumby sits facing the group. Bumby's T-shirt is a little small for him and he sits with his belly out, looking up at the adults, who, unbeknownst to him, are making a general hash of his world. Hadley feels bad for him; even if he can't understand what's going on, he's still witness to it. "Darling boy," she says, ruffling his hair. "How are you feeling?"

His nose is still a little red from the cold that came with the whooping cough. "*Bien*," he says. Hadley rubs his chest.

"You've been in the woods, haven't you?"

Bumby nods and seats his thumb in his mouth.

"I used to do that as a child," Fife says, and both of them look at her, as if they have forgotten Pauline Pfeiffer even sat with them at the table.

"You'll win the game for me while I get something from the house?" Ernest puts Bumby on her lap. Minutes later he returns from the villa with a tray of glasses.

"Gin and tonics," he says, "how could I forget?"

Drinks, now, earlier and earlier. At the stroke of three Ernest is ready to take a spritzer or gin fizz. Hadley throws back the gin and tonic surprisingly quickly. Ernest looks at her with surprise, and, she notices, delight. She sends Bumby back into the house so he won't get in the way of the game. Suddenly she feels full of the desire to win, to knock Fife down absolutely.

9. ANTIBES, FRANCE. JUNE 1926.

Bridge has ended, as it always does these days, with one of them pushing back their chair and striding into the house in barely suppressed dismay. This time it was Hadley: unable to watch, when it was Ernest and Fife's time to partner up, how implicitly they read each other's bids, how easily they banked on her losing out to the stream of cards in the dummy seat. Ernest followed her up to the house trying to mollify her. But fury—hot and sure and so seldom felt—rises in her as she climbs the stairs toward their room.

"You're the one who invited her here!" Ernest snaps.

"And I regret the day that I did!"

"Well she's here now. We can hardly turn her away."

"No we can't, and it seems like you can't stop gadding about with her either!" Hadley slams the bedroom door. "How *long* did you need to stay out on the raft? And how *long* did you play tennis with her yesterday? I am your wife! Not her. Need I remind you of this?"

"I didn't even want her here."

"I invited her because I was lonely. Because none of your friends would even come inside the house! She was the only one who'd had whooping cough."

"Bullcrap. I don't know why you did it, Hash. It makes no sense."

Hadley's head swims because he is right: it didn't make any sense. Why invite his mistress here; here, where they could have started to patch things up? What a foolish stratagem it had proved: to reconstitute the two of them by becoming a three again!

Ernest sits by the pillows, his fingers pressing his eyelids, one knee drawn up to his chest. "*You're* the one who bitched the vacation," he says with his eyes still shut. "Just as I try and stay away from her, you invite her to Antibes!"

"Oh, and aren't you *good*, Ernest? Aren't you *brave*? What a brave man to do that rather than get rid of her altogether!" Hadley wants to throw the hairbrush at his head. "You didn't want her here because you love her. Because it's too damn complicated." He doesn't say anything. "Be a man, for Christ's sake. Maybe this is why I invited her—so you could tell me you've fallen in love with her. Then you can leave me and live with her, and we can all get on with our sorry little lives! *Do you love her?*"

There's a majesty between them now that those awful words have been said. They stare at each other impressively but neither speaks. The hairbrush is still grasped in her hand. Afternoon light feathers the blinds. A shutter bangs mournfully downstairs.

Ernest looks at the ceiling. He says: "My God, I'm miserable, you know that," as if this were an answer to her question.

"Well so am I. But the difference between us is that you enjoy it."

"I hate this," he says, his eyes softly resting on hers. "I hate this."

"Liar. You revel in it. This is nothing more than material for you. You've made your hell and now you intend to live in it, and you're forcing me to live in it too. I want to go home." Her voice becomes gentler. "With you. And Bumby. To Paris. And I want to drink Tavel and eat in our café and walk along the river." She lays the hairbrush on the dressing table. She does not throw things. She would never do that. Not at him, not at her darling Ernest. "The truth is I don't know if you want to do that anymore. At least I don't know if you want to do that anymore with *me*."

"Of course I want that."

"But you want her too."

Hadley sits by the dressing table with the crystal-cut perfume bottles. They give out an ancient scent near their stoppers. Their glass planes flash.

"We're acting monstrously," she says. "This summer is shabby as hell." Hadley would like to put her head down to sleep, so that she might forget how easily she has let this woman steal her husband. She had let them court each other last year with all the appetite of adolescents. Why couldn't she have more backbone? Why hadn't she *done* something earlier?

"I can't continue like this."

"Can't we just stay as we are?" but from the hollowness

of his voice, he knows, and she knows, that he hasn't put his heart into it.

"You have to decide." She hears herself say those words and watches herself in the mirror, like a jilted woman would do in a movie, ginned and tearful. "If you want to be with Fife, then fine. I understand she is very much in love with you. I don't know if you're in love with her, or if you're merely flattered. But by tomorrow I want to know if it's her or me. None of us, and I include her in this matter, can stand much more of this."

Ernest does nothing, then he nods. Hadley comes to sit by him on the bed. She hears his sigh. Roughly he pulls her into his arms. One of those Antibes embraces. His smell and his warmth: they are magnificent. It feels as if her heart is breaking. "No," she says, and she pulls herself out of his grasp and manages to walk away so that he cannot see her tears.

Under the stoop, lavender bobs in the sea breeze. Bees gather around the shoots: they buzz so heavily, and move so little, that they look as if they are barely flying. A big hornet emerges from the terra-cotta pot—she must tell Bumby never to touch one. A headless frieze of the goddess Victory hangs behind the table. Ahead of the sculpture their cards lie folded, still in three separate piles. One hand lies open; the other two are facedown. Hadley checks Fife's hand. An ace. So she wasn't bluffing.

She hangs Ernest's bathing suit on the clothesline. Fife's

is there, black and long and raw. Pinned to the line, all three suits sag obscenely at the crotch, dripping with water onto the French tiles. Upstairs, Hadley hears Fife singing, readying herself for tonight's party at the Villa America.

10. CHICAGO, ILLINOIS. OCTOBER 1920.

Hadley squeezed past a group of men and headed over to the piano. The blue serge dress was rather tight and she warmed when she felt their gazes rest on her backside. But after months of caring for her mother, watching her decline as Bright's disease made holes of her cheeks, she felt she deserved to be the object of attention for a night or so. She was no longer her mother's nurse. Here was liquor and men and tonight Hadley wanted to get very drunk. But still she blushed a little when they looked at her; the hem of her dress barely reached her knees.

She couldn't find the friend she'd come with. The cocktail was a little strong, but she'd have to drink it until someone asked her to dance. Maybe it was distilled from corn; it was rotgut, really, and she wondered where they'd got it. Prohibition seemed to mean nothing to this set.

Hadley tried to be less fascinated by what the dancing couples were doing on the makeshift dance floor between the sofas. She didn't even have the language to name what the steps were and she felt old enough without drawing attention to herself by gawking. Behind the piano a man's voice addressed her but she didn't catch what he'd said.

"I'm sorry?" she said, turning.

"I said could I get you a drink?"

Hadley waved her cocktail glass. "I'm already well furnished, thank you."

"We haven't met."

The man came round to her side of the piano. She offered her hand. "Hadley."

"Your Christian name?"

"Yes. My grandmother's surname."

"I'm Ernest."

"An earnest Ernest?"

He winced. That was a stupid thing for her to have said. "I hate my name."

"You shouldn't. What's the next part?"

"Hemingway."

"Ernest Hemingway. That's a man's name."

The squad of dancers had broken up and a young man in tails was looking for another record. It was nearly midnight but Hadley didn't feel remotely tired, even after the long train ride from St. Louis. The room was so warm that the windows were steamed up and some of the men had loosened their bow ties. Even some of the women were smoking. A slower record started, and a couple began to dance. Something about the way they held each other, tenderly but not intense, suggested they were friends rather than lovers. "That man," Hadley said. "He's not wearing shoes."

"The sockless hop. A Midwest specialty." They watched the couple for moments longer. "You can always trust a man by his shoes," he said.

"He's not wearing any."

"Exactly."

They made it over to the liquor cabinet. At one point she lost her footing and Ernest steadied her at the hips. "Maybe you shouldn't have another one," he said, with a grin. She'd heard that people go up to the roof at these parties. She wondered if Ernest Hemingway would invite her up there: he looked strong as a butcher. She wondered why a man like this would be talking to a woman like her. "How old are you?" she asked.

"That's bold."

"I think you're younger than me, that's all. I was trying to guess by how much."

"I'm twenty-one."

"Oh," she said. "You seem older."

"Everyone says that."

"But *twenty-one*? Twenty-five would have been disappointing. Twenty-one is an outrage. You must be barely out of college."

Ernest shrugged and poured her a gin with lemon on the rim of the glass. He sunk a green olive in there too.

"Is there not a mixer?"

"Gin tastes better straight."

"Are you a Princeton man?"

"No. I served in Italy."

"Did you see much action?"

"My leg was shot up before I could see much."

"That's terrible."

"Not so bad. I fell in love with a nurse in Milan. She was called Agnes. That was worse."

Hadley laughed and tried not to seem too interested. His beauty only seemed to underline how frozen she had felt these past few years. But tonight she felt reckless and bold. She wanted to be drunk nearly all of the time if this was how it felt. "And is your heart still in Milan, Mr. Hemingway?"

"Not anymore, thank God. Please," he said, "call me Ernest."

"What do you do now?"

"I'm a writer." His eyes momentarily followed a pretty girl down the length of the corridor before they came to rest once more on her. "Or trying to be."

"What kind of thing do you write?"

"Short stories, sketches. Mostly articles. I'm a journalist by day."

"Do you enjoy it? Earning your keep that way?"

"It just keeps me from writing what I really want to write."

"And what's that?"

"A novel. Something strong. With the fat boiled off."

She laughed. "I'd like to read something you've written."

"Do you write? Is that why?"

"Not at all." Hadley had never said this before, but she decided that this stranger would make the perfect first audience. "But for a long time I wanted to be a concert pianist. I tried very hard at it. Every day I practiced. Sometimes I'd have to lie down on the carpet for fifteen minutes of every hour because I was so tired from practice. There's a cost you have to pay, to write, to sing, to play. I don't think I was strong enough to pay that price."

Ernest smiled at her. "No one ever tells you that: that there's no method. Writing's a lawless place." Someone shouted her name but Hadley didn't want to move away from him. "Someone's calling for you." He stood close to her. That he might be interested in her was almost impossible, but it seemed as if he was.

"My mother died two months ago." She had no idea why she had to say this.

"Oh"—and his smile disappeared—"I'm sorry."

"No, I'm sorry. It's just . . . I've nursed her these past months. And I haven't been out much, on account of that." Tears felt close but she wouldn't allow them. "I feel a little out of the scene. I feel like you might have to wipe the dust off me."

"I'd wipe the dust off you."

Hadley smiled into her gin, pleased to her toes.

"Were you close?"

"No. She was obsessed with politics and suffrage. She didn't have much time for me."

"You're not a modern woman then?"

"I am modern, but maybe in a traditional way. Does that make any sense?" Ernest nodded. Hadley cleared her throat and finished the gin. "Our talk has ended up rather grim. That's my fault. What I meant was it's nice to be with friends. It was a relief when mother died. I know that sounds awful. But the house—being inside it every day—it was killing me."

"Hadley!" The record had stopped. Her friend beckoned her over. "Come and play!"

"Oh, no."

"Go on, Hash. Can I call you that?" Ernest took her by the elbow back to the piano. "The whole party's demanding it!" Ernest placed her gin on the piano top with all the other half-empty glasses smudged with lipstick. He bent down to her ear. "My mother's a musician. She'd like to meet you." He smiled. "Just play what comes to mind."

"I only know classical," she said, feeling rather stunned. She hastened to pull down her dress when she sat at the stool. Hadley tried to think of a song that wouldn't sink the mood. Eventually, she settled on Bach, a sonata. It seemed to make people rueful, but in a romantic rather than melancholic way.

As she played she thought how all of the happiest times in her life had been with music. Often, in the afternoons, when her mother would take a nap and her yellow mouth would fall open in laboring breath, Hadley would take a walk around St. Louis, keeping her eyes to the sidewalk, listening to women her own age talking about men, house-work, a new pair of gloves. When she got home she would stuff a towel into her mouth to prevent her mother hearing the lonely sobs from the bathroom. Then, in the after-noons, she played the piano, and momentarily, all that sadness lifted.

Maybe she had played the nurse with more morbid gusto than she knew. It wasn't just her mother keeping her inside that stopped her—she could have slipped away in the evening. Something else in her had given up—years ago really. She'd given up on friends and dancing. The only men she had talked to all this time were her brother-in-law and the grocer at the end of the street, who would look at her over the pale rounds of the oranges with pity. She thought about what that word meant. *Spinster*. And whether, at twenty-eight, she might be called that now.

Hadley neared the end of the sonata. Ernest hadn't become transfixed with her hands at the keys or become mesmerized by her playing, nothing like that. Instead, he looked surprised when she laid down the lid.

"Put on another record, someone," she said. "It's too sad for a party." But then the room burst into applause, and Hadley felt pleased. She had done well.

When the party ended Ernest walked her out onto the sidewalk. Rain made the roads slick and the yellow leaves had been stamped into the sidewalk by the tread of boots. Ernest stood shyly with his hands in his pockets.

"That's a fine cape you have on," she said, tugging his collar.

Ernest looked rather bashful. "Women say that."

"It's a hit, is it? You look . . ." she laughed, thinking of the word: "ducal."

"Can I walk you home?"

"You could, but you've already done it. I'm staying here tonight."

He slipped an arm around her and kissed her. It was more chaste than she had imagined, just the press of his lips on hers. "How long are you in Chicago?"

"Three weeks."

"We have three weeks then."

They made promises to see each other again after she returned home. She wrote him a letter, telling him how finding him felt like liberation; like jailbreak. She decided she was going to get out of the Midwest. She was going to break free—of St. Louis, and her mother's ghost—with or without Ernest Hemingway.

11. ANTIBES, FRANCE. JUNE 1926.

Mercifully the evening has lost the day's heat. The last of the day's light comes from the sun dipping behind the trees and ends on the terra-cotta tiles in the shape of the villa's windows. "I remember this," Ernest says as he sees her in the dress she wore to the Chicago party. The fabric pulls over the width of her hips but it still fits. "I forgot how lovely it is."

Conscious of the ultimatum she has set down, they are being nice to each other. "I'd never shown my knees before. And my hair was long, remember?"

He fixes his cuffs at the window. "I remember."

"I hated it when it was cut in New York. I felt too much like a boy. But you liked it. And I knew how much your father would have hated it, which helped." She goes over to the dressing table. "He despised bobbed hair."

Hadley pulls her hair back now, brushing it with three firm strokes on either side. "Your mother never said anything about it. She was always more tactful than we thought," Hadley says. "She chooses her battles, like you."

Ernest looks at her quizzically, but doesn't comment.

The earrings clip her lobes and she loosens them so they don't squeeze. Lightly, she applies a blush and eyeliner as a friend in Paris has taught her to do. In the mirror she looks fine but still can't escape the image she has of herself as a handsome peasant who should feel grateful for rolling around with the aristocrats of the village for a precious few years. There is still much good to him, but it's this summer; it's made everyone so bad. She can feel it in herself and in Fife: how quickly they are moved by petulance or glee. Mascara spikes her lashes. It might be the first time she has worn makeup this vacation.

Hadley inspects her reflection. She wishes the bones of her chest might protrude a little, or that her cheekbones would rise from her face. She imagines that, after a divorce, she might stop eating and her friends in Paris might shake their heads and talk among themselves, saying she is *worryingly thin*. How delighted she'd be, to be worried about like that.

"What do you mean I choose my battles?" Ernest asks from the bathroom.

"Why did you never yell when I lost the suitcase?"

He comes back into the room. "This is what you want to talk about? Now?"

"Yes."

He gives a sigh. "I thought the worst had happened. I thought maybe you'd fallen in love with somebody else, or that you didn't love me anymore, or that I was losing you. Then you were crying and wouldn't tell me what was wrong." He stops at the window where she stood that morning, looking down at Fife's bedroom, thinking today was going to be like all of the others spent here.

"So you were relieved. All I'd lost was your first novel."

"Incomparable with losing a wife."

"I'm sorry"—Hadley can't talk about it without the tears threatening to spill—"about losing it."

"It's over now, Hash. It doesn't matter."

"It just seems like it's been over since that moment."

"There were good times after that. Very good times."

He smiles at her and she smiles back: good old friends as always.

As she opens the box for her amber necklace she sees the bull's ear, cured and no longer bloody. It was given to her last year by a matador who admired her red hair from the ring. The ear is as hard now as the leather of a shoe. She pulls a finger down the hairy ridge of the ear—it was meant to be a lucky charm, and for a while it had worked. It had fended off other women before Fife had come along. Hadley fixes the necklace, closes the box and feels the hasp click.

"I heard from the publisher," Ernest says, sitting down on the wicker chair and draining the last of his gin and tonic.

"About *The Sun*?"

"They say I'm nearly there."

"That's wonderful." But he doesn't seem pleased. "What's wrong?"

"I'm nervous."

"Why?"

"It has to be a success," he says.

"So what?"

"So I can afford more than one good suit and one pair of dress shoes."

"Of course it will be a success. I know no one else more likely to succeed than you. And besides, we've got enough to eat, enough to pay the rent, and our beautiful son who is well, now, and healthy."

"And we've got rich enough friends to bail us out when necessary."

She puts a last fix to her hair and goes over to him. "Don't say that." She kneels down so that she is at eye level with him. "It's the night-time blues. That's all. One day you'll be as rich as Sara and Gerald and only then will you realize you don't need it."

He takes her hand and kisses her palm. "You're too good for me."

Ernest has forgotten to correct her when she said "you" rather than "we." And her heart sinks again, even though he is kissing her now, just like he did on the cold Chicago sidewalk. Suddenly, she knows his decision before he does. Fife will win. It seems inexorable. It freezes her to the spot.

"Are we going alone?"

"Yes," he says very quietly, almost near the door, so that she can barely hear him over the evening hush. "We'll meet Fife there."

"Papa!"

Bumby's footsteps rush up the central stairway. They see, first, a small hand move the brocade, then his sandals, still dark knees, and his lovely brown face show up at the doorway. His eyes are sleepy but curious: he is not allowed in their bedroom. "Papa, I got this for you." He hands his father a red rose from the garden.

Ernest lifts him up and moves his face along his child's face. Bumby shies away from the bristles of his mustache. "*Merci, mon amour.* Now shall I give it to *Maman*?"

"*Oui*," he says, very decisively, but then his eyes narrow with suspicion. "Where are you going?"

"To a party."

"Can I come?"

"I think you're too tired for that tonight."

Hadley watches her husband and son: aghast that this could be it.

Ernest plants him on the floor. "You tell Marie you can have a *chocolat chaud* after your bath." He pulls a finger over one of his son's knees and sees the white trail left. "You're so mucky! Now look at your mother. Look how pretty she is!"

"Very pretty," Bumby agrees.

"Kiss her good night."

Hadley bends over to feel her son's lips on her cheek. "Good night, darling." Bumby gives her the red rose and she puts it in the perfume bottle by the mirror. She takes her shawl and wraps it around her.

"Ready?" Ernest asks, by the door, looking at her.

"Yes." And she follows him out into the night.

12. ANTIBES, FRANCE. JUNE 1926.

They arrive at the party later than they would have liked; Scott is already very drunk, as is Zelda. They greet everyone to reassuring murmurings: they are so pleased Bumby is through the *coqueluche*, what a strong boy he is, et cetera. Their friends say how much they have missed them, but they look tanned and golden, and Hadley suspects this might not be quite the truth. Dinner has already been eaten: claws and shells are the leftovers of a bouillabaisse. Sara and Gerald's kids are evidently still closeted away, just in case the infection has been carried on the Hemingways' coattails.

Fife is nowhere to be seen.

"We had to eat with the kids before they went to bed," Sara says. "You have already eaten, haven't you?"

Ernest says yes, even though they haven't. Hadley gives her husband a look, which is meant to say: *I'm starving, even if you aren't.* This performance shouldn't be done on an empty stomach.

Sara wears so many pearls she looks positively bandaged. Most people—and most of the people here—prefer Sara to her husband, but Hadley has always preferred Gerald. Ernest thinks him a poseur, but it's precisely this that appeals to her. Both she and Gerald seem miscast for their roles, while the others are pitch-perfect, delivering their lines pat. He is a mortal, like her, among the gods.

It had been Gerald who had laughed warmly when Hadley, at a café session in Paris, had gaily declared Ernest to be the first American killed in Italy. "Amazing news that the man himself lives and breathes next to you, eh, Hash?" She realized her mistake and blushed. "Wounded," she'd said quietly. "I meant wounded." She caught Sara giving

Fife one of those looks. But she was thankful it was Gerald who had been on hand to deliver the gentler riposte.

Everybody is sitting around the table under the linden tree looking relaxed and handsome as spring. "It's *so good* to see you two," Sara says. "Have you been awfully pent up?"

"It's good to be out," Hadley says in her best attempt at neutrality.

"And Bumby's completely out of it?"

"It's all out of him, thank God. He was just too tired to come." Hadley wonders why Ernest had to lie about dinner. Her eyes travel the empty bowls; there's a bread roll left at Scott's place.

"Well that's just wonderful. I can't *wait* to be all together again." Sara squeezes her hand and looks at Hadley, mother to mother. She has an intense stare made more so by her bangs that come just short of the brows. She is a handsome woman, though not like Zelda or Fife. She isn't skinny; could not slip, eel-like, into tiny dresses or bathing suits.

"Fantastic news, eh, Hash?" Gerald emerges from the house with a tray of drinks. Framed by the black satin sofas, white walls, and the vast vases of Sara's peonies, he could be emerging from a Hollywood set. He could play a leading man, were it not for the creep of baldness. "Cocktails!" he announces, and, as if on cue, he nearly trips on the step down from the house.

"Do be careful!" Sara says but giggles. She is never mean to her husband.

The wind carries the smell of the citrus orchard from the bottom of the garden. Heliotrope and mimosa flower by the gravel paths. Gerald puts down the tray of drinks and cookies with a flourish. Ernest looks embarrassed and barricades himself between Hadley and Sara. Gerald kisses Hadley near the lips and Scott goes for another glass.

"What number is that?" Sara asks.

"I haven't drunk a thing all night."

"Minus the aperitif before dinner."

"And the bottle of wine during it," Gerald says as he passes drinks around the table.

"So tell me, dearest Hadern," Scott says, with the moniker only he uses for her. "What have you been occupying yourself with?"

The table turns to look at her. "Oh, you know. Reading. Writing endless telegrams to my absent husband. Looking after Bumby, mostly."

"She is a doting mother," Ernest says, looking at her proudly, but then his eyes flit upward toward the house as if he has been, in a moment, transfixed.

Fife walks from the house smoking a cigarette. A vest plunges from her shoulders. Her skirt is made of black feathers, layer upon layer from the waist, and it resembles the closed wings of a swan. Their spines click against each other as she moves, her feet making no sound, as if she really did advance like a bird of prey under the lounge's electric lamps. When Hadley turns back she notices her husband is entranced, as if only he has had the where-withal to spot this goose no one else has thought to shoot.

"Darling dress, isn't it?" Sara asks, with a plump wink for Hadley who feels dumbfounded, ambushed. What can an old serge frock do next to this bird's plumage? Scott offers her a cigarette as if in consolation. She tries to recompose her features. It's just a dress. Only a dress. And Ernest has always hated women who care too much for their appearance.

Fife sits down with a broad smile. "Hello, chaps," she says. Her marcelled hair looks immovable. She must have spent all afternoon getting ready after the abandoned game of bridge. "Have I missed anything?"

Tears feel like they will breach Hadley's eyes with nothing more than a blink. How can no one else see how schlocky and cheap is this show of feathers and skin?

Hadley tries to join in on the conversation at the table: Sara still seems to be berating Scott but now it's for his profligacy rather than his drinking. "Surely you're rich by now, darling?"

"Not as rich as you. I don't think any of us can get to that dizzying height."

"I heard your last book's advance was so big you've had to drink vats of champagne just to get rid of it." Sara plays with the length of her pearls and puts them for a moment in her mouth. "Dearest, I'm only teasing you. Besides, it's old Hemingstein who's going to have to worry about this soon." Sara drapes her arms around Ernest's neck and kisses him on the cheek. Storm clouds gather on Scott's face. He'd rather be teased than ignored.

"Do you think so, Sara?" asks Ernest like an ingénue.

"You'll have girls walking around Paris talking like Brett Ashley in no time."

"What are you talking about?"

"Talking? Isn't talking simply *bilge*? Doesn't Brett say that? Did you steal that from me?"

"Certainly not."

"*The Sun* is going to make you a star, Ernest."

"Of course it is," Hadley says, looking over at her husband. "It's the best thing he's ever done. And he's worked so hard at it."

No one speaks. Ah yes, she has forgotten that success should come effortlessly or not at all. It's always got to be playtime. Cocktail hour. As if life were always a mooning adolescence or always blindingly fun. Hard work was for other people. "I mean that it will be the great success we've been waiting for." There, Hadley thinks, half-saved.

Fife's feathers lift and fall in the breeze.

"Wonderful title," Sara says.

"The Bible gives and gives, as my mother would say."

"And what *does* the Bible give, may I ask, aside from the obvious?" A man has come up the gravel path from the direction of the sea. He comes with a basket of fruit and a bottle of perspiring wine, like a figure from a Greek myth. "Spiritual nourishment, the standard homilies, rolling papers for cigarettes?"

The man looks to be in his late twenties, with short brown hair and a neat little mustache that does its bit to hide a large mouth. A generous mouth, Hadley thinks, though perhaps too full for a man. "Harry, my dear!" Sara says, rising. "We thought you were staying in Juan tonight?"

"Oh no. It's positively malarial there this evening. I haven't ambushed the party, have I?" Harry is handsome, though his eyes make Hadley think of the empty stare of geckos when they sun themselves at the top of the day.

"But darling, we've eaten everything! There's nothing left. The kids were ravenous from being in the sea all day." Hadley notices, as the man comes over to the table, that each step has a neat girlish bounce. She can see Ernest grimace—he has never been one for queers.

Harry places the basket on the table and Hadley eyes her supper in a couple of apples. She notices his finger-nails are very neat. He kisses Scott and Zelda but shakes Gerald's hand. "You have met the Hemingways, haven't you, dear?"

"No," he says, "I haven't yet had the pleasure."

"Harry Cuzzemano, this is Ernest and Hadley Heming-way. Ernest and Hadley, this is Harry Cuzzemano, book collector extraordinaire."

"Pleased to meet you, Harry," says Ernest, holding his hand in his own as he asks, "What type of thing do you collect?"

This is when those eyes come to life. "Oh, anything I can get my hands on. Rare books. First editions. Manuscripts.

Anything with a definable . . ."—he seems to search for the precise word—"value. I'm a sucker for anything that will make a killing in a few years or so."

He flashes a grin at Hadley, as if this comment is meant just for her.

"Does it have to have merit?"

He laughs. "Just value, sir, just value. But I must say, Mr. Hemingway, I read *In Our Time*. I managed to get my hands on the Three Mountains edition. If you carry on writing like that you'll have given me quite the little nest egg. I think it was a print run of a couple of hundred or so?"

Ernest's color is high with the flattery. "I'm only in possession of one myself."

"Well, keep on to it, man. You know how expensive school can be nowadays." Hadley wonders how he knew Ernest was a father. "I can only hope your next book will have a similar print run."

"I don't wish for the same thing, you'll be unsurprised to hear."

"Any other publications?"

"The *Little Review* did something a while back."

"That should get your name out."

"I shouldn't think so. It's only read by intellectuals and dykes."

"Dear man, it's the most stolen journal in the country! America, that is."

"Suits me fine," Ernest answers. "I'd rather be read by crooks than critics."

"Very right. Very right." Cuzzemano seats himself between Ernest and Sara and pours himself a glass of white wine.

"You don't mind, Mr. Cuzzemano, if I steal a piece of fruit?"

"Not at all. Please."

Hadley eats the apple and tries to listen to Zelda's conversation with Sara but she finds herself returning to watch this man. Harry's eyes are always on her when she looks at him.

As the night moves on, dancing starts on the terrace. At one point the Murphys' kids, Patrick, Baoth and Honoria come down, rubbing their tired eyes, asking what's going on, but with an eye on the plaguish Hemingways Sara shoos them quickly away. Ernest and Scott are too busy singing along in chorus to "Tea for Two" for anyone to notice the kids' dispatch.

All evening Cuzzemano toadies up to her husband. Ernest answers his questions cordially enough. It is good to see Ernest behave well to someone he doesn't like. Sometimes he can say such astonishingly vile things she wonders if it's really him. She knows he grapples with dark thoughts and low moods but that doesn't give him an excuse to treat people badly. Most often it's the night-time when it's worst: when he enters a world where he can't find anything left that's meaningful. And then, in the daytime, Ernest is fine, and cheerful, and immensely interested in words and art and how to make a new kind of text from the bones of language. The two personalities seem as if from two different men.

Though he evidently has no good feelings toward the collector, Ernest signs a piece of paper which Cuzzemano puts in an envelope and seals with a swipe of his tongue. On the envelope he writes E. HEMINGWAY, JUNE 1926.

Later Cuzzemano scrapes a chair closer to Hadley. She prepares to be flattered. "Mrs. Hemingway?"

"Hadley. Please."

"What a handsome name. There's a South Hadley where I'm from."

"And where's that?"

"Massachusetts."

"Where do you live now? I assume it's not Massachusetts anymore."

"Oh no. I split my time between Paris and New York. They're the only places to really live. London is such a bore. Too many English to make it a city worth spending any time in."

Hadley wonders if he is queer, or married, or a bachelor. Paris is full of all three, often doing all three at the same time. Cuzzemano gives her an inquiring look, as if asking if the pleasantries have now been safely dispatched. He has teeth that wouldn't look amiss in the gums of a fish. "Can I be frank, Mrs. Hemingway? Hadley?"

Cuzzemano drops his voice.

"Sara told me about a valise, Mrs. Hemingway, a suitcase full of papers gone amiss: Mr. Hemingway's first novel, and several short stories. Make no mistake, I inquire about this not to upset you, but because your husband's work is of lasting literary merit . . . And whatever was in that valise will one day be worth a whole heap of money." Cuzzemano's eyes wince, as if pained to think of its value. "Now, my understanding is that it was lost at the Gare de Lyon? Four years ago, on a train bound for Lausanne?"

Hadley is nothing but bewildered. "I don't care to talk about it."

Cuzzemano draws toward her. His hands practically rest on her knees. "Mrs. Hemingway, did anyone have any idea of what was in there? Ernest, surely, would be so happy to see his work returned to him—"

"Mr. Cuzzemano, I thank you for your interest in my husband's work, but I think you are grossly exaggerating his place in the world four years ago." She keeps her voice to a fierce whisper. "Mr. Hemingway had not even been published. We'd barely been in Paris a year! The case was lost. Someone took it by mistake. It's all gone: stories, carbons, novel; the whole kit and caboodle. And I won't forget the horror of it." She recomposes herself. "Nor will I ever forgive myself. Now if you would kindly let the matter drop. I don't care to spend my evening furthering your enrichment."

Gerald leaves the jazz and puts on a waltz. Ernest asks her to dance but Hadley wants to listen to the piano. It has taken her some minutes to recover from Cuzzemano's questioning, and now all she wants is to be quiet among this gang who will not quit talking. Brett Ashley is right; all their talk *is* bilge.

Ernest asks Zelda instead. This is a safe choice. No one is under any illusion of the mutual contempt they hold for each other and they dance together in a difficult embrace. Zelda is stiff and unbending, and Ernest moves all of the wrong parts of himself to the wrong parts of the music. He is pigeon-toed and jokey, but Zelda doesn't find it very funny at all. Evidently she doesn't like to be caught in something so dumb and sentimental as a waltz.

The music finishes and Zelda drifts back to the table to reclaim her sherry, but Ernest still has a hold of her wrist. As a faster standard follows he attempts to whirl her around in a quickstep. Zelda looks furious and the drink spills but Ernest still has a hold of her. The Murphys, Cuzzemano, and Fife are laughing but to Hadley it looks as if everything is on the brink of turning sour; she knows Ernest when he is in this mood.

"C'mon, Mrs. Fitzgerald! Or are you only good for a cabaret?"

Zelda disentangles herself but Ernest, for whatever reason makes sense in his drunk head, pulls her over his shoulder in a fireman's hold. "Put me down!" Ernest will not let go. Hadley looks at the scene with disbelief. "You BRUTE, Ernest Hemingway!"

Scott emerges from the double doors, a bowl of fruit in his pale hands. "What are you doing with her?" he says, grabbing the figs at the top of the bowl. "Get off my wife!"

he shouts, the ends of the words lost in his chin. "I said: PUT HER DOWN!"

Scott throws a fig which arcs across the garden and smashes on Ernest's blazer. He drops Zelda and has time to duck before the next one flies through the air. Fife has leapt to his aid but then another one of Scott's thrown figs explodes on her hard white skin.

"Oh, Scott," Fife says. "What did you have to do that for?"

Ernest glares at him as Zelda shuffles back to her chair. Her lips press in a smirk. He takes off his blazer and surveys the damage: two round purple spots where the figs hit. "That wasn't right," he says.

"For God's sake, Scott," says Sara. "Why do you *insist* on behaving like a child?"

Fife strides into the kitchen and Ernest follows the sound of the feathers.

Hadley feels as if she wants to kiss Scott. What a fine sense of grievance and possession! How often had she felt like wringing Fife's neck when a dainty slipper had fallen off a dainty foot in their Paris apartment and caught the wandering eye of her husband! Back at the villa over bridge or sherry she had never felt that she could throw a tantrum—never mind fruit.

Zelda toasts Scott his chivalry and Sara looks fit to burst. Scott is too drunk to really notice anything but his feet and the kisses administered by his admiring wife. Then Sara tells him what she's obviously been dying to say all night. She calls him a selfish infant who belongs in a kindergarten. Children, Hadley thinks to herself, children are more civilized than this gang on the sauce.

When she looks back, Fife and Ernest have left the kitchen. The room is curiously formless without their figures in it. "Well," says Hadley, now that Sara has had her say and Scott sulks in the corner to the overtures of Mr. Cuzzemano, no doubt kissing up to him after the glories of *Gatsby*. "After weeks of no fun at all I think I've had more than I can take." Hadley pushes back her chair. "Will you excuse me?" She goes into the house to fetch her things.

Gerald has hung her shawl in the bedroom of his two sons. If Sara knew about this she would be livid. Patrick and Baoth sleep curled around each other. They are beautiful, just like their parents, and Hadley wonders what they'll become. Something amazing, she's sure of that: they are of this boundlessly good and clever New England stock. She'd like to kiss them good night, but if Sara caught her she'd be excommunicated entirely. Especially after the debacle with the figs. Though she is not a religious woman, Hadley thinks of a prayer her mother used to say over her at night to keep her safe while she slept. These kids are intensely lovely. They quite take her breath away.

She's about to take the stairs when she hears a noise from the landing. A bedroom door has fallen open and voices travel. Through the slot between door and frame, she finds a couple standing in the middle of the room.

There's nearly no light and their faces are featureless. The woman's bustle comes into view, all spiky feathers tearing down from her waistline. Hadley hears her own intake of air. Ernest's hand goes round between the two wings as if they have dropped open for him, like a swan's downbeat in flight. He kisses her forehead, her eyebrows, the lids themselves. A spot of fig still stains her skin. The feathers begin to tremble. She says, "Two weeks and nothing, Nesto. It's been so hard." Hadley can feel how much Fife wants him. She can see how little weight is on those legs. Then they fall onto the floor and the feathered skirt falls open. Hadley slams the door as hard as she possibly can.

She sits on the edge of the chess-tiled patio. Sara and Gerald are clearing up in the kitchen and discussing Scott's behavior and what should be done. The Fitzgeralds and Cuzzemano are nowhere to be found. A smell of camellias and oleanders wafts up from the garden. Peonies rise from pots as big as fists. This garden is something else.

So they've done nothing these past two weeks, and she realizes that it is Ernest and Fife who were under quarantine too, not just Bumby and herself. That the whole fortnight has been sexless seems even more depressing. Then the thought occurs that maybe what they have between them is only a sexual thing. She had never felt particularly adventurous in bed. Perhaps, if she could keep them apart, she might draw him off his attraction to Fife and make him see reason. She would be like Emperor

Tiberius: give them one hundred days of separation, and then Ernest would come back to her. He hated to be alone for a day or even an hour when the horrors struck; he certainly wouldn't be able to stand a hundred-day quarantine.

While Sara stacks the crockery on the shelves, Gerald sits down beside her. "It will be all right," he says to her. "You and Ernest . . . you're hitched up to the universe. You can't be parted." No, she thinks, hitched up to a fresh decisiveness, but Fife and Ernest might.

Ernest comes through the French doors looking sheepish. He places a warm hand on her shoulder. "Did you get the fig off?" she asks.

"Yes. All gone. Time to go?" His voice is cautious.

And she says yes, time to go, and they hardly say a good-bye to the Murphys who seem, suddenly, full of understanding: their features soft with sympathy, as if they had not realized quite how grave the whole thing had become.

The Hemingways set off from Villa America down to the beach. Fife will stay with the Murphys tonight. Hadley imagines there might be tears in both houses. Soon they will reach the end of the beach, weave through town, then arrive at their villa, together or apart.

This thought makes her tread slower on the sand. She feels terribly sad, because she knows that the empty spaces inside her are the same as the empty spaces inside him, because they match, because their geographies correspond. He does not match Fife, not like this.

"No seaweed," Ernest says, and they laugh, because it's funny that Gerald has cleared the beach of its algae—to have gone to so much meticulous effort to please his friends! He spent the whole of April at the task, removing the snaked green strands from the sand. Perhaps they laugh for different reasons: Ernest thinks it's silly; Hadley thinks it's sweet.

The waves leave their foam on the beach. Smells of wet rope and fish hang on the air. Draped over the landed boats are fishing nets, the moonlight crusting scales and shells on the threads. Boat masts lean in the direction of the wind. The night hides the far-off trees and the raft where they dived this morning. Nothing is visible but their limbs going forward, long and brown. "I'm sorry for acting like an ass. I shouldn't have done that to Zelda."

"It's okay," she says.

They stop. To carry on walking would somehow make this conversation casual.

Hadley delivers this to the sea, not to him: "When I saw you at the party in Chicago, I thought you were just playing up to me. Interested only for the night. I thought I was going to be a spinster in St. Louis forever. Ernest, you changed everything for me."

"That night changed everything for me as well. Of course it did."

Breakers come and go by her feet.

"If you want to go, I accept that. I don't regret any of this. What you have showed me. And what we have done in the five years we have had. It has been another class of marvelous."

Ernest doesn't say anything.

Hadley clears her throat, committing herself. "Do you love her?"

"I still feel the same way about you." The expression on his face changes completely. She can't read it. She wonders if it is love. It just might be. "But my feelings for Fife are there."

"Are they very strong?"

A pause, then: "Yes."

"Strong enough to end us?"

He doesn't answer. Hadley walks on a little farther and he follows her. They come to a brightly painted canoe with big red letters: DAME DE LA FRANCE. The warm waves come over her feet and she leans on the boat's body. She will be the one, then, to set out the terms. "This is what we will do. We will go back to Paris. You will move your things out of the apartment. You can marry Pauline, if that is your wish." Ernest looks horrified and relieved all at once. "But only after a hundred days of separation. No more, no less. If you want to be with her after that, then you have my blessing. I will grant you a divorce. But you have to prove to me and to yourself that this isn't a passing affair."

"Hash." The tide reaches his feet then pulls away. She rises from the canoe and walks up to the end of the beach. He follows, walking over the sand slowly behind her.

The trees sound out into the night. They walk back to the villa, tracing the same steps they made early this morning when they came out to the raft to swim, to play their game by the rocks, and to hope, while they held their silence, that things could always just continue as they always had been.

Near the lavender, at the villa's porch, she says: "I'm doing this for us. A hundred days, Ernest. It won't be long. You'll work out what you need after that."

Behind him their three bathing suits hang in the breeze. Upstairs, with the window open, is Fife's room. They tread quietly into the house alone.

FIFE

13. KEY WEST, FLORIDA. JUNE 1938.

Fife's house is splendid. Heads stud the walls: impala, kudu, oryx; their long horns magnificent and as hard as bark. When the shutters are open a breeze comes into the house from the Gulf carrying in the scent of tamarind, frangipani, banana.

Sometimes it feels as if the house is all moving air.

To either side of a divan or dressing table are matching spiked plants and lamp shades. Oriental rugs are just the right side of fraying and where there are no rugs the floorboards cool her bare feet. Ernest's books—he has written so many here—sit in the cabinets under the chandeliers of split glass. Copies of old issues of *Vogue* pile on the secretary.

Nearly ninety years ago, slaves built this house. Seven years ago, the Hemingways moved in, with boxes of manuscripts filling the hall; plaster dust falling onto baby Gregory's crib and his brother Patrick running through the corridors causing mayhem; shutters falling off the balcony; and Fife and Ernest sharing their first kiss under a nest of two birds where the dining room ceiling had fallen in. Her first job was to renovate the gardener's toolhouse so that her husband could get to work. Writing, Fife knew, would keep her husband going straight.

*

Fife sits in the garden with a newspaper and a martini. A map of Europe on the paper's front page has dotted lines and arrows that show spheres of influence, occupying pressures, sovereignties displaced. Europe chews itself like a child with its fist in its mouth.

What she searches for is something written by Ernest from Spain. Fife scans all of the pages. Nothing, not a single article.

Her garden, around her, is a zoo: a spray of feathers might be a peacock or a flamingo, and cats stretch and crawl over everything—she keeps it this way for the boys. During her husband's foreign correspondence this past year, the garden has flourished. Every time Ernest has gone to Spain—and this is his third assignment—Fife has attacked with great energy the weeds and roots of unwanted things. Now the garden has an unnerving bloom. But she'd let it go to pot if only Ernest might spend a little more time with her in it.

Fife calls out to the servants. Ernest returns tomorrow and she wants the food perfectly fresh for his arrival: she has planned meals of crawfish and avocado salads with chipped-ice daiquiris. Each time he comes back she convinces herself that this is her husband finally returned to her. But months, sometimes weeks, into his stay he soon announces he's going back again to cover the war in Spain. It is a world, he has told her, of oranges and shoelaces, a city where there is nothing—and she looks around at this house of splendor and wonders about his need for Madrid. But she knows Madrid has nothing to do with why he goes back.

And yet it seems so pointless for her to be in Key West without him, where they live so that Ernest can go out to fish after a morning at the desk. All Fife wants to do is boat out somewhere on *Pilar*, eat tuna steak, and swim in the coves as they did in the early years of their marriage, with the sun glittering on the sea top and the both of them half-cut on martinis. She longs for their old cherished life as newlyweds.

Closer to the servants' quarters Fife spies a silhouette in the window though no one answers her calls. She wonders if the help dislike her. Somehow, they seem to know when they've been summoned for company, even though all she does is read them the menu for the week. She can bear the look of pity from the grocer over the plantains, but she can't take it from her own servants.

At least, in Antibes, there were the three of them. Hadley had her; Fife has no one. Here, in this jerkwater island, right at the bottom of the entire country's landmass, she doesn't even have his mistress for company. This morning she went to the hair salon just to feel someone's hands on her.

"Isobel!" Her voice comes out shouting.

Light streams through the same kimono she has kept since Paris, which she wore in their first stolen mornings together while Hadley was still skiing with Bumby. What a simpler time it had been, back when Hadley had been Ernest's wife, and she his mistress.

Pink bleeding hearts droop over the terra-cotta, crisped up in the heat. Fife powders the dead leaves in the press of her fingers. A kitten arches its back into her offered palm. It's tiny: nothing but bones and fur and a wet pink nose. It mews, circling her ankle. But when she kicks it her foot finds only air; it has slunk off to the safety of elsewhere.

Martini in hand, Fife climbs the stairs to her bedroom. It feels like her bedroom now; Ernest says he sleeps better alone, especially when he's writing. Miró's *The Farm* hangs above their bed, filched off Hadley in one of the more suspect pieces of divorce loot. Or perhaps it's on some kind of permanent loan—she has never been sure of their arrangement.

Out on the balcony is the smell of curing tarpon. On Whitehead Street the lighthouse looks out onto the Atlantic and the Gulf. Ninety miles away is Cuba, where they sometimes go for drinking and dancing, where Ernest sometimes goes for peace and quiet, as if he can't get enough of that on this four-mile island where nothing much happens.

Their home is the grandest on the street: really the only stable residence in what still feels, to Fife, like a shanty-town. It towers over the shacks with their broken balconies and boarding, their frames put together with treenails and pegs. She's seen builders make a house in a day: made from the salvaged wood of wrecked schooners. Were there to be a direct hit their neighbors would be swept away in the winds and the only house left on this lump of rock would be the Hemingways'.

Beyond the high brick wall a woman wheels her icebox, selling slabs of ice for more cents than they're worth. Sailors follow. She hears hollering before they head up Duval Street, probably aiming for Sloppy Joe's. A kid is shouting out his wares: two cents a milk can, probably found in the garbage. In comes a fresh blast of the ripe sewers. Key West: Ernest calls it the Saint Tropez of the Poor. Fife calls it the Rock.

Back in her bedroom she closes the shutters to keep out the stink.

Her wardrobe is still full of her marvelous furs. She'd like to resurrect these coats and bundle up against the metropolitan cold. Fife wants to be with her set and *move* and *talk* and *laugh*; she wants to be *harassed* for her company. The chinchilla skin is right at the back of the wardrobe. She remembers the night she wore it when she first met the Hemingways. She remembers, over tea, how Mrs. Hemingway watched her husband with a certain kind of awe: as if, even within the marriage, Ernest were still a kind of celebrity.

Fife hadn't fallen in love with Ernest at that party. Oh, no. It had been by degrees, over a year in Paris in which his wife slowly bowed out—just as she had always done in bridge.

Now she catches the *click click click* of the dress from the back of the wardrobe. It still gives her a rush of happiness and excitement, as if she were in Villa America all over again. It's not the most expensive of her outfits—there are far costlier samples stolen from the *Vogue* closet—but it is the most cherished.

Without much thinking, Fife decides to try it on. Two children later and more than a decade from Antibes, the dress still fits perfectly: this in itself is a minor triumph. The feathers sound in the breeze. It is a suit of wings.

She would marcel her hair if she had the tongs, just as she had done that Antibes night; instead she paints her lips red. In the mirror's reflection she sees how soft her lids have become with age: the skin feathers the kohl line. She remembers doing all of these things that evening, while she listened to Hadley catastrophically pleading with Ernest for a decision.

Mrs. Hemingway had never exactly blended into their set: she wasn't exactly a wit or *bon viveur*. Sara had said the same thing: Hadley was a wonderful mother and wife, but not quite the companion for a wild party, or, necessarily, a wild author. Fife liked to think Ernest had found that in her. The playmate. The partygoer. Her wealth had also seemed attractive to him. She didn't care what that made her. Or him. Sara said that when they'd married, on that warm May day in Paris in 1927, their group came to look just as it always should have.

Fife remembers wearing this dress on the night she had

won him, walking from the French doors to the terrace, where Hadley sat in proper blue serge—a dress Mrs. Pfeiffer would have approved of—appropriate, say, for a child's baptism. As she walked she watched Hadley. And Hadley watched her husband watching Fife.

How hard Scott had thrown the fig hours later; it had felt like a tennis ball hit from a crosscourt lob, and how comic the moons of Zelda's rump had been when Ernest had strong-armed her into a fireman's lift.

Afterward, when they were cleaning up in the kitchen, Ernest kneeled to wipe the fruit from his dress shoes. When Fife was sure they couldn't be seen, she slipped her fingers into his mouth and the fig began to melt on his tongue. She felt Ernest tense though he wouldn't look at her. Nothing for two weeks. Not even earlier on the raft when they had been all alone. And now Ernest was sucking her fingers and grabbing her wrist: just as he had the first time he had touched her in Paris. This time, however, he held on.

Beyond the glass Sara was berating Scott, Hadley wasn't talking to anyone, and in the kitchen Fife had her fingers in Ernest Hemingway's mouth.

He let go of her wrist and touched her stocking-less ankle. His fingers slipped upward to her knee. She heard his intake of breath as his hand traveled upward. From the garden Sara smiled at her brightly.

"We can't do this here," Fife whispered.

But Ernest wouldn't stop. She leaned against the sink

watching his wife. "Nesto. Upstairs. Now." It felt right to break the quarantine at Sara and Gerald's.

Villa America, after all, debauched all of its residents.

She should have thanked Scott for throwing the fig, Zelda for being the best histrionic version of herself, the composer of that waltz who had encouraged Ernest to dance with someone for whom he had no tenderness, because after that night nothing was the same. There was never any chance of going back to the time before Antibes. Not for anyone.

Fife worries at the feathers; how lush they once felt! Now she feels an old crow. Born in 1895, what an ancient she feels next to Ernest, who only seems to look younger as the years pass. How easily he attracts women! How they come in droves, unwelcome as moths.

By her feet there are feathers on the tiles where she has in distraction pulled them from the dress. The frock looks as if it has been supper for a tabby cat. Pulled feathers skitter along the tiles. The telephone rings downstairs.

Fife has always hated the telephone; she feels a child of the twenties, at home in the subterfuge of letters and telegrams, not this bawling thing demanding attention. There's no time to drag herself from the dress so she rushes the stairs but still manages not to spill a drop of her drink.

"Hello?" she says, a little out of puff.

"Fife? It's me, Hash."

Far from Paris, far from Antibes, they are friends once

more: it is Hadley's generosity that has made this happen. They gossip for a few minutes. First about Sara and Gerald who will visit next week, then about Harry Cuzzemano who has been calling her again about Ernest's lost novel. "I tell him it was fourteen years ago. That suitcase has either been thrown to a bonfire or is in some attic somewhere. It's silly," Hadley says, "but I still get upset about it."

"It was an honest mistake."

"You know Ernest wouldn't pay 150 francs for an advertisement on the off chance someone might come forward for a reward? We didn't have any money but we would've spent the same on a *ski pass*. Maybe we could have found it. Then maybe we could have moved on."

Dressed in the very frock that robbed Hadley of him, Fife smiles at the irony. Who, then, would have been Mrs. Hemingway?

"Now I just fob him off with dead ends," says Fife. "I told him Eve Williams might have some explanation for the case."

"But she died not long after we all left Paris."

"I know," Fife says wickedly, "but it took him far longer to work that out on his own." Briefly, they talk about Czechoslovakia and Spain and the "lunacy of Europe" as Hadley puts it. They talk about their boys: what a fine young man Bumby is turning into, about how nine-year-old Patrick and six-year-old Gregory are doing at school. They gossip about Scott and Zelda because they are the easiest targets, and somehow, remarkably, their struggles seem the least heartbreaking of their set. Best not to talk about the Murphys. Or the Hemingways, indeed.

Fife asks if it is just a social call. She can hear the hesitation in her friend's voice. "I know Ernest has been away a lot," Hadley says finally.

Should Fife risk asking for help? It makes her feel ridiculous to be asking this of his ex-wife. Even more so to be standing here like an old ginned debutante. But she'd like to tell someone who knows her husband just as well as she does. "Ernest has found himself a new . . . affinity."

Hadley doesn't say anything. Perhaps this is a fact she already knows. Perhaps even Ernest has told her. They are still firm pals and write each other faithfully. "Her name is Martha Gellhorn. Have you heard of her?"

"Yes, though I've never actually met her."

"She's from St. Louis," Fife says. "He must be cursed."

"How do you mean?"

"Falling in love with all these Midwesterners. Can't be fun for any man." Fife means to sound droll but her words are a little hollow.

"You think he's in love with her?" Hadley probably means *in love* as opposed to *infatuated*; there have been those kinds of affairs too.

"I think this has been some time in the making."

"How long?"

"Last year. Well, the Christmas before it. He brought her to a dinner party, both drunk off their heads. I had to sit there all evening while he talked to this girl hauled in from Sloppy Joe's. Sara and Gerald were so embarrassed. Then, what do you know, they both end up covering the Spanish war."

"And have you talked to him?"

"We had a blazing row about a year ago in Paris. He said he would deal with it when I offered to throw myself over the balcony. I thought that meant it was over."

"And was it?"

"I think it just meant it was confined to Spain."

"Well. Europe makes fools of all Americans."

"Sounds like something Scott would say."

"Sorry, I didn't mean to sound facetious. Just that I think people behave a little more responsibly when they're back home. God knows we all acted badly in France."

Fife lets her silence acknowledge this as truth.

"Every time he's billeted to Madrid they're there together. Jinny told me they don't even bother having separate hotel rooms anymore. I torment myself imagining them: jaunting around Madrid acting like man and wife."

"How does Jinny know that?"

"Jinny! Jinny somehow knows everything. Oh, Hash, I don't know what to do!" She composes herself but holds on to the telephone with just as much grip. "I'm scared I'm losing him."

In the background there is a man's voice. Paul, Hadley's husband, is a fine man: kind and quiet and, it seems, enviably unchangeable. Since their marriage, Hadley has rather blossomed, as if all she needed was someone gentle to bring out the bolder parts of her. They had met each other while Paul was still married; in Paris they went around as a three: Hadley, Paul and his wife. None of them, not even Hadley, were innocents anymore.

Hadley sighs. "I can't think I'd be the best person to advise you. I lost him, after all." There is only an admission of fact here: as if she is explaining a bad business decision made in her youth. "Maybe the only thing to say is: he'll grow out of it. During the hundred days, I saw how much in love you were. That's why I called it off. Because I saw how much you meant to Ernest—how much it was killing him that he couldn't be with you. This thing with Martha, it sounds like an infatuation. When the Spanish war finishes it will finish off Martha too. She's someone to get him through the war, that's all. He'll not be a man of many wives."

"I'm his second."

"Well, sometimes we need a false start before we get it right."

Fife takes a deep breath. "You're a saint, Hadley. And a true friend. To us both." She is about to hang up when she realizes Hadley is trying not to laugh. "What is it?"

"I don't know if I should say. It's rather crass."

"You have to."

"The one thing I do know about Miss Gellhorn. Her father was a gynecologist in St. Louis. In fact, Dr. Gellhorn used to be my gynecologist."

"You're joking."

"All rather Freudian, don't you think? Just imagine Martha's father staring up Ernest's first wife's undercarriage."

"Is it a good sign or a bad one?"

"Very bad, of course! The affair has been damned from the start."

Fife laughs: fully now, with heart. "You've cheered me up incalculably, Hash. Though I'm not sure how."

"Me neither. Good-bye, Fife dear. Take care. And try not to worry. It will all blow over. Believe me."

Fife hangs up and sinks the last of the martini. She sucks at the tangy green olive, spitting the pit back in the glass. This is what her passion for Ernest feels like: she wants to have him all the way down to the stone.

14. PARIS, FRANCE. 1925–26.

All fall Fife had meant to leave him to his wife. Her friend, kind Hadley. That October she did try to stay away. But she couldn't conceal the elation when Hadley invited her over to their apartment. And as it grew cooler, Mrs. Hemingway's invitations only increased.

Now every night Fife would leave the office to see them: her chaps. If she'd known her friend had felt uncomfortable, she wouldn't have gone; but the invitations *were* always from Hadley. And she couldn't say no: it was only

in their apartment—when she saw Ernest with a manuscript balanced on one knee, his face lit by the coal
fire—that a stillness came to her. All day at *Vogue* she
positively vibrated with her own nerves, but as soon as
she stepped into the Hemingways' tiny apartment she felt
herself hit like a tuning fork, sounding out the right and
perfect note.

In the evenings the three of them talked books and
gossiped about the writers they knew. While she read his
work, and he waited for her thoughts, he spat clementine
seeds into the fire and watched them flame blue.

She prayed to God to put in her way a more suitable
husband.

When she should have been at *Vogue* she helped
Hadley with the dishes, the cleaning, the changing of the
bedclothes, encouraged her friend at her pursuits with the
piano. Anything to be in his space and have her hands on
his things. When Hadley needed to sleep off her cold, Fife
took care of Bumby, and Hadley would pat her on the arm
and say what a dear she was. She felt wretched and knew
she was being hateful, but she did not desist.

With Ernest, she felt that she could only worship him.
She praised his work and told him every night how famous
he was going to be, how stinking rich, how admired as a
writer and almost as a philosopher. She meant every last
damn word and she loved to see him grin, ear to ear, when
she told him these things.

One evening, she caught him looking at her. It had been

one of those evenings when they read rather than talked and Hadley was in the bedroom, nursing the cold. On these nights her imagination often strayed from the story: Fife wondered what it might feel like if he were to kiss her. Or what might happen if she innocently sat on his knee, or what it would be like to go to bed with him.

And when she looked up from this daydream, with her legs swung over the ratty armchair just as she had always sat reading as a schoolgirl, this time she found Ernest observing her. It made her feel self-conscious, as if she had been discovered bathing.

He put down his manuscript and came toward her. The fire behind him darkened his face so that she couldn't find his expression. He picked up her hand and looked about ready to snap it, but instead he pressed his mouth to the button of her wrist and held his lips there. Hadley coughed in the bedroom behind the wall, and Ernest went back to his chair and gazed into the fire, looking scared and alone.

They sat for a long time like that, no one saying much. Then Fife began talking in a hushed voice about the mystery of the lost suitcase, and Ernest admitted how sorely he still grieved for his wife's mistake. Oh, yes: Fife knew there was a special place in hell for women who did this to other women.

It was Sylvia Beach who mentioned it first. Not to her, but to Jinny. The two women were huddled into their coats at La Rotonde, surveying its patrons with much indifference until one of their set walked in. All afternoon they had been gossiping about Sylvia's customers at Shakespeare and Co.: whom she liked and whom she didn't, who didn't pay their dues on time and who was to be tipped as the next big thing. Sylvia knew just about everyone.

Fife had been up to fetch drinks when she caught the tail end of what Sylvia was saying. "—is Ernest Hemingway in any way involved?"

Several people in the café looked around when Fife came to a standstill, hidden by the curtain at the café door.

Her sister blushed. "Why do you say that?" Her face rose perfectly from the mink that Ernest had so admired above her own half a year back.

"You've no idea how indiscreet people can be: they think a shelf of books is as good as soundproofing. Harry Cuzzemano calls them the *Hemingway Troika*. It's just rumors, of course. But I wondered whether they had any basis."

"And what do these rumors say?"

"Just that wherever Hadley goes, there Fife tends to be."

"They're best friends."

"All three of them?"

"I mean Hadley and my sister. *They're* best friends."

Sylvia dropped a sugar cube into her coffee, one gloved hand stirring the cup. "Ernest has started borrowing love poetry. Walt Whitman, of all people."

"So?"

Sylvia sank her coffee. "Trust me: he's just not Ernest's usual tastes, that's all." She kicked at a couple of pigeons pecking at the crumbs of a madeleine on the sidewalk. "You know the Hemingways have absolutely no money. It's none of my business, Jinny, but I can see your sister's allure to a man without means."

A waiter in an apron tried to get around her to the terrace, and Fife was forced out into the wintry air. At the table she pretended she'd heard nothing and put down the drinks. She thought of Sylvia's words about her money, and how exotic she sometimes felt in a dress borrowed from *Vogue* in the tiny apartment of the Hemingways. So what if Ernest found her wealth attractive? Money was attractive—it meant travel, and fine wine, and good food. Above all, it meant opportunity.

Sylvia pushed the glass of Pernod over to Jinny. "Got to dash! Will you have mine?" she asked, looping her scarf around her. "Adrienne's cooking for an American book collector tonight. So rich he stinks!" Sylvia kissed them both and walked away in her quick brogued stride. The pigeons flew about her shoes like mud from under a car's wheels. As they watched her go, Fife tried to talk about something else but Jinny immediately cut her off.

"There's nothing going on between you and Ernest, is there?"

"No," Fife said. And it wasn't a lie.

On the night of the heavy rain Ernest invited her over to his apartment. They had spent all Christmas as a three on a skiing trip where no one had done much skiing. In the evening they read by the fire, or drank sherry and played billiards or three-handed bridge. As a joke they called themselves the harem. Fife slept in the room next to theirs.

Now Hadley had stayed on, and Ernest had come back to Paris for business. And soon enough, the invitation arrived from the Left Bank. Could she look over something new he had written on the train home?

Fife walked instead of getting a cab that night. She thought she might be able to exercise from herself her bad thoughts. *Be good*, she urged herself, as she walked over the Pont Neuf, *be good, you foolish girl*. But she could think of nothing but him.

When she arrived Ernest stood in the doorway: pale and tired. He greeted her almost as if she were an unwanted guest. Fife waited for him to show her the manuscript, but instead they talked about his trip to New York. They sat by the fire. All evening he seemed distracted and grouchy.

When she made to leave he idled by the door as if he did not want to let her go. She started to talk about some piece of gossip Jinny had told her when he shoved his knee between her legs and grabbed at her breasts under her coat. She struggled against him at first, meaning to stop it, remembering her words to herself on the bridge. But she collapsed into him and they made love by the fire without Ernest even taking off his pants. It was exciting as hell. Afterward he sat propped against his armchair and she against hers, still dressed in their clothes. She had desired him, in this very spot, for what had seemed like years.

*

Writing might prove, that spring, an absolution. Fife wrote letters and letters to Hadley, as if in writing to his wife she could absolve herself of guilt—but it was no good. Sometimes she got so excited about what was going on with Ernest that she forgot to tone it down even in her letters to his wife. Drunk one afternoon she slipped up and wrote a letter only to Ernest about a friend of theirs she had been flirting with, scrawling it out on a piece of notepaper and sending it off, imagining the delight on his face when he opened his private mail.

After their strange little trip to Chartres cathedral Jinny had stayed on at the Hemingway apartment for tea. Now she stood in their house on the rue Picot and peeled off her hat.

"Ça va, mon homme?" Fife asked her sister.

"I've been at the Hemingways'."

The newspaper fell from Fife's lap. "Was Ernest there?"

Jinny looked about their home as if newly sensitive to how much space the sisters kept. She seemed wound up. "I am frozen. Their apartment is tiny, and cold, and smells of dead birds. I don't know how that woman stands it. Or him, or you, or herself! You're all ridiculous."

"You're tired from the drive. Let me get you some tea."

"Oh, I don't want any more tea!"

Still in her coat, Jinny pulled out a stained handkerchief and went to the kitchen. "Barely room for two people to sit," she said to the faucet's running water. "Where does everyone *go* when you're there? Or do you just jump into bed with each other to keep yourselves warm?"

"For God's sake, stop washing that damned hankie!"

Jinny swiveled around to face her. "She asked me."

Fife felt her whole face flush. Nothing had ever been said. Not by Hadley. Not by Fife or Ernest, not even to each other. All three of them labored for everything to be always unsaid. "And what did you say?"

Jinny's gray eyes looked out of the window then back at her. "I told her you were very *fond* of each other. She seemed to get the picture."

"Wonderful."

"I confirmed only what she already knew."

"You had no right."

"I saw you praying at Chartres," Jinny said. "Are you not afraid of what you're doing? There's Hadley to consider, and Bumby too. And what about the state of your soul?"

"To hell with my soul; he is my soul! I love him, why can't you see that? I need him and he needs me. We are the same guy."

Jinny looked dumbfounded, bewildered. "What are you *talking* about?"

"He says he'll leave her."

"She's his wife!" Jinny banged the side of the sink, and

the skillet pans knocked against each other. "And you are a plaything. A bauble for when he's bored at home."

"That's not true. Why are you on her side?"

"Because she is out of her depth! Because Hadley doesn't have a hope in hell against you. She has no friends. No family. No money. Everything you have, she does not."

"I'm your sister. Where's your sympathy for me?"

"You have everything!"

"She has everything! She has him!" Fife leapt to her feet and Jinny cowered, as if she thought her sister would hit her. Instead she grabbed the tea-stained hankie and threw it hard against the icebox. It landed against its side then slid slowly to the floor. "Just you watch, Jinny Pfeiffer. I may be his mistress now, but soon I will be his wife!"

15. KEY WEST, FLORIDA. JUNE 1938.

A car door slams outside. Through a lemon slice of window she sees it is Ernest, emerging from a cab, directing the driver to the cases. Feathers go wildly around her legs as Fife rushes the stairs. He had said Wednesday; she was sure of it. He would think her mad for being in this dress; Antibes is a memory that they do not speak of.

As she flies into the bedroom she struggles to get herself out of the frock.

"Hello?" His voice travels as the front door opens.

"Coming, darling!"

But Ernest's feet are on the stairs and the buttons seem tiny; her hands are all thumbs. They won't give and the fabric rips as she pulls at it. She's too late. Ernest is opening the bedroom door and he blinks at what he sees before him.

"Fife," he says. "What are you doing?"

"I . . . wanted to see if it still fit."

She has ripped a hole in the side of the dress near the buttons. She covers it up with her hand, feeling like such a fool. "I didn't think you were back until tomorrow." His eyes go to the empty martini glass on the side table. "How was your trip?"

"Fine. The flight to Miami was delayed." He kisses her hello on the cheek. "But I guess that makes no difference."

Ernest sits down on the edge of the bed, rubbing his face with tiredness. There are a few moments of silence—it feels strange to have longed for her husband for so long and now she doesn't know what to say to him. She notices a louse crawling out from under his shirt collar. "You've brought back a friend," she says, and Ernest looks up with confusion, as if she has caught him out. Fife pinches the creature in her fingers and shows it to him. It crawls a way up her pointing finger. "Don't they treat you with a salt shaker on your exit?"

"I met a general last week. Now I find them everywhere."

"I can't wait to find them on the bedclothes."

"I stink," he says, and he peels off his shirt and pads into the bathroom to shower.

In the kitchen she waits till the gridiron is hot before assigning the louse to the flames. It pops when it bursts. As she makes Ernest coffee she admires her best china on display in the kitchen cabinet. They have always avoided throwing her expensive plates.

Upstairs the water begins to run.

The suitcases are piled neatly in the hall. She wonders if she has enough time to search them for traces of Martha. Probably not. He'll be down in a few minutes and then he'll want to eat his dinner and be in bed early with a paperback in their sons' room. She wonders what has hastened his return. With a leap of hope she wonders if Martha and Ernest have had a huge fight and he has left her somewhere in New York, done and dusted with their silly affair.

She lays out slices of ham on stale yellow brioche. What a meal for her Odysseus.

Ernest comes down washed but unshaved, wearing his shorts and a white T-shirt. He looks fantastic. It would be easier if she weren't getting older so much faster than he was. She's forty-two and Ernest looks the same as he did in his twenties. He stares at the sandwich on the table.

"You did say tomorrow."

"It doesn't matter."

Fife brings in the newspaper from the garden and notices the toolhouse light on. She must remind the servants again that they are not allowed in there. Ernest is convinced Cuzzemano has bribed them to send him his trash. "How was Spain?" she asks, handing over today's paper.

"Things on either side so bad you come to think both sides stink. Kids dead. Blood in the streets." He presses the lids of his eyes. "The food was horseshit."

"I heard awful reports. I was worried." She pours him coffee with a slug of condensed milk straight from the can.

"I can't tell you what it's like not to be surrounded by sandbags. I keep waiting for the sounds of shelling. And there isn't any."

"How's the writing?"

"The play's nearly done. But I need something big. A novel."

"You've never had a book that didn't sell thousands."

"But the critics—I want one they'll like."

Fife takes a seat opposite in her black feathered dress. She is an odd companion to an odd meal. Ernest hasn't yet touched his sandwich. "You might as well be writing for dogs as trying to please critics."

"I don't understand why they hate everything I write now."

"A handful of conceited people compared to the millions that love the books."

"I want *them* to like it."

"I'll like it."

"I know, I know. Oh, Fifey. Ever faithful." The way he

says it—it's as if the word *faithful* means shoddy. It vexes her. In fact, she feels a certain recklessness— if Ernest didn't care about this marriage, then perhaps she didn't either. Fife leans over and takes a bite of his untouched sandwich. The ham is delicious even if the bread is hard.

"Hey!" he says, but she can see how he enjoys her mischief.

She takes another bite. "Hey *what*, Mr. Hemingway?"

Ernest tries to grab at the sandwich but she holds it from him and makes her face seductive. "It tastes so good." Ernest rolls his eyes. "Oh, I'm just a starving reporter who hasn't had piggy in months. What have you had these past few weeks, hmm? Cabbage and broth?"

He leaps up but she runs away: she darts left around the dining table and he goes right; she goes right, he goes left. They're like the cats she saw playing by the birdbath this morning. As she runs to the garden the feathers on her dress make a mad sound and the cats scatter as they come. Her feet slap the pool tiles as Ernest grabs at the sandwich but Fife takes the last bite and it's gone. Ernest shakes his head. "I've had nothing for months!"

"Serves you right for abandoning me."

They stand close. He puts one hand between her legs in the feathered dress. "I remember this dress, Fifey. You killed me with this dress." He goes up farther. She smiles at him; he smiles back. She wears no underclothes. "Just like France," he says, his eyebrows raised.

She thinks this—this!—is the joy of her husband returned to her. Ernest grabs her wrists. "Now, what do we do with the boys when they've been up to no good?"

"No, Ernest." She grins. "Don't!"

But he has already swung her into the pool.

The cook exits the servants' quarters right on cue. "Mr. Hemingway. Hello, sir."

"Hello, Isobel. Mrs. Hemingway has been a very naughty girl," he says. Fife wonders what she must look like, a bird drowned in its bath. "Don't mind us."

Isobel shakes her head as if she will never understand rich people and the stupid things they do. The cook goes back into the carriage house.

"You're soaking wet," Ernest says, when Fife climbs out of the pool. The feathers drip onto the tiles. He pulls at the bow of the black ribbon she still wears in her hair. He does it very gently, as if he were skinning fruit. "My little boy." The corners of his lips rise, acknowledging it. "How long are the kids away?"

"The month."

"So we have the whole house to ourselves."

Fife wants to say: be rid of Martha first, then you can have your wife. She wants to tell him he can't have the both of them. Instead she lets out a long breath as he kisses down to the hollow bit of her neck and he says, "I have been thinking about fucking you all the way home from Miami."

16. KEY WEST, FLORIDA. JUNE 1938.

Since his return from Spain, Ernest has been working in the mornings, then fishing or swimming in the afternoons; the evenings they spend together. There are no telegrams delivered at odd hours, no phone calls to St. Louis, no dispatches from Madrid. China sits un-thrown in cabinets. Dusk is no longer the signal to begin the hot assaults that both have perfected in different parts of the house during the long warm days. Ernest hasn't been like this since he began his trips to cover the Spanish war.

He wants her, now, all the time: Ernest wakes her by kissing her and they go to bed having taken off most of their clothes downstairs. It reminds her of the early years of marriage when things had been so marvelous. On their honeymoon they had gone to the south of France to walk the salt marshes and swimming beaches. Magical; to be living for the first time like man and wife after so much time sneaking around, and Ernest told her how cockeyed in love with her he'd been these past few years. There was a Gypsy festival in the nearest town that week and she had stained their faces with berry juice and they had swigged red wine from pigskins. At home that night it was as if the dark masks freed them, and they had done some strange and wonderful things to each other in bed. Appetite—

that's what they had for each other—and it had always felt, to Fife, as if they had it in abundance.

Now it feels like their second honeymoon. In the first few days of Ernest's return, they are never out of the pool. Guava trees and weeping figs crowd the decking. The sapodilla leans in, its rich bark leaking gum. Fife perfects her dive, remembering with shameful pleasure that flop Hadley had committed to the waves in Antibes. Ernest practices a dead man's float.

His scars are pinker in the water. There is the gash on his forehead from Paris, his calves shot up from gaffing for sharks, the burst on his knee from the war. She has never met anyone so prone to accidents, to cocked guns and roads swerved down.

Mostly Ernest stays in the shallows, watching as the water lifts around her. The adrenal feeling of hitting the water keeps her going; Fife has always loved the sensation of diving. She remembers the day out on the raft in Antibes, diving only for his pleasure. But she remembers, too, when she had asked him to go up to the rocks once Hadley had left. He had looked at her strangely, as if he were a character in a book and he was thinking of what his character would do next. Then he had said no. The moment had been profoundly depressing: Ernest, evidently, could take her or leave her. She, on the other hand, wanted him always. He had once told her that love was never about the powerful and the powerless. But Fife can't think of what else might constitute a marriage.

*

On her last dive she swims over to him in the shallows. She thinks about knocking him over so that water will surge up his nose. Instead she pushes his ankles apart and blows bubbles that rise on his skin. Ernest pulls her up by her shoulders only to push her head back down.

"Water's gone up my nose," Fife says, as she surfaces, in a cartoonish voice.

She pulls herself to the decking as the sinus thump begins to ease. Ernest watches her. Those marvelously seeking eyes: as if once again she's an object of fascination. What has she done to make her husband come back to her?

"Your mother wrote. She wants to come down and see the boys."

Last night, they had talked to the kids on the telephone and both Patrick and Gregory had jostled with each other to talk to their father. Whenever one was speaking the other was speaking too, and Ernest had put his hand over the mouthpiece, laughing, saying to her: "I can't understand a damn thing either one of them is saying!" And then he turned back to the telephone: "Boys!" he said. "One at a time now!"

Wrapped up so much in each other, neither one of them had been as attentive to the kids as they might have liked. She had always just assumed, because they were boys, that she could leave them to do their growing up in private. It wasn't like daughters, where you had to school them in how to behave, and tell them what not to do. In their first few years Patrick and Gregory had been practically raised by their nursemaid, or Jinny, while she had gone off wherever Ernest wanted to go: Spain, Wyoming, safaris in Africa. She could manage being away from her sons, but not her husband.

It's not that she doesn't love them; it's just that there is always so much to do: editing Ernest's work, instructing the servants, restoring the house; then there were the trips with Ernest when he wanted to go quail shooting, or deep-sea fishing, or to the bullfights in Spain. She was his wife; it left little time for her to be a mother as well.

"My mother doesn't want to *see* the boys. She wants something else. Money. More money. She can go to hell." Ernest swims over to her and he pulls at her suit so that it snaps against one warming buttock.

"Nesto."

"I'm not allowed to touch my wife?"

"Not that. Your mother. I think she's lonely without your father."

"Maybe that's her fault."

He rests his head on her belly. Fife traces water from his ear. "Do you really think she could've stopped him?"

"No. Doesn't mean she didn't drive him to it."

"He's the one that pulled the trigger."

"And he was a son of a bitch for doing it. A chickenshit coward."

Ernest's weight drops down again to the water. When

he emerges on the other side she says: "He was ill. People don't kill themselves over nothing."

"He got blind to drown out Mother's voice. God knows I would have done the same." Ernest paddles at the water then looks up at his studio, as if the answer might lie in his work, or his ability to write through it. "All that worrying about money. Why not ask me for help?"

"There were so many years when you didn't have a dime."

"He knew you did. Your family could have bailed him out of life's biggest fixes."

"Please." Fife rolls onto her back to feel the sun on her. She won't tolerate his habitual carping about her family's money. It doesn't make any sense, not when he feels no guilt about using great bags of it. "There's no one to blame. It's just sad. That's all."

The water gives a sucking noise as Ernest pulls himself up to the pool edge. "I don't think she should come. Now's not a good time." He wraps himself in a towel and wetly pads to the kitchen. The sound of chopping ice comes from inside the house. Two p.m. Cocktail hour.

When he returned from his father's funeral a decade ago, Ernest spent his evenings working. Sometimes, when Fife went to his study with a gin and tonic at the end of the day, she caught him looking at the page with so much sadness that he might have been staring at his father's dead face. To have died in such a manner. To be the son of a suicide;

it seemed to dispossess Ernest of the idea of himself. He would take the drink and then give her the half smile he used when it was only just the two of them. But his mind was another place altogether.

A package arrived some time after Ernest's return. Their address was written in a firm Midwestern hand. Wrapped in brown paper with his mother's schlocky bows, the package sat in the den for days. After some time Fife saw the box's base was wet, a dreadful smell coming from it. He had to either open it or throw it away, she said, but it could not remain in here forever.

When the package was finally opened, they found the source of the stink. Ernest lifted a dripping chocolate cake from the packet, its icing blued with mold. He raced with it into the kitchen, dropping great chunks of it as he went. But an altogether different object had been warming under the cake this past week.

Ernest read the note aloud. "'You said you wanted it, so here it is. For you and Pauline. Enjoy. From your loving mother, Grace Hemingway.' I guess she meant the cake." Ernest picked up the handle of a gun. "Not this." It was a Civil War handgun: a Smith and Wesson. Mold furred the trigger that had last held his father's finger.

"It stinks," he said. And he went back to the kitchen to clean the gun of Grace's cake.

Fife wonders where he has put that gun, where it sits in Ernest's collection of arms. It would look small next to the long shots that killed bison, lion, elk; this tiny thing that had killed his father.

In the shadows, in the garden, the scent of citrus spills. Dusk is coming. She follows the smell of lemons into the kitchen. The gin and tonics stand blue on the countertop. She hears him quickly closing a drawer in the dining room.

"You're up," he says, coming into the room with his edgy grin. "I've already sunk a couple of these. Post meridiem. Now we can break out the strong stuff!" He chases the ice cubes in the glass with a long spoon.

Out in the hall is his fishing gear: rods, the live-fish box, and the hat he likes to wear on *Pilar*. He takes a drink then says, as if there hadn't been a break in their conversation: "Hadley's father shot himself as well, you know."

"I know," she says, following him back into the dining room, placing her hand, cold from the iced drink, on his neck.

"She was only thirteen. Put the gun behind his ear while still in his nightshirt. We are a cursed generation. All these children without their fathers."

He holds her hand against him.

"You're not a child anymore, Ernest. You're a father now. So," she says, thinking if she can steer his thoughts back to work she'll be able to snap him from this dangerous melancholy, "tell me about this play." She lays out a spread for them, of hams, cheeses, grapes, and pineapple. They drink their cocktails and then one more each as Ernest tells her about his character, stuck in Madrid, faced with a rather large decision to make.

17. PIGGOTT, ARKANSAS. OCTOBER 1926.

Hadley said she would commit to a divorce if they agreed to one hundred days of separation. On day seventeen of her exile, Fife found herself in the family car being driven back to her old home. Mrs. Pfeiffer had begun her spiel on the station platform, only pausing to direct the driver to her daughter's trunks. On the drive home her mother had really found her stride: Fife must, at all costs, avoid sundering a union God Himself had made. Hellfire and brimstone were waiting for her in the Ever After if she would insist on this path. "Your mother will wear you down," Ernest had warned, begging her to spend Hadley's required exile elsewhere. "You won't come back to me and then I'll be all alone." Fife had only laughed at the absurdity of that notion.

She tried to keep busy: learning Spanish and keeping up her French and doing exercises to keep herself toned. On day zero she was determined that Ernest would think her more beautiful than ever before. She walked around the town and cycled when she could, anything to avoid her mother.

Fife tormented herself with how easily Ernest might run into Hadley in Paris, stay on at their apartment for a glass of wine, play with Bumby, be entreated into staying the night . . . and then the rest of his lifetime. She was banned from seeing Ernest, but Ernest was not banned from seeing Hadley. Maybe his wife had been far more cunning than either of them had ever given her credit for. Jinny was her eyes and ears in Paris. She told her sister to see Ernest as much as she could.

Late into the separation Fife took her old bicycle onto the mud roads to the west. Outside, she saw the trees only as swatches of color, the sky gray. All morning she had felt wretched. Her mother's words accompanied each turn of the bicycle wheel: *You have broken a home. You have trespassed against God. You have sinned.* In the cotton fields she tried to out-pedal her mother's admonishments but they would not go away. *Marry Ernest and you cannot pay back the price of this sin.* She rode through the town square, past the liquor store where she and Jinny used to flirt with the owner for thimblefuls of rye. *Let Ernest be a father to his child and a husband to his wife.* Back home she abandoned the bike at the porch.

Each room in the house that afternoon was unlit and the air hung motionless. "Mother?" She checked the chapel— often she might be found offering a daytime devotional— but her mother wasn't there. No noise could be heard in the rest of the house.

Shadows settled on her things in her room. It was as if

someone had been going through her possessions. In the sewing room a reading lamp was still switched on. On the table where her mother kept her tapestries was one of Ernest's books: *The Sun Also Rises*. The book was open and facedown, but had not been started. Instead, it was creased at the dedication page. *This book is for Hadley and for John Hadley Nicanor.* Little Bumby's real name.

Outside, the sage brushed against the boarding. A moth was in the reading lamp, its wings fluttering against the soft cloth shade. Fife held on to Ernest's book, and the moth beat its wings faster. It sounded like blood beating in her ears. Above her mother's sewing things there was a portrait of the Virgin and Child: a look of fierce calm in Mary's eyes.

For Hadley and for John Hadley Nicanor.

Fife then regarded herself with terrific shame. All summer they had acted horribly, as if only the three of them were involved. But what was going to happen to Bumby?

Her mother must have heard her sobbing because minutes later she hurried into the room and held her as she wept. Fife felt heartsick for everything and everyone: herself, Ernest, Hadley, Bumby. She said *I can't, I can't, I can't, Mama, I love him, I love him, please, please don't make me.* She could feel how she shook in her mother's firm embrace, as if she were experiencing a delirium.

From then on, Fife woke with a quiet horror of herself. Even the sight of a feather on her mother's church hat reminded her of the gentle menace of that dress. For days she did not write to Ernest but stayed in bed, knowing what she had to do, and thinking at the same time how awful it was to do it. She thought about all the days at *Vogue* when she went home instead of seeing the Hemingways: how miserable those nights were. And now she would have to stay in Piggott and marry some man from the country club. The portrait of the Virgin now hung above the bedroom bureau. Mary and the baby stared at her, a vigil for the penitent. Her mother was right. But how could she go on living without him?

When she wrote to Ernest now the words were only about Hadley: her kind open face, how savage they had been, the sheer lunacy of Antibes. She remembered with revulsion how she had contemplated slipping between the sheets with them in their marriage bed. Oh, Europe had deviled the lot of them!

But if Fife could stay in America, perhaps it wasn't too late. If she never saw Ernest Hemingway again, she thought, she might not do the devil's work. Still, she crossed out Hadley's hundred days on the calendar: fifty-eight, fifty-seven, fifty-six . . . The Virgin and Child stared down at her. Reproach was in her eyes.

A telegram arrived on day fifty-five. HADLEY HAS CALLED OFF EXILE STOP WHEN CAN I EXPECT YOU? EH. In his subsequent letter Ernest explained Hadley had gone to Chartres to do some thinking and had decided to cancel the separation. Divorce proceedings were already set in motion; Fife should come back to Paris as soon as she could. This was, Ernest said, entirely what Hadley wanted.

Knowing that it had been Hadley's decision, Fife's shame lifted, quickly and easily. She was going back to France and to home. She was going back to marry Ernest.

Thank God, Fife thought, for Chartres cathedral.

When she saw him again, at the port of Boulogne, she said she would never leave his side again for the rest of their lives. Only later did she wish he might have promised the same.

18. KEY WEST, FLORIDA. JUNE 1938.

In the first week of Ernest's return Fife scours the gossip columns. She looks for a "bust-up between our seasoned Spanish reporter and a girl correspondent." She looks for the story that says the screeching heard from one room in their hotel "was said to be louder than the bombs that fell on Barcelona that day." The newspapers would never break this story—but sometimes the private lives of celebrities were hinted at, glossed over. Fife looks for the scrappiest piece of gossip—anything to confirm his relationship with Martha is over. There's nothing. This must be a good thing, she decides. Already, this week, she treats Ernest's infidelity with positive retrospection—Martha was just a passing infatuation. Still, she calls Sara Murphy.

Sara's voice sounds even richer on the telephone than it does in person; she has the voice of a movie star. Fife imagines she might be lounging on a divan drinking Scotch and wearing a man's housecoat. In another room Gerald would be painting. Sara has always been as close to her idea of glamour as any of her friends.

"How's Ernest?" Sara asks. "Is he back?"

"He came back Tuesday."

"Any concussions? Gunshot wounds? Did he blast off his toes and not even realize?" Fife tells her he's completely well. "Really, I have never met anyone so accident-prone. He's always getting himself into these damned scrapes."

"He's fine. In fact, he's quite the changed man."

Fife looks into the living room to check Ernest is out of earshot. He is the type of man who can be involved in one conversation and be monitoring another across the table as well. "He's more than fine, actually. He's come back with a sense of . . . I don't know . . . interest, really. As if he's broken it off in Spain."

"And did he?"

"For all I knew I thought he was out there with *her*. But he's come back with a new . . . ardor. He's so attentive and sweet. Fetching me breakfast in the morning and working hard in the days. He keeps on gazing at the palms as if they mean something. He won't leave me alone. It's magical."

There is a stiff silence on the other end of the line, then Sara says: "What did he say? When you asked him?"

"About what?"

"If he's called it off with Martha."

It's irrational, she knows, but she finds it distasteful that her friend would mention this woman to her by name. "I haven't *asked* him if things are *off* with her."

"Broach it with him then."

"If we did it would ruin the whole—" Fife was going to say illusion. But it's not illusory, despite what Sara says. "It's like he's come back to repair us."

Another pause. Is this what she called her friend for? To be disabused of hope? Perhaps Fife was indeed looking for the gallows, and Sara is wheeling out the stocks.

Her friend says: "You *have* to make sure Martha is out of the picture."

Fife wants to scream. She wants to tell Sara how the brush of a cat's coat against her leg last week only reminded her of how little she's been touched.

"You can't get into this if you're not sure she's out of it. I'm not saying this to hurt you. I'm saying it's going to feel a thousand times worse because Ernest has given you cause to hope. Then what will you do? When he goes back to her?"

Sara is wrong. She is sure of it. Ernest has returned to her from Marthaland.

"It won't happen again. I know it."

Fife says she'll call them back to confirm details for next weekend. "Don't forget the cereal boxes," she says, but rather sadly, as if she weren't talking about preparations for a party. Fife replaces the earpiece to the telephone and looks at the receiver nervously, as if it's likely to shape-shift into something beastly and alive.

Outside, the evening is warm. Fife takes the iron steps up to the studio and taps lightly on the window. Ernest looks up and smiles. She motions a drink with one hand and he nods his head; something about her mime makes him laugh.

In the kitchen she makes herself a gin and tonic, and leaves a Scotch and lime by his pages, kissing the crown of his head. He looks like he's still going at the play; she wonders when he'll ask her to read it. For a decade she has read and edited everything he's ever written. Deep in his writing, she won't disturb him. If she loves anything more than him, it's his words.

Fife sits instead at the table by the pool, listening to the tapping of Ernest's keys. Spanish moss gauzes the trees and a peacock walks the yard. The bird was given to them by Jane Mason, a mistress before Martha, and every time it comes into view Fife would like to pull out a long rifle and shoot it in its skull. It didn't last for long with Jane: six months or so, a few years back, and she had, until Jane's arrival, understood her relationship as a happy one. They still went everywhere together: quail hunting in Wyoming, bullfights in Hendaye. And when they weren't together they wrote such long letters that it was as if the other person were still there. She missed him whenever he went away. During Ernest's absences she was liable to burst into tears quite randomly, whether it was crossing the street, or eating chocolate peppermints.

And then Jane had come along, with her blonde hair and delicately blue eyes, and Ernest started making unexplained trips to Cuba. But Fife had never felt seriously threatened by Jane. Jane was too unstable: she had broken her spine after jumping from her balcony after an argument with Ernest. Ernest always liked his women happy and healthy, and the affair—if that is what it had been— seemed to end just as soon as it had begun.

But Miss Gellhorn, hale and hearty, was no meek Miss Mason. Up at the studio his hands work at the typewriter's keys. The bitterness of the gin meets her nose each time she drinks. An ice cube splinters in the fizz—it sounds like a breaking bone. Fife pulls her hands through her hair, feeling the last of the day's heat in it, and drains off the last of the cocktail.

What a pull he has! What a magnetism! Women jump off balconies and follow him into wars. Women turn their eyes from an affair, because a marriage of three is better than a woman alone.

19. KEY WEST, FLORIDA. DECEMBER 1936.

At half past seven that evening, Gerald, Sara, and Fife sat watching the bean soup grow colder while they waited for Ernest. He had, so far, neglected to show any sign that he was on his way to the dinner that sat before his empty space in the dining room of 907 Whitehouse Street.

But Sara was not a woman to hold her tongue. Her spoon was cocked, as if, given the invitation, she would splash it as soon as she could into the bowl. "Perhaps we should start."

"Ernest will be here soon enough," Gerald said. He looked even more uncomfortable than his wife, whose eyes darted dangerously to the door at every noise. Gerald applied his tongue to his top lip, as if sealing the gum of an envelope, and put a hand over Sara's. "The boy said he'd be back in ten minutes."

Fife rose to open a window but even with it open no air came into the room. The poinsettia she'd cut from the garden that afternoon was limp and the linens drooped from the tabletop. Fife took her seat once again.

"It's been twenty minutes already, for God's sake," Sara said in a fierce whisper. Her butter knife fell from the table. "I'm starving." Gerald returned the knife to his wife's plate. He gave Fife an apologetic smile, which looked as if it meant: *Marriage! Who'd recommend it?*

Fife watched the Ernest-less space opposite. He'd been

restless recently: unhappy with the reception of one of his short stories. The horrors had come in the evenings more and more: these climbs into a sadness that transported him far away from her. And the cabinet of alcohol—which she could spy now behind Sara's softly sweating shoulder— had to be resupplied twice a week. He had always been a drinker, but not like this, not out of some compulsion to bury some part of himself.

"He's been unhappy these past few months," she said to Sara.

Her friend had a hard time changing her expression from outrage to sympathy. "Oh? Why's that?"

"I think he feels stuck. In the creative endeavor. The last book didn't do well."

"It sold gorgeously, as I understood it."

"That's not the point. He wants the critics to love him. Somehow he's fallen out of grace with them. He calls them knife throwers."

"I remember the young man who would've been delighted with selling a thousand copies." Sara's hand started massaging the spoon again. "Now it's tens of thousands, and still he can't be happy. More, more, more: that will be Ernest's death knell."

The room was dangerously warm for keeping people's tempers in check. "Well," said Fife, now regretting starting this line of conversation at all. "You know what it's like. Especially when he gets into these low moods."

The door opened and the three heads turned expectantly. So he was here, and there was nothing more to worry about aside from the small matter of manners. But Isobel wandered in to take the plates and was surprised to see the food untouched.

"Not yet," Fife said. "We will wait for Mr. Hemingway to arrive."

Fife watched Sara and Gerald sit uncomfortably as the soup continued to cool—if there could be any heat left in it—in the shallow white bowls. Even in the evening light, the drive gave off a glare as if it were summer noon. The bottle of white wine beaded with moisture, and Fife saw how much of it she had drunk. She could imagine the bloom of tomorrow's hangover.

The garden gate squeaked and the Murphys stopped their talking.

"Here he is," Fife said. So they had been suffering under the tyranny of Ernest's timekeeping, and nothing more! When Fife stood she had to lean her fist against the tablecloth to steady herself. Gerald caught it and gave her a forgiving smile.

Fife went from the house past the fountain out front. Ernest was at the fence posts, wearing his T-shirt and roped shorts. He wore no shoes: this barefootedness was a recent habit. As he came through the gate he wore a strange expression, as if he had been preparing to ambush his own house rather than walk straight into it. His mustache went beyond the corners of his mouth.

"You're late," Fife said, her stiletto heel sinking into the gravel. In her full summer dress she felt ridiculous next to him. "Sara and Gerald have—"

"Ah, Fife," he said. Then he worked himself up into a smile: the one he used for show. He leaned his bulk against the post and folded his arms: he looked drunk out of his head. "I thought Mr. and Mrs. Murphy left this morning."

A woman then appeared behind him. She wore a small black dress and low heels. She had bronzed legs, toned arms, hands just the right size. Her hair was loose in a blonde bob and was swept heavily over one eye. As she came closer to the gateposts Fife was reassured she was not as handsome as she had thought. But she was young, quite young. "This is Martha Gellhorn. She's a writer. Here on vacation with her mother."

"In Key West?"

Ernest smiled. "Where else?"

Martha put out a tawny hand. "Ernest has told me all about you."

Fife gave Martha a varnished smile. She then addressed herself to Ernest: "You," she said, "are very late for dinner."

"Is there enough for another?" He walked up the drive and didn't wait for a response. "I'll ask Isobel for an extra place." He left the two women out on the gravel path, looking anywhere but at each other.

*

After dinner that night the rain clouds burst and the temperature of the room instantly fell. "I should go," Martha said, as if the storm had induced the awareness that she was not wanted here by any save Ernest.

"Coffee?" asked Fife with little enthusiasm. Isobel had already served the sherry and cookies which no one had touched. Martha shook her head.

"I'll get you in the right direction," Ernest said, picking up two umbrellas from the elephant stand in the hallway. As she watched him Fife remembered the nights he had accompanied her home in Paris. And was it there? Did she make it up? Or did she see Martha Gellhorn lick her lips like a cat waiting for a sparrow?

Later Fife helped the cook clear the table. Sara had gone to bed, pleading a headache. Rain came down in sheets, graying the world outside the villa, spraying the banyan trees and the big crowned palms. Fife drank two tepid glasses of water to flush out the wine. Then the gate swung open for the second time that night.

Cigar smoke wafted into the hall. Gerald was outside and she heard him offer Ernest a smoke. Fife moved to the living room where she could hear them better. Gerald said something that she couldn't hear over the rain, but Ernest's reply came back perfectly clear: "Oh, for God's sake, man!"

"You've only just got rid of Jane and now . . . who even was that girl?"

"Leave out of it, Gerald. She's a writer!"

Fife had only ever known Gerald as a mild-mannered

man and here he was, braving Ernest as if it were nothing. "She's trouble, don't you see? Don't you see how sick everyone is of all of this?"

"Not all of us are as blessed as the heavenly Murphys." Ernest's voice was low and edged with threat, as if he was about to sock his friend in the jaw. "This has nothing to do with you."

The front door opened and with it came the smell of rain and cigar smoke. Ernest stood looking at her, knowing full well she had heard all of this. For moments they looked at each other dumbly until Fife took the plate she was holding back into the kitchen, leaving her rain-soaked husband making a puddle of himself by the doorway. And the cook had shot her a knowing look.

Martha stayed in Key West for two weeks that winter. In the days, Fife hid herself away in the toolhouse, since Ernest had no need for it, while he chatted to Martha about writing, war, and Spain. Only when Martha had caught her weeping into the sofa cushions did she take the hint to get out of Key West.

Just as Fife thought they had been left in peace, Ernest chased after her. He didn't mind telling her they'd had a steak in Miami and that they had trained their way to Jacksonville with a bottle of merlot for company while Ernest made up some business trip to New York. Fife wondered if they shared a carriage room. It killed her to think of his hands on her skin, her young body unscarred by babies.

Martha sent her a letter from St. Louis that January addressing Fife as *Cutie*. In her tone of lithe boredom Martha wrote how she was going to commandeer a boat, or head to the Himalayas—wherever might amuse a girl like her. She said Ernest's writing was hot stuff. Martha wrote how swell it was of Fife not to mind her hanging around for the past two weeks, becoming an installation, like one of the kudu heads pinned to the walls. And if she were to keep a journal, the letter continued, it would be chockablock full of nice words about Fife.

Would it now? Fife thought, folding up the letter which she did not reply to, because the words in return would not be so fine about you. She had never enjoyed the sight of a kudu head again: those spiraling antlers reminding her of Miss Martha Gellhorn: writer, war correspondent, husband snatcher.

If only it might be Martha's head that could be displayed on a spike.

20. KEY WEST, FLORIDA. JUNE 1938.

Still their détente continues; still terrible news comes from Europe. What happened, Fife wonders, as she eats breakfast with the newspaper in front of her, to the Europe they once knew, where the only violence was the noon light of

Antibes? Hundreds are bombed in Alicante, Czech troops mobilize at the country's borders, and a madman in Berlin does just as he pleases. Maps are on each of today's newspaper pages and fracture lines are everywhere: Europe, a broken bone.

Ernest pads past her, coming from a bedroom they have once again shared. He sips at her coffee but winces, forgetting she takes it black.

"Do you think this is it, then? Another war?"

Ernest nods at a photograph of Chamberlain. He's so gaunt there are holes in his cheeks: he has the look of a scarecrow in a collared shirt and dickey bow. "Not if he can avoid it."

Fife follows him out to the back door where the sun blazes. His study is dark as an inkwell even in the Florida sun. "Will you be able to pick up the Murphys next Thursday?"

"The Murphys?"

"They're coming for the Thompsons' party, remember?" Fife steps out into the garden. "I told you when you got back." The pool's current reflects on his face so that she can't quite make out his expression. "We'll have to make something. I was thinking Titania and Bottom. I'll go as the queen and you as an ass. I doubt you'll find it too difficult."

"Next weekend's no good."

"Why?"

"It might be too much for them."

"Nonsense. It's just what they need." Ernest seems to

be sorting something out in his head. He is about to speak then reconsiders. "What's wrong?"

He stops, a hand on the iron railing. "It's just going well with the writing that's all."

"Should I call it off?"

But her desire to please seems to irritate him and he shakes his head. "No, no, Fife. Let them come." Ernest climbs the staircase and leaves the door open for the draft. Sounds of typing travel downward. If Martha is in his writing—if Fife can even detect her in the margins—she'll use the manuscript as kindling and throw a match to it. Or she'll sell it to Harry Cuzzemano for a dollar.

"I'll clear out the boys' room then," she shouts up at him, trying to remember the good mood she woke up with. But he's already writing, and he doesn't respond.

In the garden the lighthouse catches her eye and winks in the morning light. It makes her stop just a moment on the threshold of their house. She has told Patrick and Gregory a story that a little boy lives in that lighthouse alone, a boy from the city, with short black hair and dark eyes. When the boy felt alone in the night-time he would slip from the lighthouse, when it was still dark, and come down to the beach to talk to the sharks. This boy knew the sharks made his job easier because they kept the boats from smashing into the rocks, and he would feed them the fish he'd caught that day. For many years she could catch Patrick and Gregory staring up at the lighthouse, hoping to find the boy with big dark eyes staring down at them from the top window. She has not, she thinks, always been the terrible mother she thinks of herself as; this story had been a good one. Perhaps she might write it out so that they could have it when she cannot be with them.

Ernest continues with his own story upstairs. She goes back inside to get the second bedroom ready for the Murphys.

In the boys' room Fife throws Ernest's clothes in the laundry, amazed at the stink. Shirt after shirt comes up from the suitcases like nets of fish. Loose paper is everywhere, including one of her telegrams: *Come back darling, the studio is ready and there's an abundance of food.* Spare pens, a gas mask, a newspaper from when he'd docked in New York. A bottle of whiskey rolls across the floor, not a drop left. At the bottom there's a wrapped package from one of her favorite boutiques. A gift! What a return to form this is for Ernest.

Inside the wrapping paper is a blue dress, quite lovely, with two pockets on the lap and cross-stitch on the front. Really, the happiness of the past week, it's almost outrageous. She's never felt so high—aside, perhaps, from the time they were sneaking about Paris, when she would wait for the touch of his hand below the table at a dinner party. It had seemed, to Fife, as if Hadley saw Ernest as an astonishingly amusing party guest, but had never really expected him to stay long past dessert. It was as if Hadley had never felt that Ernest was hers; whereas Fife has never felt Ernest was ever anybody else's.

When she had come home from the hundred-day exile, Fife and Ernest were the talk of Paris. When they walked into the Closerie des Lilas or the Select, it made her feel special: to be Ernest's fiancée, his almost-wife. That vertiginous happiness: it reminded her of a party trick her father used to do when she was small. Very carefully she would step onto his hands from a raised table and he would carry her like that, on his palms, displaying her to a crowded room of aunts and uncles, like a statue on a plinth. Her father would shout, "Hold it!" when she wobbled, but she would soon fall off into the waiting arms of her mother. But while she was up there she loved to see the glowing cheeks and clapping hands of her family. And that's how she felt with Ernest: adored, and elevated, but with the faintest feeling that she could, at any time, lose her footing.

Fife hangs Ernest's gift next to the feathered dress and goes back into her sons' room. Ernest's work case is now the only one left. Friends have been bored stiff every time Ernest tells the story of how Hadley lost all of his work— stories! Carbons! His first novel! But the consensus is that nothing sacred had been lost. Ernest had moved on to such great work that people almost thought the loss rather a stroke of good luck. It had sharpened his writing.

But just as soon as Fife gathers the laundry she drops it back on the bed and walks over to that suitcase. The glass of the chandeliers sounds in the breeze. She's not supposed to touch his work case, not after Hadley. But the sounds of Ernest's typing travel from the toolhouse and she watches her hand pull back the zip. The case eases open.

Inside are pages of notes. A Loyalist rag. His horsehair shaving brush. Two paperbacks on war. Then there's another book and Fife's heart starts to race. The title is *The Trouble I've Seen*. The writer's name is embossed in gold. And her hands begin to shake.

A wire paperclip holds a photograph of Miss Gellhorn to the flyleaf. It's a press shot. There is the curved Picasso nose and the same apple cheeks. It feels outrageous that a photograph of this woman might be inside her house. Fife smacks the book shut then thinks again. She slips the portrait from the clip and turns it over, where the studio's name is watermarked against its backing. On this side there is Martha's handwriting. And the words are devastating.

The rain has the sound of static as it hits the car roof, as if the water has electrified the air. Knowing how treacherous Key West roads can be, Fife takes them slowly. She won't let her timely death release him. She didn't say to Ernest where she was going or even that she was leaving. She's dying for him to worry.

The air is chaotic with rain, salt, fish; the clouds low and edgeless, barely higher than the fog. Palm leaves buckle under water. Tarpaulin sags over conch shacks. People run under tented jackets. The roosters that so provoke her as they cock about the roads stay by the shops, their cold eyes surveying the wash. Mud, thin as sauce in the downpour, flies out from her wheels. When Fife nears the ocean she sees the whitecaps of the waves splash over the pier. Maybe a hurricane is coming. She drives out to the sponge docks and the empty open-air market. Along the roads the black mangroves and buttonwoods are lashed by rain.

Fife drives past the bordellos and hair-straightening shops; the women stare moon-eyed at the rainstorm outside. All she can think is how she hates this jerkwater town. She hates her husband. She hates Martha Gellhorn. The ice cream parlors are packed with islanders and tourists who have escaped the storm, but the thought of fruit ices—sweet soursop, sapodilla, sugar-apple—makes her feel nauseous. Fife drives, wondering what on earth she is meant to do.

Saint Mary, Star of the Sea, the only Catholic church in Key West, is a white building with high walls. Inside she wets her brow, genuflects, then sits at a pew. The air in here is velvety next to the loose stuff outside. One of the stained glass windows is a crude Virgin and Child: it reminds her of the portrait from Piggott, and the painting in Chartres.

How vehemently in a French church had she prayed for

one husband to leave his wife! And now Fife may well be losing the same man in her own church. It seems to her that these are, now, the irreducible components of marriage: theft, possession, recompense. And Ernest's affair with Martha: this may well be her reckoning.

On the back of Martha's photograph was her handwriting. Much worse than the dedication was the date:

Nesto,
Be mine forever!
Marty. May 27, 1938.

Just weeks ago. She was a fool to think it could have ever been over between them.

This church is so much smaller than the French church where she had asked God for Ernest Hemingway. Ambitions have narrowed along with these walls. Now, she only wants Ernest to love her, or to stay, even if he does have these passing affairs. Outside, the world is baptized in a spring rainstorm. Fife marvels at the depth of her unhappiness.

What do you want of me, she asks God, as she sits on the moth-bitten pew and looks up at her Christ. Atonement? Have I not atoned for Hadley? Must I accept Martha now as my just punishment? I am sorry, she says, oh God, I hurt.

In the quiet of the church the only offering she can give Him is sorrow.

*

When Fife gets home it's as if everything has changed. The bedroom is full of afternoon darkness. She switches on a few lamps but the pools of light do little to wake the room. In the wardrobe there is the blue dress. She will incinerate his gift in the fire can outside. Or take a pair of scissors to its skirt. She doesn't want it, not when she knows Martha and Ernest were together not less than a fortnight ago. Down the dress are mother-of-pearl buttons. When she looks at them closer she realizes they have melted onto the cotton. To the touch they are cold and ridged. Something about the ruined buttons makes her want to burst into tears.

"Ernest?" she shouts down the staircase.

Isobel answers from below: "He's gone out, ma'am."

Fife throws the dress back to the wardrobe. Clouds stack in the sky outside. She fixes herself a drink under the cook's silent watchfulness. But Fife won't say anything because Isobel won't say anything. Why does this woman never talk? It's infuriating the way her servants treat her.

Fife knocks back the drink and bounds up to the toolhouse. She rattles the door. No reply. She goes in anyway. The garbage overflows with the play's discarded drafts. Lottery tickets and magazine wrappers litter the floor. The typewriter is black and gleaming, its shape a curled-up cat. On the shelves are Ernest's books. Fife plays with the idea of slipping one of the signed books from the shelves. She could do it to poor *Nesto*. She could open the window and throw the play's pages to the cats. Or make one call to

Cuzzemano and have it all, conveniently, lost. After all, maybe Hadley had done the same thing. Maybe that story about the valise being stolen was just another piece of fiction and Hadley had tossed the case to the garbage. When Ernest wanted, he could do an outstandingly good impression of a shit. She could imagine how much a woman might want to teach him a lesson.

Fife sees the papers on his desk, piled up neatly next to the typewriter, the title page on top. The play is called *The Fifth Column*. When she turns to the next page there are only four words on it. My God, she thinks, he's done it: he has broken my heart.

To Marty, it reads, *with love*.

In the bathroom upstairs the mirrors butterfly her face. She looks like a child in the reflection, twinned with depthless images of herself. An infinite number of wronged women stare back at her with doleful black eyes. Her short hair, black as tar paper, blanches her face. Her head begins to ache. *Nesto*. She only wants her husband. If she does not have him, she'll kill herself, or him. She takes a sleeping pill and swallows it dry. All she wants is to stop thinking. She steadies herself on the cold ceramic of the sink, as if to hold on against the brain's whirring circus: the whole tottering lot of them—Fife, Martha, Hadley—a wheel of wives and mistresses, mealy grins and doughy skin and wet holes all just waiting for the joy of being fucked by Ernest.

Fife switches off the lamps in the room. Her headache sounds: *woomph, woomph, woomph.* The bedsheets are so heavy. After this afternoon's storm, the evening slides into a honeyed dusk. She would like a Parisian sky, with nothing in it but cloud, and the rain would be the consistency of sleet. She'd like her marriage not to fall apart in these hot summer nights, with the sweet smell of the banana trees wafting through the hurricane shutters. Outside, the night bugs hit the fly screens.

The next day she looks for Martha's dedication but it's not on his desk. That evening they eat at the Thompsons': crawfish, plantains, Cuban bread. The night is jovial but she can't join in and Ernest looks preoccupied. *Be mine forever.* The date: *May 27, 1938.* Fife skewers the crawfish with her knife and slowly chews. And for the first time since his return, Ernest sleeps in their sons' room.

21. KEY WEST, FLORIDA. JUNE 1938.

The Murphys arrive on Thursday with their daughter Honoria: she is a fine girl who resembles her mother. Sara and Gerald are as dignified as ever: tanned, rich, good-looking. Despite everything that has happened they look in such good health, as if the decade since Antibes hasn't left a mark. They leave their taxi in white suits that wouldn't look amiss on a tennis court. "Mr. and Mrs. Diver!" Ernest says, because he knows the reference will vex them: "Welcome!"

Fife whispers a terse "Ernest!" before he helps them with their bags.

After they have unpacked, Ernest, Gerald and Honoria take the boat out; Ernest has found a perfect spot where the sailfish are sweet. His hauls are becoming more and more colorful by the day: bonitos, yellow fish, barracudas, and amberjacks.

The women stay back at the villa to make the costumes for tomorrow night's party. Sara looks like she's going to melt with the joy of the summer heat.

"Your pearls," Fife says, "you're still wearing them."

Sara bites into the string. "Of course," she says. "They need the sunshine as much as I do." Her friend stays quiet for some time as if reheating by the poolside is a serious business.

Later she brings silver paper and tin cans from her room and they sit under the umbrella assembling their costumes with cereal boxes. "Robots," Sara says. "For the party."

"Wonderful."

"Oh, we're just recycling from one of the Paris parties," says Sara. "Do you remember that time when Zelda stripped in front of the band, and the trumpeter didn't know what to do? I remember his cheeks ballooning as she took more and more off. Scott didn't know whether he should put a stop to it or join in." Sara laughs and looks genuinely cheerful. "What did you and Ernest go as?"

"I went as Aphrodite." And now it's Fife's turn to laugh. "But I didn't go with Ernest. Hadley did."

"Oh, of course." Sara fiddles with the costume. "It's so easy to get all the time muddled. It feels like yesterday and yet a long time ago as well. I always assume you and Ernest were together for the whole time in Paris. It felt that way."

"We were barely there as a couple."

"The twenties in Paris. What fun." There is a tinge of irony to Sara's words. To Fife it seems as if that decade had been constant playtime, but as if, too, they had forgotten to look over to the school gates, where the faceless adults were waiting to tell them something grave. "We had a fine time, didn't we? A fine, brainless time."

Sara sits in the chair with all limbs akimbo for the sun. The poor snowbirds, Fife thinks: starved of light. "We used to be avant-garde and bohemian," Sara says. "Now I feel washed-up, out of the scene. Where do things happen anymore? Not on the East Coast, that's for sure."

Fife clips fabric roses to hairpins and weaves them into the long blonde wig. She once dyed her hair blonde, just to catch Ernest's eye. Sara wraps one of the cereal boxes around her chest, measuring for size. She glues the sides together and sets them upright in the sunshine. "These will be our chests. With buttons to make us speak and have things like emotions. Though I fear I already have far too many of them."

She begins to paint the boxes silver. "Sometimes, you can't believe they're gone," Sara says, as if from nowhere, but it must never be out of nowhere for her. Fife remembers how strictly the quarantine was carried out during Bumby's *coqueluche* to protect her kids; but Sara's youngest son Patrick had died a year ago of tuberculosis; and her eldest, Baoth, had died from meningitis in '35. Somehow, Sara's mania against germs makes her loss seem even worse than it already is. It makes Fife want to telephone her own boys to just check that they are well. How blessed we are despite everything, Fife thinks, when the Murphys have been so robbed. Thank God, too, for Honoria: who is such a delightful young woman that Ernest has become quite wrapped around her little finger.

"How's Gerald?"

"Oh, coping."

"Is he still painting?"

"He does what he can. I think depression gets in the way a lot."

"It's understandable. That he'd feel like that."

"Of course our grief is very *understandable*." Sara fixes her robot head to the boxed trunk. "Doesn't make it any easier, of course, knowing it's so very understandable." Sara steps back to survey her work. "Gerald paints," she says as she's chopping a can in two, then fixing the halves as eyelets to the box, "for a week or so, then he gives up. It's not a question of talent; it's more a case of seeing the purpose in doing it at all. I try to encourage him but there's little point if he draws no pleasure from it. What's the point in art no one else is going to see if it's not even fun to make? Might as well not bother. Look at Zelda. I think art can do very bad things to a woman's head. Just look at what it does to men."

"I think Zelda would have ended up there with or without her writing," Fife says. Neither of them says *sanatorium*.

Sara puts the finishing touches to her robots, which sit like two little kids themselves. "Scott always thought money was a great immunizer. But look where it's gotten him. It's ruined the Fitzgeralds. If they'd had half the money they would've had double their luck. Absolutely."

Sara sips from her drink. "Scott was always a deeply intelligent idiot. That week in Switzerland, when we all thought it was the end for Patrick, I counted them up. There were four novelists in the room that day. And I was sure that no one would ever write of it. They were too cowardly to write about what was real." She pauses and her voice sounds near to cracking.

"And yet it was like something out of a story. The ice melt on the mountains. The light on the snowcaps, the smell of pines. It was so quiet. I remember hearing a tree come down and wondering how far away it was. What the sound of timber might be like if you got your ear close. You know, I just wanted to be out in the cold. To get away from my dying son. How awful: to want to be away from your child. But part of me couldn't stand it anymore."

Sara picks up her brush and composes herself as she paints. She gives Fife a small, ironic smile. "Well. Good fortune harasses us all, does it not?"

When the costumes are nearly complete and Fife has fixed up a couple more cocktails, Sara says: "And so, dear Fife, what news of the Spanish Front?"

"I was afraid you were going to ask that."

"Oh dear."

Fife goes into the house to fetch what she has found this past week. When she returns, Sara looks up, one arm around her chest as if these European memories have made her cold.

"What do you have here?" Sara leafs through the pages of Martha's book. "We knew she'd written this."

"Look at the photograph. Clipped to the back."

Sara reads the inscription. "Oh," she says flatly, closing the book, laying her thin hands on the dust jacket. "Where did you find it?"

"In his work case. The one I'm not meant to fuss with to avoid a Hadley-style disaster. The date is the day they docked."

"Oh, Fife."

"Then I found the dedication for the play he's writing."

"It's for Martha?"

Fife flinches. "*Marty*—that's what he calls her. And it's made *with love*." Sara sighs and puts the book to one side. Her robot men stand behind her like sentries. "I remember when I had some say in this. I went to Paris last Christmas thinking I could find out what was going on. When I went to Sylvia's she couldn't cover up the fact that she'd thought me out of the scene. Sylvia knew about them, just as she'd known about me and Ernest before anyone else."

"You can't extrapolate the end of your marriage from a thrown look of Sylvia Beach. You do realize Sylvia probably hadn't seen you in a decade? Maybe she didn't recognize you."

"I told Ernest at the hotel where he could shove those books. I even offered to throw myself off the balcony if he didn't propose to *do* something. But nothing's changed. And now we're all in the same fucking jam as six months ago. Hell, let's call a spade a spade. We're in the same jam as Hadley and I were in a decade ago."

Sara crosses her legs. On the chair she looks as neat as a folding knife. "It's ridiculous for him to continue with Martha and be with you at the same time. You must give him an ultimatum."

Fife leans forward. She attempts to be as precise as possible. "Hadley gave Ernest an ultimatum that night of the party. I heard them from my room. She forced him into making the decision. And look what happened to them. *I* didn't win Ernest; *Hadley* lost him. Sara: I won't make the same mistake."

*

The telephone sounds from the house. Fife drops the wig and goes into the hall where Gerald had so robustly defended her two years ago.

"Pauline. Hello."

Her skin crawls when she hears his voice. "Mr. Cuzzemano. I've told you to stop bothering us."

"Pauline—"

"No one calls me that. Please stop."

She is about to put down the telephone. "Mrs. Hemingway, I am not calling about the suitcase." Something about Cuzzemano's voice makes her still her hand. "I am calling about a different matter altogether." There is a pause on the line, a crackling. She remembers what he said to her, at the party at Villa America, when no one was listening: *Miss Pfeiffer: I know you are fucking Mr. Hemingway*—in an attempt to blackmail her of Ernest's things. Fife had laughed and said, "Darling, you wouldn't find a person around this table who *doesn't* know I'm fucking Mr. Hemingway. Even his wife is on very familiar terms with that fact."

"Mrs. Hemingway," Cuzzemano says, with oily delicacy. "If there's any way, any way at all, you might procure any of the . . . aftereffects of Miss Martha Gellhorn, I would be able to pay you handsomely. Handsomely! Or any letters written by your husband to his . . ." He clears his throat with theatrical poise. "Affinity. Just look in his drawers, in his correspondence, for any of their love letters. You'd be anonymous: no one would even know—"

"Good-bye, Mr. Cuzzemano—"

"Know that I am here if your situation changes, and if my proposition becomes more attractive—"

The telephone rattles in its cage.

Sara has clipped back her bangs and her head is at full tilt to the sunshine. She is in the company of her robots, one of whose arms has fallen off and with it some of the paint, revealing the TOASTED CORN FLAKES lettering on its side. She opens one eye. "Who was it?"

"The grocer. We're late on a bill."

Fife makes daiquiris for them both. She thinks, as she stabs at the ice, of giving Harry Cuzzemano just what he wants. A small part of her wants to revel in her husband's ruin if Miss Martha Gellhorn is still around. She thinks again of the inscription. Those words. *Nesto. Be mine forever.* What did *forever* mean to that woman?

Ernest comes home with Gerald and Honoria that evening, tired, the stink of fish on them, zinc still on their noses. Fife imagines herself as one of his sailfish, hooked in at the mouth. He'll let the line out, let it slacken for a while. He will do this once, twice, three times, letting the fish go, as if it were free, before reeling it in and gaffing it on the boat. What a strange dance it is, until she comes in bleeding, reeled in by the nickel-plated rod.

They eat in the dining room that evening: her and Ernest, Sara and Gerald. Martha is their fifth guest at the table: invisible and mute but loud as hell.

22. KEY WEST, FLORIDA. JUNE 1938.

They arrive at the Thompsons' party gorgeously dressed. Sara and Gerald make the most perfect robots. No one in Key West high society—if there is such a thing on this Floridian backwater—has ever dreamed of such costumes. The locals are dressed as pirates or sailors, mermaids or Hawaiian girls; nothing like this mechanized couple from up north.

Sara and Gerald are all silver boxes and geometrical shapes, with tin cans on their heads for goggles. They have a wobbling gait when they walk; Honoria screeched in pleasure when they had clomped down the stairs, but still declined the invitation to join them.

Ernest and Fife are Bottom and Titania. Fife wears flowers in a wig of blonde crimped hair; painted flowers climb her chest and ivy wraps her arms. She wears a bra of shells and a grass skirt; she is half mermaid, half fairy of the woods, but they did well for making it all yesterday.

Ernest's donkey's head is stuck with fur; tufts of it hedge his eyes. They should have made the eyelets bigger: Ernest complains that his lashes scratch his eyes. His lids are at constant blink, as if he is trying to send a message to the world in code.

The guests at the party are a little more understated. There are white Key West fisherman who have painted themselves darker to look Cuban: with their loincloths they look more like a group of oversized Gandhis than dockyard Cubanitos. Peacocks and cats roam among them.

An Adolf Hitler marches past with a little mustache. He seems a bad-tempered man; it turns out later he is one of the Thompsons' cousins from Jacksonville. "Give us a goose step, Adolf," says Ernest.

"Or a *Heil Hitler*, at least," says Gerald.

Adolf resists. Fife wonders why he chose such a costume if he didn't want to join in. "Go on," she says. "Tell us how Europe has to be a good boy or else you'll eat it up!"

Sara joins in. "Now, now, Adolf, indulge us! Quick march. Pretend I'm a Czechoslovak ready for a ravaging!"

Adolf squeezes the paper cup, his silly mustache adding to his peevish refusal to join in. "If Herr Hitler is so under-confident he'll never get on in the world," says Gerald, whose face is so sweaty it's rubbed off the mask's gray paint. His lips are quite pink. "Did mother not love you enough, *mein Führer*?"

"Do shut up, love. The poor man's already lamenting his costume choice." Sara pulls Gerald by one of the goggles which breaks off from the mask. "Oh, Gerald," she says warmly, "you do look ridiculous."

"No more than you do, my dear. Besides you've *ruined* my costume."

"It was a pile of crap anyway."

"This was made by the hands of a New England socialite! How dare you!"

"You'll just have to make do."

"Fife, tell me if you want me to send this coarse old woman home. No wonder I never invited her to meet my mother; I couldn't introduce her to the servants without blushing."

Gerald kisses his wife handsomely on the mouth.

The sight of them together makes both Ernest and Fife smile. They've not been the best versions of themselves these past few years. Not like Sara and Gerald, the stoics among them. Living well, they insisted, was the best revenge. And sometimes, Fife could almost be convinced that this was true. Later, she watches bashful Adolf in an elegant waltz with a tall woman, perhaps his wife. Perhaps he wasn't shy. Perhaps he just didn't like being bullied by this group of semi-Europeans from up north.

The two couples take turns with husbands and wives; they still drink as much as they did in Paris, though now they marvel at their hangovers. At least, tomorrow, Fife will not think about Ernest and Martha. The four friends will sit by the pool eating, nursing their heads, then go off to bed. The hangover: such a cure, she thinks, for overthinking.

Ernest keeps on adjusting the mule mask. He seems nervy and his eyes look sore. He flings her about the dance floor when it's their turn to dance, and then lets off a donkey's bray that makes the robots and his fairy queen laugh. But he keeps on doing it, won't relinquish the game, until Gerald tells him to shut up, and Ernest walks off. Fife remembers Gerald's words from that dinner party two years ago: *Don't you see how sick everyone is of it?*

There has been a request from the floor and the band starts up a slower tune. The piano begins, and the trumpet over it. Couples dance as close as their costumes allow. Sara is taken up by a bald Gandhi, and Gerald takes Fife in his arms. Over his shoulder she sees Ernest in the kitchen, rifling through the cupboards for something stronger.

The singer's voice rasps as she begins "All of Me." It is a lovely number, so melancholy and blue. The song is so full of sadness, it nearly knocks the breath from her, as the singer offers her lover just about every last part of her to take away with him as he leaves her. The trumpet now begins. The singer pauses to watch him and her hips kick at the beat. Fife wonders whether she grieves for a man she loves, or had once loved.

Other words circle in Fife's mind: *Nesto. Forever. To Marty, with love.*

"You look very beautiful with your hair like that," Gerald says as they dance. At this angle she looks up at his full neck and chin, and she loves Gerald for his middle-aged plumpness.

Fife rests her head against his shoulder. "You're nice to me. You always have been. But then you're nice to everyone."

"You are funny, sometimes." They stop. She feels her shoulders give. "Are you all right?" Gerald asks. He leans in to her. "Are you crying, Fife?"

"No, I'm fine," she says. "Everything's fine." But she feels as if Ernest is about to take all of her, just as the song says, her heart, her mind, her mouth, every last one of her limbs. As she turns away from Gerald she notices the singer, too, has tears in her eyes as she just about manages to sing, through her tears, the last refrain of the song. It is a requiem, and it fills the night.

Rain comes for the second time that week. The guests—who are hot and disheveled from the Charleston and the hop, with the Cubanitos whiter and the mermaids less scaled—rush under the garden's canopy to wait for the downpour to end. Everyone looks happy and drunk, smeared in each other's face paint.

The New England robots are sitting on the other side of the enclosure's wall, laughing and pointing at the food: turtle stew, jewfish, plantains. Fife watches her friends pile their plates, then she catches Ernest slip through the crowd. He turns back momentarily with a watchful look then walks down the side of the house. Fife follows him, dodging around the guests whose faces are rosy under the red bulbs.

Ernest is in the back garden, talking to a woman in a black dress. She wears a cat mask with perfectly pointed ears. Her hair is done up in a neat chignon, and the string leaves a shadow line where it cuts her golden hair. When Ernest goes to pull the woman's mask, she bats him away.

Is this why he didn't want the Murphys here? Because he'd invited his mistress to vacation with them?

Her mother had told her once that even when she was a baby Fife could be left alone on a chair and would never fall off. "Like an angel on a pinhead," her mother had said. And Fife wonders what's wrong with her; why she is sitting so still, watching events unfold and doing nothing. She must do something; she cannot sit still forever.

Ernest and the woman laugh as they shelter under the eave until the woman says something and looks ready to leave. Ernest watches her walk away, but his stare is one of accomplishment, as if, later in the night, he will come to possess what he appears to be losing now.

Fife moves, knowing she has to be bold to get this right. She sees Ernest warning her off but she catches up and with one movement she pulls the woman's mask so hard she can hear the elastic give. She is all ready to confront the face she'd found at the dinner party, and in the photograph, but it's not her. It's not Martha. The mask sits on the woman's head like a hat. And Fife feels like such a fool. "What are you doing?" Ernest says.

This unknown woman gives an edgy laugh.

Fife stares at them, incredulous, before turning on her heel and running from them both.

Gerald and Sara's eyes are on her as she bolts through the party. She heads for the beach, letting the air fill her lungs. A car swerves to avoid her. On the beach she feels the sand fill her shoes but she won't stop until she reaches the shore.

Yards from the waterline, she comes to a stop, watching the black water turn white as the breakers reach the sand. She hears Ernest coming after her. "What's gotten into you?"

"Oh for God's sake." She rips off the wig. Her scalp has been itching all night and she wishes now she had claws so she could scratch with a deeper trawl. "I found your dedication, Ernest. *For Marty with love*, is that it? I saw what she wrote to you in her book. Why did you bother coming back here, and being so nice, if you were still writing love notes to each other?"

Back at the house featureless faces stare down at them on the beach.

"Fife, don't make a scene."

"I will do what I want. Since that's what you do all the time, isn't it?"

"No."

"You're pathetic. You're worse than pathetic. You're a psychopath!"

"Fife!"

"Why toy with me as you have the last two weeks?" She stops, genuinely interested as to what the answer could be. "It's made the god-damned disappointment so much worse." Fife bites into her lower lip. "You have broken my heart, Ernest, over and over again. At least, while we were enemies this past year, you couldn't do that anymore. But this couple of weeks, even while everyone was warning me; Sara, and Hadley—"

"You brought Hadley into this?"

"Surprisingly enough she could empathize with the situation." Fife puts up a hand. "If you leave this marriage, Ernest, you'll marry Martha and then you'll find you just want another one. You always love at the beginning, when it's easiest to love. And if you go through life like that you'll never get past the start." Fife waits for him to say something but Ernest stares morosely at his boat shoes. His hands hang unmoving.

"I can't have three people in this marriage. At least tell me you're in love with her. Be brave. Or are you a hero only in war?" Waves break mournfully by their feet. Fife counts each breaker. Ernest doesn't say anything. "Are you in love with her?"

"I don't know."

Something in her collapses. What is it? Dignity perhaps. "Please don't leave me," she says, though it breaks her heart to have to beg him like this. But she adores him. She has never loved a man more than she has loved Ernest; she knows she never will again. "Stay with me."

Ernest looks back up at the house. The partygoers have gone back inside. He looks back to her. She thinks he may relent. "I can't," he says at last.

Fife suddenly feels very tired. She remembers the song. Well. She will not let Ernest Hemingway take every last piece of her.

"I won't divorce you, Ernest. Not for a long time, if that's what you're hoping. You can go to hell, for all I care. I won't let you marry that woman." Fife spits out her name at last. "Martha Gellhorn. If we hadn't had this week, I would let you go much more easily. But you gave me grounds to hope. And you'll be punished. I swear it."

Ernest makes a grab for her, and Fife—not quite consciously—socks him on the jaw. The shock of it—because it can't be the power—makes him stumble into the surf. "You chickenshit coward!" she screams. "I could kill you!" And for a moment she thinks she might just take his neck and hold it under the surf. She would rather kill him than have him be the possession of a woman who is nowhere near her equal. This is why her love is better than Hadley's, better than Martha's. No one, ever, will love him like this: enough to see his brain smashed into rock or his lungs fill with brine. Ernest picks himself up, nursing the jaw, and brushes the sand off his pants.

"You bastard," she says, "you don't even know what you've lost."

Fife starts by pulling books from the shelves, looking for whatever might hurt him the most. She puts them into piles of signed and first editions. She opens the books she thinks are most bankable and starts writing down information: the book's edition, publication city, date. She looks for his marginalia; his graffiti would add another zero to the selling price.

Later on, sounds travel up to the toolhouse. It's the Murphys, returned from the party. They sit by the poolside after Gerald has made tea. Ernest must still be at Sloppy Joe's.

Fife watches them, ginned and alone, in Ernest's study above. Down by the pool they sit in what's left of their costumes: a cereal box here, a spring there; both have lost their eyes. "So it's over? That's it?" This is Gerald. He nurses his mug between his hands. "Why does he have to be such an ass?"

"I think he tries hard not to be cruel. Then sometimes he's so savage, you have to stop excusing him." Sara starts ripping Gerald's robot costume to shreds.

"What are you doing?" he asks her, laughing.

"I'm finding your heart and leaving my initials there. So every woman around will know you're mine." Sara has now completely de-robotted Gerald and she kisses him on the chest near his heart.

Fife slumps down by Ernest's desk. It kills her to see this. She imagines how many other women there will be, sitting at their typewriters somewhere in the Midwest, or reading a Hemingway book in their fine English lawn, or on assignment in China, not knowing that they'll be plucked from obscurity to be the next Mrs. Hemingway.

From the pool she hears Sara's voice again: "Promise me you'll never go away."

"I'm not going anywhere."

Fife gets up. The pen's bleed has thinned the paper

for Cuzzemano. She screws it up in her fist; she cannot do it.

When she leaves the toolhouse she sees Sara and Gerald are asleep on one sun lounger, curled into each other under the Florida night sky, surrounded by the remains of their robots. And around them, walk the peacocks.

MARTHA

23. PARIS, FRANCE. AUGUST 26, 1944.

The Pig, they say, has liberated the Ritz.

In an altogether different hotel, Martha lies in bed, imagining Ernest on his favored bar stool ordering martinis for his troops. He'd be thinking, no doubt, about his life here in the twenties, when he was poorer and happier, a man only once married. His Paris life is a memory Ernest loves to slide over and over until the place is smooth and cool with his affections. Today he would surely be longing for the sawmill apartment and his lost Saint Hadley: a woman all the more exquisite for her generous retirement of the title *Mrs. Hemingway*.

A title Martha has come to hate.

Martha has always felt more affection for the Mrs. Hemingway she robbed. At least Fife had the guts to hate her; she had no time for Hadley's mousy surrender. To be so good seemed a calamity visited upon the poor woman. Apparently Hadley and Fife are even pals still: by Ernest's accounts his two ex-wives chat regularly on the telephone, talking of children and the proper care of Ernest. Martha and Fife have never spoken since that vacation in Key West. Why would they? She has a proper respect for the rules of this game.

Ernest cradles the memory of Hadley as he would a

baby. Fife he castigates as the devil. After today, Martha wonders which one she will become.

In bed she tends a bottle of whiskey; the alcohol keeps her straight-thinking. Her journey to Paris yesterday was not an easy one and she feels a pain in her chest—it might be a broken rib. When she arrived at the Hotel Lincoln this morning, typewriter, knapsack, and bedroll in hand, the concierge had told her with great enthusiasm the story of her husband's escapades when he saw the name in her passport. Apparently, Ernest had liberated the Ritz with a troop of soldiers, sending the men from the Luftwaffe and their whores scurrying from their beds.

None of this should be a surprise to her: Ernest loved being in the limelight wherever he went. Boxer, bullfighter, fisherman, soldier, hunter; he can't go anywhere without playing the hero. Often, over the course of these years, she has longed for the plain friend she made in Spain.

More of the whiskey helps her nurse her outrage. Martha hates the way he throws himself around a city with all the swagger of a warlord. She hates, too, that other people can't see past his phony heroism. So he has liberated the Ritz! Of course he would.

The Pig knew it was the one place that wouldn't have run dry.

But today Martha will show him he can't trick everyone. Today she will be the one to rip open his idea of himself, and she will do it with claws. Because today they are done and through, and she will throw away the name Mrs. Hemingway with as much gusto as his ex-wives slavered over it. Today, Martha will leave him.

The air in her hotel room is insufferably warm. An odor wafts in of scorched wood, of things having been burned. She has left the windows open so that she can hear the cries of the Parisians, but also so that the panes won't smash if the fleeing Germans were to indulge in leftover shells. Gunfire only briefly interrupts the singing of "La Marseillaise."

Martha wears her pajamas, the same ones she wore when she was evacuated from a Helsinki hotel five years ago. She had asked Ernest if he would come with her to cover the Finnish war, thinking it might be good for them to re-create the dangers of Spain. But Ernest said he wanted to shoot duck in Sun Valley. Funny that it had been Ernest who had first lit her interest in the battlefield while his wife brought them cocktails in the shade of mimosa trees and banana palms, and now it was Ernest who wanted to make house while she went off to war.

Martha rises from the bed. Flags drape from the opposite building and boys cock about the pavements with carbines, as if they had single-handedly driven *les boches* to the gates. Well, good for them. The recriminations will come later—who colluded, who resisted—but not today. Today everyone is jubilant.

In the bathroom the washbowl faucet creaks with the old plumbing. Her hair could do with a wash; the Jeep's fumes are still in it from last night, but instead she rolls the curls to her neck. She pulls on a white shirt and her army jacket with the "C" for correspondent. Martha uses some black-market lipstick she bought in London and wonders where she will find her husband. Who knows? Perhaps he is planting a flag at the Arc de Triomphe. She wouldn't be surprised to hear Ernest has freed the whole City of Light single-handedly.

In her satchel she gathers her things—notebook, purse, and hotel key. For luck she takes an extra shot of the whiskey. She will watch how Paris frees itself: take notes, heed its guidance. Fleeing the shadow as the wife of one of the most famous writers in the world: is she mad to leave him? Her father would have thought her mad—but then her mother had thought her mad for marrying him in the first place.

The concierge gives her an oily smile in the lobby. He looks desperate to talk more but Martha hurries on through the revolving doors. As she steps into the iced light of Paris she is immediately kissed on the lips. The man—he is rather handsome and tall—says, *"Vive la France!"* before strolling toward the crowd on the Champs-Élysées.

People kiss and drink on every corner. Perhaps each family saved a bottle of something good ready for this day. Men, as always, are first on the streets. A man released, she thinks, is worse than one imprisoned, and she does up the top button of her shirt. Spiked on their own glory, they eye her with an abandoned look; it might scare her, had she not seen it all in Spain. Kids hide in the shade by tanks and women wear the most enormous hats, the size of buckets. It seems quite the perfect day for her own liberation. Martha sets off into the city to break the news to Ernest Hemingway.

24. KEY WEST, FLORIDA. DECEMBER 1936.

Martha went to Key West to meet her hero, not marry him. In fact, the island had been rather an afterthought that Christmas holiday of 1936, somewhere to go after they'd run out of things to do in Miami.

All she wanted to do was talk about books with him. Perhaps pick up some tips. In her own writing she tried hard to manipulate the words so that they were cool and dry—just like his—as if worked by a mason from hard stone. She had even included a quote from *A Farewell to Arms* in her first novel: "Nothing ever happens to the brave." But if she weren't brave, she thought, as the Gellhorn family disembarked the ferry, surrounded by mangroves, sea grapes, and the most enormous palms, then she definitely would not meet him. And so she had worn the little black dress that her mother had said showed her off in the very best light.

They spent the day walking the key. As she walked

around the island she formed a vague outline for a travel piece about the persistence of the Depression here though it was nearly a decade after the crash. Raw board hung from the houses and everything looked in need of paint. Chickens roamed the streets, and the smell of garbage and the sewers was everywhere. Bordellos did a brisk trade and nobody seemed to mind. Everywhere there was abundance: banana, lime, coconut—fit to burst off the trees with a snap of the fingers. No wonder the Depression hadn't left: without work you could just as well eat by shaking down a tree. Still, the kids looked about as happy as they did in any other American backwater.

When they passed the Hemingway home—it had to be his, it was the biggest and richest-looking house on the whole key—Martha spied prowling cats and a water feature behind the high brick wall and locked gate. Her mother read aloud from the tourist map; the Hemingway home was on the attractions list. From what Martha could see, the garden was piercingly neat and well kept. The house was grand, its shutters open to the breeze coming off the Gulf. A woman's voice traveled over to them from inside the garden. "Fetch the scissors will you, Sara? I'm going to attack this poinsettia."

Mrs. Gellhorn looked up from her map and gave Martha a bright smile as if they had overheard something deliciously secret. "Oh, Martha, it's Mrs. Hemingway!"

Martha led her family onward; she thought them superior to the tourists come to gawk at the author's private quarters. Perhaps, she thought later, she should have knocked and introduced herself there and then. Perhaps, if she had met his wife first, things might have turned out a little differently.

By the afternoon they were hot and tired, and Mrs. Gellhorn suggested a drink. It was dark inside Sloppy Joe's and the bar looked like something salvaged from a boat wreck. Fans did little to move the air. As the Gellhorns sat themselves at a table, Martha had a memory from some magazine article that this might be the author's haunt, that Mr. Hemingway might even be here, killing the hottest part of the afternoon alone.

Because she'd imagined him being here, she had assumed he would not be. But there was Hemingway, looking older than the photograph of him she had tacked up on her college wall, coming directly from the pool table and seating himself at the bar. He was scruffier too. He wore a dirty T-shirt and basque shorts with a rope tied at his waist. Barefooted, as well. The barman, whose dark hands had been juicing limes, put a glass of greenish liquid in front of Mr. Hemingway without him even placing an order.

"*Un highbalito*," he said, and the author smiled and read his mail.

Martha straightened her back and cocked her head in a posture of listening to her mother while the scent of the limes spilled into the air. From the bar she felt herself observed.

Her mother was deciding volubly on the relative merits of a daiquiri or a gin twist in a louder voice than Martha would have liked when the penny dropped. "Oh!" her mother said, barely trying to temper her excitement or lower her voice. "Mr. Hemingway is at the bar, dear!"

Mrs. Gellhorn then looked up above Martha's shoulder. He must have come over. Martha willed the heat to leave her face. When she turned, she was as bold and as richly voiced as she could muster. "Mr. Hemingway," she said, standing, and put out her hand before he put out his. "I'm Martha Gellhorn. A pleasure to meet you, sir." She tilted her head; she had decided her beauty was best at this angle. And indeed he seemed pleased by the look of her.

Martha introduced her mother and brother, and Hemingway pulled up a chair to join them. "What are you drinking?" he asked Mrs. Gellhorn. "Have you had one of these?" Her mother took the offered glass and sipped at the drink. "I call it a Papa Doble."

"That's going to knock me sideways for the rest of the afternoon," Mrs. Gellhorn said. "I'll have one." She passed it to Martha.

Her mother was right: the drink was strong as hell and delicious.

"Skinner," he said. "Papa Dobles for everyone."

"Thank you, Mr. Hemingway," her mother said.

"Only the IRS calls me Mr. Hemingway. Please call me Ernest. Or Papa."

Though he might be a decade or so older than Martha,

there was no way she was going to call him Papa. Ernest would do just fine.

They talked at first about Key West and what they had seen and what they thought. Ernest admitted he thought her brother was her husband and laughed when he found out he was not. Everyone was quickly drunk by dusk and Martha thought it wonderful that they all were sitting there in the presence of a genius. *The Sun Also Rises, A Farewell to Arms, Death in the Afternoon*—as well as all of the short stories that writers studied for the inner trick of them. But there was no trickery: only the plain words put there as if they had always been there—like pebbles cooled in a river.

Martha, at twenty-eight, had only one book she was proud of; the rest of it, she thought, was the foulest *crotte*. She wanted to ask Hemingway questions without sounding like an ingénue: how does one edit one's work and know what was good and what was bad if one thought the whole thing, invariably, was rotten? When should one soldier on, and when should one just throw it to the trash?

They ordered more drinks and Skinner continued to work at the limes. At one point the barman shot her a meaningful look. Perhaps Ernest was expected at home by Mrs. Hemingway.

Later, when her mother and brother argued about the best route back to the hotel, Ernest addressed her privately. "Are you in love, Miss Gellhorn?"

Martha took a sip of her Papa Doble and laughed. "Why do you ask?"

"You look flushed. And happy."

"No," she said. "I am not in love."

"But you have been?"

"Of course."

"Who was he?"

"A Frenchman."

"Did you leave him or did he leave you?"

Martha drained the last of the drink. It really did taste wonderful. "I am not a woman apt to be left," and then she laughed at her absurd words. "I left him."

"I see." When he smiled he looked more like that college photograph. "Why did it end?"

"He wanted to marry me."

"And you didn't want to marry him?"

"No. His wife didn't want him to marry me."

"Ah," he said. "Wives are apt to feel like that." He finished his drink. What number was it for him? The man could drink like a fish. "How old are you?"

"Twenty-eight," she said.

"By that age I'd married my second wife."

"And how'd your first wife feel about that?"

"Not very pleased."

"Ah, wives are apt to feel like that."

"Touché," he said, then he stared at her for longer than was polite. Maybe because she was drunk Martha went ahead and stared right back until it was Ernest who looked away and she swore she caught Skinner, now done juicing the limes, roll his eyes.

"Why are you wearing your shorts like that?"

The frayed rope belt flopped on one side of his pants, like a snake sunning itself. "Because I like to."

"You look like you've just pulled your pants on and are about to take them off again."

"You might have just hit upon my plan."

But now her mother and brother were listening again and Ernest changed the subject. "Have you ever known war, Martha?"

She shook her head.

"I think you might like it. I met a woman like you in Italy in the Great War. She was a nurse at the Milan hospital." He paused for a moment as if lost in the memory. "I imagine you'd like living on the knife-edge."

"Did you enjoy it?"

"Some of it. Some of it was terrible. I remember after a munitions factory blew up and we were sent to recover the bodies. There was hair everywhere, tufts of it, clinging to the wire. The dead had faces like blown-up balloons. Lumps of flesh with bits of bone, that's all they were after the hit." Ernest's eyes had gone hard and smooth. "It took three days to clean up. I vowed that I'd never think war a good thing after that. And I don't. But there are good things about it for writers: it makes every minute seem a million bucks and all you want to do is kiss all the women you meet and hunt for the truth and write good words. Think you could do it?"

"Aside from kissing all the women, yes, I think I could."

"I'm going to the war in Spain. You should think about it. Where will you go after Key West?"

Martha shrugged. "Back to St. Louis."

"Both my wives are from there. You're from a noble tradition." His eyes search her face. "The Blonde Peril. That's what they'd call you on the Front Line, Miss Gellhorn."

Ernest insisted Martha eat with them that evening back at the villa. When they walked up to its gates, she was followed by the memory of her shyness that morning, hiding behind the brick wall.

Pauline Hemingway sat through supper pinched about the mouth and drunk but in a sour way. When Martha addressed her as Pauline, Sara Murphy practically spat out her bean soup. "Dear girl," she said, "nobody calls Pauline *Pauline*. It's *Fife*. From Pfeiffer: her maiden name"—she gestured to Ernest—"before she married this wretch."

"What do you think of Key West?" asked her husband, Gerald.

"I think it's the best thing I've found in America."

"I daresay," said Sara into her wineglass.

"If all the world were sunny there'd be much less trouble going on."

"There's a Midwesterner for you," Ernest said. "Hadley was the same."

Fife flashed her husband a look.

"What lovely flowers," Martha said, nodding at the arrangement in the center of the table. "What are they?"

"Poinsettia," said Fife a little sadly.

"Do you know the florists in Paris used to dye their flowers to make them brighter?" This was Sara. "I remember the streams in the gutters. Like rivers of blood some days."

"I lived in Paris," said Martha.

"What were you doing there?" asked Gerald.

"I was a journalist."

"For whom?" asked his wife.

"Anyone who'd have me. Often *Vogue*. I had to feign an interest in the French hemline."

"Fife was a reporter for *Vogue* too!" said Ernest.

Fife offered a thin smile. "Pass the salt please, Gerald."

During the meal Gerald kept on trying to make things jolly while Fife refilled everyone's glasses with miserable vigilance. Martha got into a wonderfully heated argument with Ernest on the merits of Proust while Sara Murphy positively glared at her throughout.

By the time his wife plunged the knife into the roast chicken, Ernest had positioned his hand on the inside of her now very warm thigh. Martha had quickly removed Ernest's hand before answering the question "Leg or breast?" with only the minimal amount of choked laughter.

At the end of the meal two little boys came into the room wearing heavy pajamas that looked sweltering in the heat. "Aha!" said Fife. Her face completely lost its watchfulness and became open and clear. It was at this point that Martha saw, for the first time, the woman's beauty. "We thought we heard mice upstairs, but it turned out it was you two!"

She tickled the little one's tummy and put the biggest boy onto her lap. Fife looked up at Martha from the crook of her boy's neck. And just minutes after positioning his hand on her thigh, Martha watched Ernest look at his wife with love.

The little boy climbed onto his father's lap. "Papa, who's this?"

"This, Gregory, is Miss Martha Gellhorn." Ernest leaned over to her. "I would ask you to shake his hand but as you can see . . ." The little boy had his thumb in his mouth.

Martha laughed.

"Miss Gellhorn's a writer. Like Daddy. And a very good one at that."

"You know in Germany they'd have to join the Hitler Youth at ten?" Gerald said.

"Ridiculous," said Sara. "I would never let Patrick go." The Murphys shared a look and Martha wondered what it meant. Gerald put his hand over his wife's and squeezed it. Sara's look was frozen somewhere.

"Hitler's a madman," Gerald said. "He belongs in the bughouse. We're lucky to be here."

"Lucky," Sara said. "Yes. Lucky, lucky."

"I think you've had enough fun for tonight, boys," Fife

said. She gave her eldest a kiss which was promptly wiped away.

When they left, Fife called in the cook to clear away the dishes. After Papa Dobles, white wine, and a whole day of sunshine, Martha felt just about in danger of falling off one of Mrs. Hemingway's exquisitely made dining chairs. And with the perfect timing of the rainstorm, it meant she could easily refuse coffee.

The next day Martha showed Ernest some of her work as they sat in the garden surrounded by exotic flowers for which she had no names. Fife had taken her on an exhaustive tour of the garden and Martha had hummed along, aiming for some genuine enthusiasm, but it was as if Mrs. Hemingway didn't understand that all of these things might have more importance to a woman in her forties than one in her twenties.

Ernest went at the story she gave him with a black pen, showing her what words could be lifted. "The bones," he said, following one of the sentences with his finger, as if helping her to read it: "That's all you need."

They were a cozy little family over the next few weeks. He edited her work, reading passages aloud so that they could hear the rhythms. In their conversations she felt valued and important: someone with whom to discuss ideas and test the weight of things. There might have been flirtation, but nothing more than was ordinary between men and women who looked good and wrote well.

More often than not Mrs. Hemingway spent the day indoors or up at the toolhouse. She said she didn't like the heat.

One morning Martha stepped into the house for a glass of something cold. "Bring me one too!" Ernest shouted and she noticed a shadow pass the toolhouse window.

In the kitchen she poured herself a lemonade and wandered over to the photographs of the Hemingways, neatly set out in their frames on the side table. There were lots of pictures of their sons, as well as the boy from the first marriage, Bumby. She wondered what Ernest was like as a father: probably absent most of the time and then, when present, exhilarating.

At the end of the table was a group shot with Ernest in the middle. Martha recognized Gerald and Sara and Fife, who looked rather startled in the magnesium flare. The other woman must be Hadley. Ernest had told her that they'd spent a holiday together in Antibes: wife, husband, mistress; the whole kit and caboodle. To Martha, it sounded as if they were all knocked out of their heads. This situation, she felt, did not even compare. After all, she was bedding down with a handsome Swede she'd found at her hotel. And even if Ernest did have romantic feelings for her, she did not have any for him. Martha replaced the strange photograph back on the side table and wondered why Fife allowed it in the house.

Then from another room came the sound of weeping.

In the living room the curtains were closed and at first

Martha could only see the animal skulls. Then she saw Fife on the sofa, facing the cushions. A big pile of *Vogue* magazines piled up behind her. When Mrs. Hemingway turned around, her eyes were raw and hopeless. "For God's sake," Fife said, very slowly, "why are you *still* in my house?"

Outside, where the white light sang again in her eyes, Martha said to Ernest, "I think you need to see to your wife. I think she is upset."

The next day she had herself well shot of Key West, of her Swede, of the Hemingways. It had not been her intention for Ernest to catch up with her for steak and fries and a bottle of merlot in Miami. Nor had it been her intention to start what began in Spain.

25. PARIS, FRANCE. AUGUST 26, 1944.

Martha heads south on the Champs-Élysées toward the Left Bank and Shakespeare and Co. If Ernest's been anywhere in Paris, he'll have been to rue de l'Odéon to find a good book.

Where the Louvre meets rue de Rivoli, there is a barricade at one end smoking, just visible in the streaked light of the summer morning. When Martha draws close she sees the dam is made up of bedsteads, park railings with roots still attached, and a door with its handle scorched.

There are holes in the ground where cobbles have been lifted for the barricades. On the wind is the smell of the lavatory. A man motions for her to stop. He has a leathery face and an easy snarl. "Can I pass?"

"You're French?" he asks.

"American."

He smiles at her warmly. "But what a fine accent for a little American! What are you doing in Paris?"

"Reporting on the war." And, she thinks, divorcing a husband. "I'm a journalist."

"Journalist for whom?"

"*Collier's.*"

He places his hand on her forearm. "Tell them what is happening here," he says. "Leave nothing out." Dirt has gathered in his nails, and his hands are black with oil.

She says, "*Vive la France!*" and walks away, trying to wipe off the muck from his touch.

"*Vive les Américains!*" he shouts back.

The source of that latrine smell is just up ahead: a urinal, pulled from the metro, has been lifted onto the embankment of scraps. Its pearled hole gleams with a yellowy wash. Martha walks by it—but when she turns to share the joke with the Resistance man, he's staring openly at her retreating behind. It's not dissimilar to the look in Italy her officer gave her a few weeks ago. Oh yes, she has had her own affairs these past few months. Ernest merely had to bare his teeth and his ex-wives and mistresses would be willingly swallowed whole if that were his pleasure. But she is different from the rest of those women, those lapdog wives.

Soon she's close to the river and can see the oily flash of sunlight on the Seine. On the Île de la Cité there are crowds of people, sitting and drinking on the grass in the shade of Notre Dame. Breakfast picnics have been made from whatever food they have. Accordionists compete against each other for thrown coins. A man in a low-brimmed hat stands on one corner, chanting: *Chocolate, American cigarettes, matches, chocolate, American cigarettes . . .*

As Martha walks over the last bridge, she rehearses the lines Ernest will in all probability use on her to win her back. "Rabbit . . . come back to me, we are stronger together . . . we can't live through the horrors without each other." She thinks of all the hateful things he's ever said to her: the times he's called her worthless, ambitious, on the make, a bitch. She remembers the time he slapped her after she'd driven his Lincoln Continental into a tree, the time he'd cabled her when she'd been on assignment: ARE YOU A WAR CORRESPONDENT OR A WIFE IN MY BED? (And she'd written back: WILL ALWAYS BE A WAR CORRESPONDENT STOP WILL BE A WIFE IN YOUR BED WHEN I CHOOSE STOP YOUR WAR CORRESPONDENT, YOUR WIFE, YOUR MARTHA.)

She thinks of how, months ago, he had cadged a flight with the RAF over to England, leaving her to make her own way to Liverpool from America on a freighter packed with dynamite. What a kind gift that had been from her dearest husband. Every hour spent on the ocean crossing she had worried the dynamite would blow up. She wasn't even allowed to smoke on the deck. But it was seventeen days to think things over, seventeen days to realize her marriage had come to its end.

After she docked in Liverpool Martha traveled south to London, where Ernest was in hospital. He'd been admitted after an automobile accident, probably motoring along in the blackout like a drunk loon. She had been ready to tell him they were through: that she was sick of his drunken accidents, his misadventures, his precious little care for her, or himself. But for minutes she watched him asleep in the dusty room. A great bandage circled his head and made a thicket of his hair. How tired he looked, poor thing—and how different from the man she had met in Sloppy Joe's, who had charmed her with that electrifying smile over a cocktail named after him. Now, his face was fleshier. He was no longer so handsome; he could no longer turn a room.

Ernest slept under a vase of tulips and Martha pulled a petal from one of the heads, wondering who had brought them. Despite all of Ernest's faults, he was always quick to charm people, quick to love those who were real and honest and genuine. Blood smeared the bandage, and Martha wondered just how he was going to survive himself. And, without having said a word, she slipped away.

Now, as she walks over to the Left Bank, she knows today must be the end for them. As she heads toward

Shakespeare and Co., Martha lets all of the other bad memories run their course. Ernest is a great talker; she must not be seduced into staying.

Today, books return to Paris. Two women cart boxes and clothes baskets down to the sidewalk. A man follows them with light fittings, paintings, manuscripts, tables, chairs. Martha keeps herself from view as she watches them go up and down to a third-floor apartment above the shop. The letters of the shop's sign are only just visible: SHAKE-SPEARE AND COMPANY. Everyone looks hot and rather happy.

Martha and Ernest had come to Shakespeare's on one of their breaks from the Spanish war and Sylvia had embraced Ernest as if he were a man resurrected. It was in this store that Martha had fallen in love with him. For a year or so she'd thought that having each other in Spain was only about survival. Maybe it was the books on the walls, the way Sylvia looked at him adoringly, the way he said "Marty, Paris," when they looked over the city's gray sloping roofs, but it was in this place that everything seemed to fit. Ernest had captured her heart not in Sloppy Joe's or in Madrid, but among the books of Paris. *Nesto*, she'd later written on the book of hers he'd bought from Shakespeare's: *be mine forever*. And at that point she had meant it: the word *forever*.

A bell rings her entry. For a moment Sylvia Beach stares at her blankly. Sylvia is famously warm to everyone but today, evidently, she can't remember who this is standing on her doormat.

"Martha!" she says, remembrance coming back quickly. There's a hint of mustache as Sylvia kisses her. "Adrienne, come here quick, Martha Gellhorn is here!"

A tall woman with a stiff smile enters the room carrying a basket full of books. "Martha, dear," she says, putting down her load. "How good it is to see you. Let me get you something to drink." She returns from the pantry with a glass of water spiked with grenadine. "Sorry there's nothing more potent. *Pas de gin, pas de whiskey, pas de vodka.*"

Martha laughs. "*Pas de problème.*"

Adrienne seats herself by the cash register. The carpenter is still installing it onto the desk, and the keys jingle as if he is putting through receipts for thousands of francs. "What happened here?"

Sylvia raises her quite bushy brows. "An unfortunate episode with a man from the Gestapo."

"How do you mean?"

"Let's just say he thought he deserved his copy of *Finnegans Wake* more than me."

"I never knew Fascists went in for Joyce."

"Oh, yes. He asked how much it was and I said it was my own personal copy. Then he said if he couldn't have this book, he would remove all of them."

"And?"

Adrienne laughs: it's rich, mischievous, smoky. "In two

hours we put everything into hiding. We cleaned out the whole shop—*les boches* never found a thing."

The carpenter announces he's finished and Sylvia settles the bill. Sylvia, in particular, seems older, her features a little harder, as if she has known hunger these past few years. "How has the war treated you?"

"Kind in some respects. Unkind in others."

There are some moments of silence before Sylvia speaks again.

"We had a fine system during the war, didn't we, Adrienne? I'd forage for berries and fruit. Adrienne would line up at the bakers. We became as obsessed with food as we had been with books. And even books didn't matter so much anymore. We considered eating them, at one time. Or smoking them, at least."

"You were in Paris for it all?"

"A brief spell in Vittel—"

"The watering hole?"

"Well, it's not quite the spa experience when you can't get out."

"An internment camp?"

"For American Lady Expatriates." Sylvia says it delicately, as if she is mocking herself. "It wasn't so bad. First they drove us out of Paris but they didn't know where to put us. So they put us in the zoo at the Bois de Boulogne."

"The zoo?"

"No idea where the animals had gone. I was in the

baboon house, which I quite liked. All that monkeying around."

"That," Adrienne snorts with French derision, "is a ridiculous joke."

Sylvia cracks a smile. Perhaps this was why Ernest had always warmed to her, this refusal to take anything seriously. Though he has made so many enemies from friends, Sylvia Beach he had always loved. "They eventually moved us to a converted hotel in Vittel. English aristocrats, artists, tarts and nuns . . . countless chambermaids too—I never did work out what they were there for. They considered the whole thing a rather luxurious holiday. Rightly so."

Martha notices Adrienne has looked away, unable to keep up with the comedy of Sylvia's storytelling. "Adrienne has been here, however, keeping stock of things. Just to make sure we'll always have one foot in the marketplace of suppressed literature."

Martha wonders how bad it was for Adrienne, stuck in Paris without Sylvia; she seems to find the whole story decidedly less comic. "And you, Martha? Where have you been?"

"Oh. Anywhere the Front is."

"You're still reporting?"

"Of course."

"Now listen, Martha, Ernest's been here." The mention of his name makes her feel strange. Shakespeare's is a treasured place, and it's beginning to dent her resolve. Suddenly she feels an urgent need to find Ernest and make sure he is all right. Her emotions all morning have veered between outrage and a mad desire to be close to him; she wishes she could feel more constant in her thoughts. "I knew he'd come here first."

"Why, of course, dear. 'Paris without a good book is like a pretty girl with only one eye.' Who said that, Adrienne?"

Adrienne rolls her eyes and takes the empty glass back into the pantry. "Balzac, *chérie*," she says, with the sound of the faucet running in the back. "But he said it about dinner without cheese."

"Martha," Sylvia continues, still excited, "your husband practically liberated the shop! I heard a familiar voice shout, 'Sylvia! Sylvia!' then I heard the whole street begin to chant my name. It was joyous, dear: really so thrilling. He went up to the attic to clear the rooftops of German snipers. Then he made sure the store was completely secure and afterward we all celebrated with brandy— then he said he was off to liberate the Ritz cellar. Wonderful!"

That longing Martha felt moments ago seems to have sunk somewhere near her ribs. Everywhere she goes she finds herself in the shadow of Ernest's propaganda. It is exhausting: her husband's need to self-aggrandize. In her articles she writes about small stories, about things observed up close: in his reportage there is always Ernest, the great writer, standing in the middle of the story like a fat dictator orating in a square somewhere.

Sylvia asks where she is staying. "Oh. We're staying

separately." Sylvia's eyes look nervously to Adrienne. "It was a mutual decision. And Ernest? Where is he?"

"The Ritz," says a male voice from the back of the shop. "I hear he saved them as well." The man she had seen outside the shop walks into view.

"Oh, Harry," Sylvia bursts into a smile. "I forgot you were there! Have you been eavesdropping all this time?"

"You didn't hear me come down?"

"Martha, do you know Harry Cuzzemano? He's a book collector. He's known your husband for years."

"Only by reputation."

Harry Cuzzemano steps out from the bookshelves. A long scar runs from eye to chin, the sutures still visible. "A pleasure to meet you, Mrs. Hemingway."

"Any success yet on Ernest's suitcase?"

He gives a hasty laugh. "Oh, I gave up on that quite a while ago. Apparently it may not have even happened."

"Oh, I doubt that. I think it's very true indeed. Gosh, just imagine if someone finds it before you. What a waste of time that would have been."

He flushes. Sensing danger, Sylvia intervenes. "If I found it, I'd sell it back to Ernest for a mint. We'd own our own island in Antigua. Imagine, Adrienne!"

Martha has been caught by Cuzzemano inspecting his wound. "Mortar attack by the Americans a few days ago," he says, quite quietly. "Friendly fire." He raises his eyebrows as if his words carried some private meaning between them.

"I must go, Sylvia. Must intercept Ernest before he rescues another damn landmark."

"*Trop tard*," Adrienne almost sings.

Sylvia picks out *Finnegans Wake*. "At least take something to read."

"Isn't it your only copy?"

"One of many," she grins. "No one should be cajoled into the selling of their books."

"A happy lesson for us all," Martha says, looking at Cuzzemano, whom she has only ever spoken to on the telephone in the most colorful language she remembered from her playground days in St. Louis, and which her father, Dr. Gellhorn, would never have countenanced at home. Martha thanks Sylvia, gesturing with the book.

"Just remember not to try too hard with understanding it," Sylvia says. "Like people, they're best not to be too thoroughly understood."

Martha crosses the sidewalk and stands at the barricade of rue de l'Odéon, behind a pile of old furniture, an oven, and some garbage bins. She watches Sylvia and Adrienne deep in conversation behind the shop front. Sylvia is furiously shaking her head and mouthing the word "Non!" Martha's presence has somehow upset the balance of the shop.

She shoves the Joyce into her satchel and strides over the Pont Neuf in the direction of the Ritz. Funds of contempt are readily there for Ernest, but in this shop is the memory of how wonderful they had been together, all bundled up like refugees from Madrid, their faces flushed with lunch of red wine and partridge, their love lean from Spain. As long as they were shot at, as long as the food was dusty mule sausages, and they could hold each other in the nights as houses blew apart around them, they were happy.

In Madrid, Martha had felt a little shy of him. It was as if his wife's presence in Key West, months before, had made them feel at ease with each other in Fife's tropical garden. But in Madrid Ernest watched her over dried bread and coffee in the hotel, and when the shelling came after breakfast he'd say: "Aha!" wiping his lips with a napkin. "Here comes dessert."

Soon, as a matter of habit, she would follow him up to his room in the mornings because it was in here, he said, that they would be out of the sight lines of the snipers. As the bombs began to dance in Madrid, Ernest put on a mazurka. Sometimes they would talk and sometimes they listened to the music. On the breeze through the window came the smell of cordite, blasted granite, mud. Though nothing yet had happened these past two weeks, Martha began to feel as if the other reporters looked at her knowingly. She basked a little in the limelight he lent her. Otherwise, she was a nobody: she hadn't yet written a single article about Spain.

Weeks in she knew to walk carefully around the dark shapes of the men cleaned from the flagstones. In a destroyed house one morning she found a boy. Sandbags stood by the door but the bomb had forced the roof in and she found the child under the table in the kitchen. The boy's extinction made Martha quiet that night. Though the other correspondents seemed to notice, no one pressed her on it; who knew what anyone had seen that day? She kept herself separate from the others as if her aloneness were the only way to honor the dead child. At some point she fell asleep while the rest of the gang drank whiskey and some of them danced. When she woke she saw everyone had gone and Ernest asleep in the other bed. Three floors down, the death carts rattled.

The next morning Ernest was sitting by the open window, watching people line up for food though there was hardly anything in the shops but oranges and shoelaces. When he saw she was awake, he came away from the window. He pulled back the blanket and held her in the single bed close to him. "Rabbit," he said, "I want to marry you."

That evening she saw him write a cable to his wife. Only two words: EVERYTHING MARVELOUS.

But their obligation was not to his wife or even to each other in Spain, but rather to observation: to watch the refugees come in on their creaking carts, the fat dogs and dead mules, buses opened by bombs. They watched people walk off with parts of houses: doors, window frames, and tabletops. There were holes in houses like broken skin. Only to observe and put it all down in words: that was their job here. And Martha, slowly, began to do this: to watch, and to write. People back home thrilled to her reports from Spain.

They should never have left the war, Martha thinks, as she comes to the end of the bridge and prepares to meet her husband in the Ritz. War was the one thing that had kept them alive.

26. HAVANA, CUBA. 1939–40.

The house rose from the hills. The palms that flanked the villa were as enormous as aircraft carriers, and the facade of the building was webbed with vines. Martha turned back to check the driver was still down at the gates; she felt a little nervous about being in the big house alone.

She peered through the windows into the living quarters—a bathroom, the kitchen, some bedrooms. They would need a study each. Inside, there was a smell of old water and in one of the rooms a pond-sized puddle. Blown-in leaves gathered at the skirting and enormous flower heads knocked quietly at the windows as if asking to enter.

In another room—which would be her bedroom, Martha decided—the vines grew so thickly around the window they made a curtain. A tarnished mirror still hung on the wall and she caught sight of herself in her sundress and sneakers. Would she be able to do this? Be mistress of this house? A cat wandered in and looked unblinkingly at her reflection. For years their home had been a single room in a Madrid hotel. Here there was space and quiet and peace. Here they could live and write books and not fear that someone's head was in the sight lines of a sniper.

In the pool the still water was covered with algae and the tennis courts were overgrown with weeds. The whole place was falling apart but to Martha it seemed close to paradise. Standing there, in the Finca's wildness, she remembered Ernest's house in Key West: how neat and well-tended it had been behind the brick wall and iron fence. Apparently the wall had been Fife's idea—to keep the world out, and, Ernest said, her husband in. But Martha would keep this home open: let nature crawl over it.

"I've found it," she said to Ernest, back at their Havana hotel, which was swamped with his things. In jest, she had started calling him the Pig. "I've found our new home." It was called La Finca Vigía. The Watch Tower. It somehow seemed right; as if part of the house's role was to stand guard against Ernest's flotilla of wives, sailing down the Straits of Florida, come to reclaim him.

"Let's make a colossal mistake," Ernest announced, one day in July, as they sat by the Finca's poolside. They were celebrating the end of *The Bell*'s final draft. As a finishing touch he had penned the dedication: *This book is for Martha Gellhorn*. He'd wanted to dedicate the play he'd written to her a couple of years back, but Fife had found out, and this was Martha's recompense. She preferred it this way. The play was fine; but this novel was magical.

They sat in the shade of the jungle leaves she'd hewn back the week before, and Ernest's face was now lit with all the daiquiris he'd had since lunchtime. He stood up from the lounger and knelt on one knee. She felt a surge of terror.

"Marry me, Marty," he said.

She stared out at Havana, white as a cloud beyond the wetlands and sugarcane. "You're already married. Don't you remember?"

"Soon I won't be."

"You should be so lucky." Martha took a sip of the champagne though a headache had been forming since lunchtime. "You'll be clawed in that woman's grasp for a long time. There'll be bits of you stuck to your wife's fingernails at the end of all of this."

Fife was still simmering her miseries in Key West. Ernest must have been a real shit for her to be so angry with him still. It seemed she would resist divorce as long as she could manage. Martha knew it to be some kind of punishment for Spain.

"She said if I'd been more honest in the beginning she would've let me go easier. There's a damn Catholic for you." He gave her that smile that made his top lip disappear under the mustache. "But I couldn't resist you, Rabbit. You know that. Marriage, Marty! It'd be splendid."

"It would ruin things," she heard herself saying. In the

corner of her vision the jungle leaves teemed, growing like the tissue of some cancerous thing. She'd have to chop it back again. The champagne gave off a waft of apples and the headache began to pulse once more. "You have to learn how not to get married, Ernest."

She needed to shake out the restlessness from her legs and she spoke pacing from the other side of the pool. "We can do what we want like this. You can go to Key West and see the kids and Fife. I can get out on assignment. Marriage would wreck us. Both of us." Jungle leaves spread around his face. The way he looked at her· his expression was crestfallen and disbelieving, as if he had previously convinced himself of a positive answer. But marriage, she thought, was for women who wanted to stay put and play tennis with the neighbors and have cocktail hour on the lawn in full dresses. Martha didn't want any of that. She wanted to be with him traveling from war to war. They were correspondents, not stay-at-home pals.

"I'm sorry. It's just not right for me."

"Don't you love me?"

"Of course I love you. But that doesn't mean I want to marry you." She felt angry at him: for ruining the nice time they were having, for commenting on the situation. Couldn't he see things were better left unsaid? "I just don't know why you had to bring it up."

For weeks he wore a look as if she'd kicked him in the guts. His eyes followed her around the house though he said nothing. But she would not apologize for trying to keep them alive. Martha had never promised him anything, least of all marriage.

They'd been at the Finca now for nearly a year. No bullets powdered their walls. They did not have to interrupt making love to dash for the hotel shelter. They did not wake in the middle of the night trying to work out the closeness of a falling bomb. They got on with their writing and went out on *Pilar* and drank daiquiris at the Floridita. But that summer Ernest wore a heavy look.

When she could bear it no longer, she sat him down at the dining room table. In an attempt to appease him, she had made his favorite lunch: shrimp salad, fresh from the icebox. But when he saw the pale pink dish he looked no happier.

"What I meant the other day," she said, trying to explain, "is that it's a tricky thing trying to do my job and still be a good woman for a man."

Ernest looked at her broodingly. "If nothing happens, nothing changes."

"I don't think marriage would be good for me."

"Marriage is excellent for me."

"Yes, Ernest, you're a pro! You'll have ten widows by the time you die at a hundred." She wanted to make him laugh but he wouldn't even smile. "Come on, Ernest. Who wants to be married?"

"I do."

"Why?"

"Because I want to marry the woman I love. To show the world it's us against them."

"You've done it before and it didn't work."

"Third time lucky. This time it's different."

"Why?"

"Because I've learned—divorce is too expensive." Ernest smiled but then his expression turned serious. "Because I'm cockeyed crazy about you, Rabbit. Because you're braver than me, and funnier, and a better reporter, and young, and you're so blonde it's like waking up next to a dandelion. Because you're damn beautiful and fearless as hell. Because I love you. How's that for a reason to be married?"

"Oh, Ernest," she said. "They're good reasons for *you* to get married. But not for me." She came over to where he sat and perched on his knee. "Let's live in sin and keep the servants disapproving. We wouldn't want to deny them gossip, would we?"

Ernest said nothing. Martha went back to her seat and watched him chew the shrimp slowly. The look in his eyes: it was something close to admiration, and something close to fear.

Later that summer Martha found the book she had given him, and the dedication written on the photograph. She stared at the word *forever* in the bedroom she had only sparely decorated. She had an odd fantasy that if she were called up again for an assignment she'd be able to clear out of the house in no fewer than ten minutes. She felt like a bird on a perch: at home but also ready to take flight. She did want this life to go on *forever* on this hill above Havana. She didn't want to lose what they had here, where Cuba seemed to her a kind of heaven away from staid America, and a Europe intent on slaughter.

If love was all that was needed to marry, then perhaps there was love enough indeed.

Thirteen days after his divorce, she married him in the dining room of the Union Pacific Railway in Wyoming in November 1940. The dinner was roast moose. She made a speech and joked that their honeymoon would be inspecting the fortifications of the Chinese Communists. There were only a few guests—it had been whoever they could round up with two weeks' notice—and they laughed, thinking the China thing was a joke. The moose was flavorless and chewy.

On one of his hunts Ernest shot a couple of pheasants and sent the meat home to Key West. He didn't really think what his ex-wife might do with the spoils of his third honeymoon. "Oh, Ernest," Martha admonished him from their bed in the hotel suite, lying naked in the fresh white sheets with that day's newspaper between her legs, "you really shouldn't have." She could just imagine the look of horror on Fife's face when she saw Ernest's honeymoon kill. It gave Martha a hint of shameful delight.

In the newspaper there was a notice of the Hemingway marriage a few pages in. "A pairing of flint and steel," the journalist had written. She wondered which of them was which, and which one of those things was tougher.

27. PARIS, FRANCE. AUGUST 26, 1944.

American officers and French Resistance fighters swarm the Ritz lobby. Their fatigues look out of place next to the heavy furniture and gold-threaded curtains. The hall rings with the sounds of wooden clogs; no leather, apparently, for the soles. Martha is glad Ernest isn't down in the lobby or at the bar. A divorce is not best served over a daiquiri.

At the front desk the concierge offers a smile. "Number thirty-one, Mademoiselle," he says when she asks where Mr. Hemingway is staying. "May I call ahead?"

"Tell him it is Madame Hemingway." She adds: "*Sa femme.*"

His cheeks color. "Very good, Madame 'emingway." Ernest must be behaving very badly to make the man so nervous.

A group of officers walk by as Martha waits and she feels their eyes run the length of her. She overhears the concierge whispering. "*Oui, je suis sûr. Elle m'a dit 'Sa femme.'*"

Finally he smiles and gestures toward the stairs.

As soon as they begin their climb the concierge forgets his nerves and won't stop talking. He describes again what she has already heard: the legend of Monsieur Hemingway's daring recovery of the Ritz from the Krauts. "And afterward our barman asked Monsieur Hemingway what he would like to toast our freedom, and he replied, 'My usual, Benjamin!' It took Benjamin an hour to make them all martinis, but we were all so happy."

Light climbs with them as they go; these windows let in all the day. Many of the balusters have been lost, perhaps to Resistance barricades or Luftwaffe fires. "But what need did the Ritz have of being freed? Were you in the habit of housing Germans?"

The concierge's eyes swing to her press badge. "One has little choice when the Luftwaffe ask for a room, Madame. They can be very persuasive." They walk along the corridor and then come to a stop outside number thirty-one. "Here we are."

He hovers for a tip but Martha simply wishes him a *bonne journée*.

Noise comes from inside the room: there's the sound of a champagne bottle giving up its cork; men laughing; bolts of guns catch as they're cleaned. Here we are, she thinks, D-day once more. She prepares herself one last time to do what she has come to do: thinking of the car, the slap, the dynamite freighter. Martha sucks in her breath and knocks on the door.

Footsteps approach but the background noise doesn't fade. When the door is opened it is Ernest who appears, Ernest with a bandage still wrapped around his head.

"Rabbit." He looks almost surprised, as if he expected her to lose heart between the concierge's telephone call and the door. "You're here."

It almost winds her to see him, and she feels the same inrush of love for him that came to her in the London hospital. She wants to say, *Yes, I'm here, darling Ernest*, but instead she says, "It's been a while, hasn't it?" She means to sound neutral but she can hear the loneliness slide into her voice.

Ernest must recognize it as well because he looks relieved. "Look at us standing here like great apes. Come in." He stops. "Hold on. Let me get them out first."

Behind him are Resistance men and Americans. One lies on the chaise longue, his dirty boots on the brocade and a flute of champagne in his oil-blackened hands. Ernest tells them in both languages that his wife is here, the famous war reporter Martha Gellhorn; have they heard of her? Pride fills his voice. They collect their carbines, maps, polished shoes, taking sneaked looks at her as they file from the room. As they go, some greet her as Mrs. Hemingway, as if curious to test that name on their tongues.

"My band of irregulars," Ernest says.

Martha walks into his bedroom: so much grander than her room at the Lincoln. "What's the membership fee?"

"A bottle of liquor. Scotch gets you the most stripes."

A tray on the desk has an opened bottle of Perrier-Jouët; green light filters through it. Typical. Plenty seems to follow Ernest wherever he goes.

"Let me just freshen up," he says, with his oiled hands in the pose of a man arrested. There's an after scent in the room: something on top of the motor oil and boot polish, synthetic and sweet. Perfume? Perhaps. Maybe he has been entertaining whores in here.

Maps cover the dressing table. Documents are everywhere and what looks like a long roll of lavatory paper spilling from underneath the papers. At the window, down on the street, women gather, surveying something. Martha leans out but can see nothing but long skirts.

Ernest returns from the bathroom with his hands cleaned. When he sits on the candy-colored bedspread, he looks happy and childlike. On the pink satin bed are army rifles and hand grenades. Another champagne bucket is on the nightstand: she wonders if the ice had time to melt before her husband finished the bottle.

Martha points at the bottle of Brut. "How'd you get this?"

"The hotel cellar. I plan to exhaust its stocks."

"And then?"

"Then I'll move on to the Lanson."

"That's not what I meant."

"I know." He sits on his hands and leans forward, looking up at her sitting on the window ledge. "Were you over for D-day?"

"I came over on a Red Cross boat."

"Officially?"

"No. Officially I locked myself into their toilets." Ernest

gives her a gargantuan smile. When he's in the mood for it, she knows he loves her bravery. "How's the head?"

"They won't let me take this damn bandage off."

"Lose your head and you'll lose your livelihood."

Ernest looks vexed. He hates it when they talk about his drinking. The breeze stirs the net curtains, and the sounds of talking drift upward from the Place Vendôme. More women have turned up and a few are arguing. When Martha turns back to the room, she notices Ernest's press badge leans against a handgun.

"You brought your father's gun? From Cuba?"

"Figured he'd like me to put it to the head of a Nazi. Seeing as the last thing it was kissing up to was a chocolate cake."

"The Geneva Convention, Ernest: you're a reporter. Not a soldier."

A siren sounds and he comes over to the window as they both check the skies. They've done all of this so many times before; in fact, it all seems part of a comforting ritual, a memory from when they were in Madrid, together and unmarried.

"Want to go down to the shelter?"

"Not really."

The people out on the street don't seem in much of a rush either.

Ernest puts on a mazurka on the phonograph. The old fox; it's their music from Madrid. She can hear the record skip where it's scratched; she had thrown it at his head during one of their more heated fights at the Finca. She wonders what the argument was about. Booze. War. Women. The old trio.

Ernest, too, watches the record spin then looks at her with his marvelously frank eyes. "You look lovely, Marty, sitting there, with the sun in your hair. I've missed you so much, Rabbit."

If he doesn't touch her, she thinks, she'll be able to stay her course. But he comes near, standing next to her, so close she can hear his breath, can hear him swallow. Gently Ernest moves a strand of hair away from her face and puts it behind her ear. She summons all her will, but then he kisses her where her throat joins her shoulder. "Tell me you've missed me."

"Pig," she says. "Of course I've missed you."

"You've been so far away. We can be together again now."

"Ernest."

"In the war again, just like old times."

"Ernest—"

The siren stops. A false alarm, perhaps. On the street people look up at the skies inquiringly. Martha turns to tell him what she has come to say, that there can be no future for them, not anymore, but he is by the bed, now, transferring the ice from one bucket into another. He pours himself a glass of champagne from the open bottle. "What I'm trying to say—"

"Is that you need a drink? Me too." He sounds jovial but

when she watches him pour the second glass she sees his hand shake.

"How much are you drinking?"

"I pour champagne over my cereal in the morning and spike my tea with gin." Ernest massages the temples of his head under the bandage. "I don't want to fight about this now."

"All we've done," she begins, "is fight these past few years."

He hands over the drink. "Because we're the same guy. Because we're both writers."

"That's not a good enough excuse. Seventeen days I spent on a boat loaded with dynamite and you cruised over on a plane. You could have got me a ticket."

He throws back the glass nearly finishing it in one. "I didn't want you here," he says. "Why would I pay for a ticket when I didn't even want you here in the first place?"

Martha leaves her glass untouched and picks up her satchel. She feels just about done with his dreary selfishness. "I don't—"

"Marty."

He pulls her back with the strap of the satchel so that she sits on his knee. He holds both her hands, playing his thumbs into her palms. "Rabbit. Remember Spain. We need war so that we can feel the force of each other. Let's not go back to Cuba. We'll follow the Front if that might bind us better. There'll always be a war for us to go to. We're a team; we're helpless against each other. Decency can't set us apart." His thumbs are still pressed into her hands. "You talk as if it's already bitched. But will you think about it? Whether we might start again?"

A gun fires. There is the sound of clogs running. Doors bang. Parisians retreat inside. "Not so different from Madrid," she says, and smiles sadly for all that has been lost since then.

"We're safe as long as we're not."

"I don't know if I want that to be true—even if it is. Ernest?"

"What?"

She looks at his scarred hands and bandaged head and stands. She must get away from him or she will never say the words. "I don't think we're good for each other anymore."

He looks blindsided. "I love you," he says, almost bitterly, "like a fucking dope." Ernest gets up, but only to finish off the glass she hasn't drunk. "Just consider what I've said. A fresh start, Marty, and we can live wherever you want us to live. We can live in a trench if that would make you happy, Rabbit."

She tells herself to say no, to tell Ernest that she has done all the considering she can do, but instead Martha nods, because she is a sucker for the love of Ernest Hemingway, and it is all she has known for these past seven years.

She kisses him on the cheek and nearly knocks over his drink. It reminds her of when their plane had taken a nose-dive on their Chinese honeymoon, and he had made the other correspondents laugh when the plane righted itself and he said, "See, didn't spill a drop!" Only afterward did he look around to check she was all right. She had stared out of the plane window, as all the correspondents around her laughed, wondering just who it was that she had married. Alcohol; she is some mistress indeed.

Martha gathers her things and makes her way to leave, passing the huge bathroom with its twin sinks and a bidet big enough to wash a dog. She is at the door when a gust of wind comes into the room, knocking the maps from the table. The long roll of lavatory paper she spied before falls and bounces on the carpet, unrolling everywhere.

"Ernest!" she says, almost laughing.

Martha bends to pick it up and it is then that she notices there is writing on the paper. It is Ernest's handwriting, in black ink, set out on six squares of the toilet tissue. "Here," Ernest says, his voice tight with alarm. "Let me see to that."

But Martha has already seen what he has tried to conceal. Written down the length of paper is a love poem. There are black holes in the tissue where the ink has liquefied the paper. Martha reads until the end while the curtains flap around Ernest at the window.

The poem, Martha sees, is called "To Mary in London."

"What's this?" she asks. "Who's Mary?"

"She's a correspondent for *Time*." He says it plainly and without guile.

Martha slowly folds the tissue back on the table. So that

explains Sylvia's look this morning: the look hadn't meant she had forgotten about her, only that she thought Martha had been replaced. Perhaps Sylvia may have even met this Mary, whoever she is. Martha stares at the paper, unable to take her eyes from the ludicrous poem. "I don't understand you. You say you can't bear to lose me, but all the while you're writing poems to another woman?"

Ernest looks at her beseechingly but says nothing. The net curtain flaps around him as if he is a groom surrounded by his bride's lace.

"Mary who?"

"Welsh."

"And who is this Mary Welsh? Is she your lover? Your mistress? Your next wife?"

Ernest looks about to say something but doesn't reply. Martha thinks how typical all of this is of him: he wants his wife, he wants his mistress, he wants everything he can get. He is not so much greedy for women as blind to what he thinks he needs and so he grabs at everything. Wives and wives and wives—Ernest doesn't need a wife; he needs a mother!

Despite herself, she feels livid. How can he do this to her? Above all things it is embarrassing—embarrassing for everyone to be in yet another public jam of Ernest's making. "Why beg for me back if you already have someone else?"

Ernest shrugs. He goes over to the cabinet and pours another drink. More silence now. "Go ahead, Ernest. Drink it down. Forget about it. It's past noon, so you can have as much as you like; isn't that your rule?" All she is presented with are his shoulders turned to the window in the direction of the street. "You're ridiculous. You're worse than a child. Try and extricate yourself from something before setting yourself up with someone else. It might be a finer way for a man to act. It's over, do you hear me? I've just about had enough of you!"

Before she closes the door she spies his father's gun, a dark spot in the room like the cobbled holes in the pitted streets. Ernest still hasn't turned around to look at her. "Don't," she says, as she leaves the room, "do anything stupid."

Out on the street, Martha walks toward the ring of women she saw from the bedroom. They are armed, now, with pans and knives. One of them wields a butcher's cleaver. Between their skirts she sees a marc felled on the cobbles. Its withers are glossy, its mane dark. Plates and burlap sacks are offered around for a leg or hoof or hairy muzzle. Martha stands back as a woman cuts a let into the mare's throat and the blood flows into the waiting holes of the cobblestones.

28. HAVANA, CUBA. APRIL 1944.

The Overseas Service was not, it seemed, going to reach this part of the world. All Martha could get from the box was static and an evangelical church broadcast from Jamaica. The tuning would be driving Ernest crazy, but she wanted news from Europe, and she wouldn't stop until she got it.

The Finca had, by now, been made hospitable; the flowers and vegetation held back. The scum of the pool had been lifted; the jungle growth cut back weekly—but housekeeping was not, Martha could admit, her natural forte. And when she was writing it was she the servants bothered, not Ernest; it was she they consulted about menus and marketing. "Go and ask Mr. Hemingway," she would say, shooing them out of the room as if they were children pulling at her skirts. "I am working."

But the bougainvillea needed to be kept in check, the menus needed writing, and the butler needed to be reminded not to suck his toothpick so indolently all day. When the days here were good she felt knocked down by her happiness; but when they were dull she couldn't cheat their slowness.

Over the radio static came the sound of chipping ice from the pantry. Earlier and earlier Ernest went to the sauce to let out the pressure of the day. He came into the living room with two coconut cocktails. He looked like any other Cuban bum in his dirty white T-shirt. She was about to admonish him, but remembered she had already done so earlier today and held her tongue. Calling him the Pig was now only half a joke.

Out of the corner of her eye she watched Ernest waiting for her attention. She took her time, still testing the dial. In came fishing news from Florida, a local educational channel in Havana, until she heard the bells and the clipped English of the broadcaster. *This is London calling.*

"I'm so happy I bought you that radio," he said, at last handing over the drink. "There's nothing like having the news freshly shrieked at us."

"It's either this or four days late on the mail boat."

"The Reich soldiers on whether we hear the news or not."

They sat in silence to listen to the broadcast, sharing the sofa but sitting apart. The three books she had written here, in the peace of this house, were lined up next to Ernest's on the bookshelves opposite: *A Stricken Field, The Heart of Another, Liana.* It was a good place to write, and a terrible place to be bored, though writing three books in five years was not a bad achievement. Scrambling around for a title one day for that little volume of short stories, she had come across a letter from Fife to Ernest. It had been another bruiser, but it had ended quite thoughtfully, with the words "the heart of another is a dark forest." It had struck Martha as quite the perfect little phrase, and she had happily lifted it as a title. She wondered if Fife might have chanced upon her book in her local store. It would have been, she imagined, quite the surprise for little Fife.

When the broadcast ended, Martha went for a shower, leaving her husband on the sofa while a band struck up a salsa number on another station. At one time the tune would have had them both on their feet. Neither of them could dance, but both, once, had loved to dance with the other.

The shower drowned out the music. As she soaped herself for the second time that day, she reminded herself again that she was happy. What a life this was! Of ice cream in coconuts, gin and tonics on the lawn, saltwater swims in the mornings and tennis in the afternoons.

But sometimes it felt as if she were being buried. The trellises wrapped themselves around the house. The flowers in the garden looked so big they could swallow a cow. Sometimes she felt as if she were drowning in martinis and flowers. Only yesterday she had found orchids growing out of a tree trunk. Martha had returned with shears, planning to get at the orchid from the root, but it was only then she'd noticed how many there were: whole clusters of them, and bales of silk growing between the fronds. She couldn't possibly get at it all. That afternoon she had crawled into bed, dreaming of catastrophe in a cold climate.

She remembered on her first day here how she wanted to let nature in, remembering how Fife had immured Ernest behind the brick wall in Key West. But this was ridiculous; the house was being swallowed whole!

And Ernest! Ernest acted like one of the servants—a hireling himself. It felt as if he constantly kept on trying to make her happy here: to smooth her out, as if it were a matter of patting down the creases of a dress. He had sent her off to Antigua, Saba, Barbados, to report on submarine warfare; anything that would give her work but keep her close. But all she found were postcard beaches and summer without cease. Only when she had finally escaped to England last year had she felt that familiar feeling; of being in war, and being at home.

Martha returned to the living room in slacks and a shirt. Ernest was in her study. She was sure that he would lose something, or put something out of order, and she had told him very clearly she did not want him in her office. He was staring at her big map of Europe, with his hands held behind his back as if he were looking at a painting in a gallery.

Not knowing what else to say, she finally blurted, "You know, I detest being sensible."

"Oh, Martha," he said, at first gently, but then she heard the ironic politeness in his voice. "Where is it you'd rather be? With the dying here"—he jabbed his thumb in the direction of Germany—"or here"—France—"or here?" The last one was London.

Yes, she thought, London sounded very nice indeed. The broadcaster's English accent had given her a vision of an apartment in Mayfair: bombs blasting off above her, getting down the copy for a story, perhaps in bathrobe and gas mask.

Martha left him in her office. In the living room she tried again for the wireless but he caught up with her and turned it off at the dial.

"I hate being cautious and good and settled," she said to him, wondering why it was so hot in this room, why the house never cooled down. "This luxury," she said, looking around at the settled misery of their possessions. "This bolt-hole! Don't you tire of it?"

Ernest brought his scarred leg up to the chair. "This is what war does, Marty, it maims; it kills. You think you're going to find something different, as if you're special. But you won't."

"Balls! When we first met, you said I should go to war."

"And you've done it now. Bravo!"

She went over to the window: outside, the cane fields glowed in the Cuban dusk. "I think you're holed up where you're comfortable," she said to the glass. Her own reflection in the window was indistinct and faint. "I think you're scared of leaving."

"Are you calling me a coward?"

"What I am saying is I am unhappy here. I don't want to live as if wrapped in mothballs."

"Martha Gellhorn," Ernest laughed savagely. "War reporter and masochist. You've got no fucking clue, girl."

Martha opened the front door and went outside to the broad stone steps. She needed air. They'd had this argument over and over. It was her own fault, perhaps, for ever thinking she was going to get the response she wanted. Outside, their cats lay waiting for pigeons. An orchid extended its thin mauve neck. Birdsong went on mindlessly. All around her, Cuba ripened.

Ernest came out to the veranda with a drink. He handed it to her without a word and then sat down on the cane lounger. There was a wheezing sound, then a snapping, and the chair collapsed into nothing more than kindling. With his knees thrust up around his ears he looked like a child. His face looked thunderous, until he saw her laughing.

"Piece of good-for-nothing junk," he said, and he picked up a bit of the chair and threw it to the garden to the comical screeching of a cat. Martha laughed again. "Now tell me why you'd want to be anywhere else?" Ernest said, gesturing at the Finca—their sumptuous ruin.

He sat down by her; his T-shirt smelled of the cocktail. "What can I do for you, Marty?" His words were gentle now. Poor Ernest. He had never loved another more than he himself was loved.

She put her arm around him. "Let's go to Europe."

"I'm an old man."

"You're forty-four. You'd flourish again."

"It'll be cold. The food will be terrible. I'll be used up and no good."

He took a sip from her drink and handed it back.

"You'd be of use to me."

"I can't be your maid, Marty. I can't be your governess."

"Then be a reporter again."

"*I don't want to*, Martha. If you stay here we could start a family. Try for a daughter."

The thought of children only made her flinch. Last year, she had terminated another pregnancy. Ernest tried to persuade her to keep it, having gotten it in his head that it would be a girl. But she told him she'd be no good as a mother. She had not been—and never would be, she felt—in the mood for mothering. "Not that again. Please."

Ernest scooted in front of her and put his hands on her knees. Please, she thought, let him not be loving. She could handle him as boorish and bullying, but not gentle and meek. "Rabbit. I know we've worn each other down. I know we haven't been the best version of ourselves always, but God never promised an easy life to two writers trying to live together. Rabbit, please."

Martha looked at his soft pleading face but held her nerve. She took a big draft of the drink. The gin was flat and strong. "I have to go."

"Fine." He stood up. "Take your weltschmerz and go find the pulse of misery elsewhere. The war will look as fucking miserable as it always has, you spoiled little bitch."

So here it was: Ernest's return to fine form.

He picked up his drink and went into the house, kicking the rest of the collapsed chair over the stoop. "You writer bitch!" he said from the house, his voice loud with vehemence. "You can make your own damn way to England, then!"

Martha unpicked a curl of soap from the diamonds of her engagement ring and flicked it over the side. She watched two birds nesting in the tree above and downed the drink in one. The rapid night fell on Cuba. Not for her the life of the writer's wife. She was off to war.

29. PARIS, FRANCE. AUGUST 26, 1944.

Martha leaves the Ritz and heads back to the Champs-Élysées. Was that it? Was that her grand removal from the Hemingway camp? This morning she had imagined her liberation as glorious as the Parisians' today. Instead, as she heads west to the Tuileries, what keeps coming back to her is that poem, spooling over the side of the bureau like the loop of a dream. A poem for Mary, whoever she is. Why did Ernest have to do it like this? This big strapping man stomping about the city—and yet he couldn't seem to spend a week, a day, even an hour on his own. Between divorcing his ex-wife and marrying her he'd left thirteen days; it seemed he was a man who couldn't bear being alone.

At the Tuileries the flower beds are empty, the plants probably eaten. A scorched tank still smokes. Martha stops at the park café for lunch where she spoons down a bowl of thin broth and orders a coffee, though when it arrives she realizes it's not coffee but toasted chicory and a few grains of saccharine. As she sits outside in the bright light she lets this morning's full derangement slowly become clear: in the same day that he was begging her to stay, he was writing love poems to his mistress. It really shouldn't surprise her, since Ernest without a woman would be a writer in want of a wife. But she feels betrayed by Mary's unexpected entrance, as if her carefully rehearsed script has been snatched by a troop of fools intent on making this day a farce.

Martha had heard a rumor in London that Ernest might be *entertaining* someone at the Dorchester, but she had put it down to wartime nooky and thought nothing of it. After all, she has had her own fair share of indiscretions since Havana. She thinks of those yellow tulips in the London hospital. Perhaps they'd been a gift from her— from Mary Welsh. Or is it Walsh? But for Ernest to be writing poetry—and love poetry at that—it must be quite serious indeed. Martha almost admires him: what a feat, she thinks, to want to marry every woman he fucks. He is so good at being in love that Ernest Hemingway makes a rotten husband.

Martha smokes a cigarette to mask the coffee. It tastes as if liquefied from bark. She watches the world go by. The Parisians all look so happy, but Martha feels a rueful spectator to the memories of the past. She remembers how many times she and Ernest had gotten blind on gin and coconuts in Havana; how they had spent one night inventing a dance called the Hem-Horn Step, the both of them too drunk to remember the moves each time they attempted it. She remembers how, after a terrible time with the writing, Ernest had taken her out on *Pilar*, and, looking out over the sea, he had said, "This, Marty, is the only thing that matters." And he coaxed her out of a misery so peculiar and so vague that only writing could cause it—and only another writer could understand it. That afternoon he named each tuna he hooked after every reviewer they'd both come to hate. And that night they roasted the cream of the New York critics on their barbecue back at the Finca.

Most of all, as she finishes up her K-ration cigarette, Martha remembers his love for her. Perhaps it had only been her own ambivalence that had made his love so sharp and so angry. "I love you like a fucking dope"—how he had seemed to spit out those words, just an hour ago at the Ritz, as if he were in some part disgusted with himself.

And now it's all ending, Martha thinks, with a shock she hasn't yet felt about the end of her marriage. Everything bad is coming to a close, but so is everything good, and she feels wretched and bleak. Oh, Ernest! Why, she thought, did he have to do this to her as well? But there could never be two people at the close of his marriage. No, she thinks, a little bitterly: it always had to end on a three-card winner.

*

As Martha walks from the park her hand is shaken vigorously and she collects a hundred embraces when they see her correspondent's badge. De Gaulle is due at three and already people are gathering on the boulevard with a bottle of calvados or plum liquor. She'll need to get her story quickly before the boulevard is flooded with drunks and jubilants.

Since her D-day stunt Martha has been in hot water with her boss at *Collier's*. To sweeten him up she's decided to give him a light piece on Paris fashion. That is what Americans want to hear from Europe: not the state of the Jews, or the work of the Resistance, but what has happened to the French hemline. Well, she thinks, let them have it. In any case, she needs her work to take her mind off Ernest. Whenever she has been sunk with worry of one kind or another, it has always been reporting that has proved the most effective anesthetic. *Travail: opium unique*—this has always been her motto.

Martha finds an assistant in one of the fashion houses. Behind the glass he hangs flags around mannequins dressed in fur and brocade, buttons and lace. It's as if Paris is an exotic bird next to London, where she saw no fabric on sale—no buttons, no lace, no beads. When she knocks on the window, the man jumps and palms his hand over his heart. Paris is still jumpy. He eyes the badge on her arm.

He leaves his mannequin sunbathing half-nude in the August light. Martha offers him her best smile and then goes in for the kill. "So what were the Krauts like as customers, Monsieur?"

He instantly bridles. "I am only the window man," he says. He watches the boulevard nervously as if he fears the mob might turn on him. Martha tells herself to go gently: all she has to do is find out what ladies did with their rayon rations.

"What could women buy, Monsieur?"

The man gives a guarded summary of their shortages— no metal hooks, no eyes, no leather for soles. He tells her about the craze for enormous hats because they could be made from scraps and leftovers. She thinks she has enough down to spin something together, a little froufrou article that her boss will love. Martha thanks him and starts to make her way back to her hotel, where, for an hour, she will forget the mess of marriage to Ernest and she will sit at her typewriter and just *write*. She might start her piece with a portrait of the couturier's, then give the panorama of the city itself: the booksellers down at the Seine, the rich women in their palanquins, the *semelles en bois* that made every Parisian sound like a two-legged horse. Keep it simple, she tells herself.

A hundred yards away, Martha realizes she has forgotten to take the man's name. She jogs back to the fashion house, but from a distance, Martha sees he is talking to someone else outside the store. Another reporter.

This is irksome. *Collier's* will only want her story if it's an exclusive. She's about to march over to this journalist to tell her to quit it but she stops short. There is something familiar about this woman, who is her own age and has blonde hair curled close to her scalp. She's very neat in blazer and shirt, though the suit can't hide her full chest. Perhaps Martha knows her from Madrid; perhaps she was a fellow resident at the Hotel Florida and they have break-fasted together over orange halves.

Martha watches this reporter from behind a newspaper kiosk. No, Martha thinks, changing her mind, she is some-one from the New York office of the *Post* or the *Times*. The shop man's *froideur* has all but gone under this woman's warmer attentions—there can be no question who has snagged the better interview. He even laughs. At the end of the interview the journalist hands over her card and intro-duces herself in French. The shock of the name makes Martha go cold. It's her. It's the woman of Ernest's poem.

Mary Welsh hardly looks a war reporter. Her breasts are unshaped by a bra and she has big soft blonde curls that are not well kept from her face by bobby pins. When she listens, she tilts her head sympathetically—she is prob-ably used to soft-soaping people for the gossip columns or women's pages. She is attractive, Martha thinks, to a degree.

An overweight American reporter comes to talk to her just as she is putting her notepad away. Mary looks

delighted to see him, whoever he is. They talk on the boulevard corner, their faces close and intimate in the crowd.

"Do you want to buy something?"

Martha looks blankly at the newspaper seller. "What?"
He asks her again if Madame would like to buy a newspaper. "No."

Martha has nowhere else to hide aside from the kiosk.
And so, with little forethought as to what she will actu-ally
say, she strides over to Mary Welsh. It is an ambush. But
it is also unplanned. "Mary?" she says, but she can't be
heard. Horns sound where a crowd has gathered, and
people are shouting that the general is arriving. A police-
man blows his whistle, trying to keep some sort of order.
"Mary!" she is forced to say again.

"Yes?" The woman looks at her with a blank expression.
The fat man blinks. His face is pink and wet in the heat.
"I'm Martha. Martha Gellhorn."

The man's eyes glitter with something like fear; she's
glad her name can still do this. He gives Mary's arm a
squeeze. "See you tomorrow." The way he says it, it's as if
he's wishing her luck, as if Mary is entering battle. Martha
wonders if Ernest's relationship with this woman is
common knowledge; perhaps she is the only one in their
circle of reporters who has been left in the dark. She would
hate to be thought of as a chump by any of them. The man
nods at her before walking away and for moments the two
women watch him go.

"I know who you are, Miss Gellhorn," Mary says. She puts her knapsack on both shoulders and smiles, as if she is completely at ease in the company of her lover's wife. "You don't remember me, do you?"

Martha feels forced onto the back foot; she thought she would be the one to steer this. "Remember you?"

"We met in Chelsea. Earlier this year."

Martha realizes where she has met her: not in Madrid or New York, but in London. They were introduced at a *Herald Tribune* party but Martha had been too busy pressing a couple of Polish pilots for information to pay much attention to her. The only thing she remembers about this woman is that she had taken a particular interest in her fox stole—but their meeting that night couldn't have lasted longer than a few minutes. And she had never entertained the idea that Ernest might be fashioning this woman for a wife. Martha and Mary, she thinks: biblical sisters, war reporters, and now companions in Ernest's shareable bed. And so the sorry wheel turns again.

Mary lights a cigarette and stands with one hand on her elbow. She looks biddable—as if her whole body were ready to do whatever was desired. How Ernest would enjoy that. "How long has it been going on?"

Mary shrugs. "I don't know what you mean."

"Don't play the innocent."

Mary gazes at her shoes but she looks far from culpable. "Ernest said you were very much out of the scene. He said he was alone in London, and that he'd been alone for months."

"Seventeen days I was away!"

"You didn't look so alone at the party where we met."

"That is immaterial. I want to know what has been going on."

"We've had lunch and drinks, that's all."

"What kind of overtures is he making you?"

"I hardly think it's your business."

A group of students approach, ringing their bicycle bells and wearing ski hats despite the August temperatures. They're chanting one of the Liberation songs and some of them, inexplicably, have toilet brushes that they pump into the air with abandoned glee. Martha wants them quickly out of here; her temper is high and she wants answers. They wheel past, forcing Martha and Mary to the side of the shop front.

"Does he talk to you of marriage? I assume he does."

Mary nods. It might be the shade of the building, darkening her features, but she finally has the decency to look a little guilty. "He's not serious."

"Oh, he's deadly serious," says Martha. "I have no doubt that he will very swiftly want to marry you. Is that what you want?"

"Marriage? To him? I don't know." Mary looks at her other hand with some misgiving. "The problem is," she says, "I'm already married."

Martha notices, now, the wedding band on Mary's finger. Suddenly she has the desire to burst out laughing. How absurd! How *perfectly* ridiculous! Hurrah for Ernest, since once more, in a new decade, cuckolds and fools are made from each and every one of them.

One of the students prods a toilet brush in her direction. He frowns, mimicking her expression, and then he traces a smile on his own lips. Involuntarily, she laughs.

"Well, that *does* tend to complicate things," she says to Mary. At least, Martha thinks, Mary might have a little more sass than the virgin brides of Hadley and Fife.

"Look, Martha. Can I call you Martha?"

She nods. Mary gestures over to a bench just vacated down the side street. The two women sit next to each other rather awkwardly, a little far apart. "Martha, what I'm trying to say is that I wouldn't have stepped on your toes if I thought you were still about. Ernest made very firm insistences that *you* were finished with *him*. Not the other way around."

Her temper, which had felt hot and sharp just minutes ago, has lifted, and she listens to Mary's words of truth. She does not want to be married to Ernest anymore. All around her are thrilled Parisians, crammed in at the balconies above them, wearing homemade flags, and kids perched in trees and streetlamps. The occupation is over, and Martha can't find it in herself to deliver the bruising to Mary she'd come here to give. Instead, she feels an urgency to be honest. Mary, a reporter herself, might even understand this strange predicament: of loving this man but wanting, even more than that, absolute liberty.

Martha sees a little girl up in a tree, with scuffed knees and blonde hair, searching for General de Gaulle. It reminds her of when she was a little girl, and how she had once hid herself in the ice man's cart until long into the night. When her parents found her she could only reply that she had wanted to see the world. Motion. Flight. Martha had always craved it.

"I'm sorry for coming across abruptly before," she says to Mary. "I didn't mean to be an ass. I was upset. You see, I have only just become acquainted with your relationship with my husband . . . with Ernest. And it has come as something of a shock."

"I'm sorry," says Mary.

Sitting beside this woman, a woman to whom Ernest has already dedicated a poem, Martha recognizes Mary suddenly for what she is: her ticket out of here. This morning she saw that Ernest won't let her break things off if there's any chance he's going to be alone. What he fears is loneliness, and whatever brutish thoughts he has when he is left untended. Only if he is assured of another wife will he let his present wife go. "All I want is to be shot of it," Martha says, slowly, to Mary. "I want my own name in my passport. You're right. I don't want to be Mrs. Hemingway anymore."

"Would you so little recommend it?"

"Marriage to Ernest?" Martha laughs. "No, that's not

true. I have had," and she says this without a shadow of a lie, "the most wonderful time. It's just over—for us that is. It's the end of something, that's all."

Mary nods and offers her a smoke. Lips that have shared Ernest's now share an American-issue cigarette. Martha looks to the wide leafy boulevard where, she imagines, tanks will soon pass, and everyone will sing in ecstasy for their freedom. "Any advice?" Mary asks, saying the words into the smoke. "If it were to happen, that is."

"I don't know . . . Enjoy yourself?" Martha smiles. "It's not every girl who gets to call herself Mrs. Hemingway."

Mary laughs. "All a bit strange, don't you think? Us sitting here discussing this?"

"Oh no," Martha says. "Paris is where this sort of thing happens to Ernest, where women knit together his fate. He thinks he is the one making all the choices." She finishes the last of the cigarette and presses it under her boot. "He is not."

They sit awhile watching the preparations, then Mary makes her excuses, saying she has copy to file before returning to cover the parade. They walk down the Élysées together, Mrs. Hemingway and Mr. Hemingway's mistress. Before they say good-bye, Martha remembers the look Sylvia Beach gave her at the bookshop this morning. "May I ask, Mary," she says, just as they are about to part, "have you been to Shakespeare's with Ernest this trip?"

"The bookshop?" Mary asks. "Yes."

"Did Sylvia ask who you were?"

"I think Ernest just said I was a friend. Why?"

"No reason," Martha replies. "What's the piece you were doing, earlier on?"

"Just a quickie on Paris fashion for *Time*."

Martha smiles.

"What?"

"Looks like our stars have aligned again." Martha scraps the idea for the article; she'll let Mary get there first. They push through the crowds and stop off at the tobacconist to see if they can get more cigarettes. Martha holds out the door for her and lets the other woman in.

30. PARIS, FRANCE. AUGUST 26, 1944.

Mary is waiting in the Ritz lobby when Martha arrives, having made her way through streets of celebrating Parisians. Mary's cheeks seem drawn tightly against the bones; there is none of the mischievous woman she had met earlier this afternoon—whom she had thought she would never meet again.

"Mary." Martha sits down next to her. "Whatever is the matter?"

Earlier that evening, just as Martha was about to sink into a bath after what had felt like the most emotionally hectic day, she had received a distressed call from Mary at the Ritz. "You've got to come here," Mary said. Martha's heart beat hard, remembering the little gun propped against Ernest's bureau. "Ernest is losing it. Please, head over straightaway!"

Now Mary sits quite still on a sofa in the lobby. The Ritz is eerily quiet compared to the noise coming from outside. "Oh, Martha," she says, biting on her lip. "I don't know what to do!"

Martha steers her to the bar. She orders Mary a stiff drink and then one for herself. "Tell me slowly what happened."

Mary takes a large draft of the Scotch. "When I came back home this afternoon after meeting you, I found Ernest in the lobby having an enormous argument with a man called Harry Cuzzemato."

"Cuzzemano. Go on."

"Ernest was accusing him of all sorts of things. Theft, harassment, how he'd hounded him for that suitcase. The poor man shook like a leaf. Eventually I managed to pry him off Cuzzemano's neck. When we got back to the room, I got him to lie down."

Mary's hands still shake—she will need to fare better than this if she's to put up with Ernest's moods. Martha has known him to swing from tenderness to tyranny in the course of only a few minutes.

"Finally he fell asleep and I decided to type up a poem he wrote me. I thought he'd like to wake up to a gift." The whites of Mary's eyes are silky with fear. "And because it was written on *lavatory paper*, Martha. When I showed him the typed poem, he seemed pleased. He began to read it aloud then he stopped: he said I'd missed something. Then he said it was just a couple of lines and that we could check it. I didn't know what to say! I'd thrown the paper into the wastebasket as soon as I'd finished. I ran back to my room but the bin was empty. The maid smiled when I asked her, saying, 'Don't worry, Madame, the papers will not reach the Sûreté.'

"I had to tell Ernest the original had been lost. But Martha, he's been down there ever since! Scrambling through the garbage, convinced he's going to find it. He won't listen to me. You've got to talk to him."

Mary finishes her drink and Martha chases hers down too.

Objects emerge from the cellar dark: prewar suitcases left by tourist refugees, folded flags, old menus, jars of mustard, and bottles of vinegar. Lined along the wall are dusty bottles of champagne—so in his twelve-hour stay Ernest hasn't completely decimated the supply. Martha calls out his name. There's no response.

She winds her way around the cases and calls out to him again. He must be down here if Mary says he is. She imagines him squatting behind one of the valises, his breath rifling the air, his eyes more adjusted to the dark than hers. She doesn't want to be scared out of her wits just because Ernest thinks it would be a good practical joke to frighten her. She tries to calculate how much he might have had to drink since the champagne at noon. "Ernest! For Christ's sake: answer me!"

She notices a line of gray light at the side of the cellar and follows it outside.

A man stands with his hands deep in the garbage cans. Somehow, among the empty wine bottles, broken wooden crates, slimed scraps of food, Ernest still has the air of a man in touch with the gods.

His hands drop from the trash cans, greased and mucky. He cracks that hobnailed grin. He isn't alone: two of the hotel staff stand some way up the alley, too respectful of Monsieur Hemingway to intervene. He's the Ritz's sweetheart. How must he seem to them, she wonders, only hours after rescuing the hotel with his *martini-tour-de-force*, now up to his elbows in the muck of rich men? "Marty."

"What are you doing, Ernest?"

"I've missed you so much, Rabbit." The words slur over each other. His arms hang uselessly. A ripe smell of garbage comes off him. She leads him to the curb where they can sit.

Martha doesn't say anything until he's calmer. "Are you all right?"

He stares at his hands. "Mary lost the poem."

"I know."

"Where is it, Rabbit?"

"You know all documents are burned if they're thrown away."

He looks at her. Mania pushes into his eyes. "Nazi

swine, what if they stole it?" He puffs himself up then he almost rolls on the ground before managing to stand. Like a bear with a sore toe, he crashes about the alley, kicking a tin can against the wall. "What if Cuzzemano has it? He's been down here, I know it, trying to find anything he can. He would have these damn hands if he could chew them off!"

"Ernest, please. I doubt Cuzzemano has a deal with the chambermaid."

"Then it's that bitch's fault—Mary! For throwing it away." Ernest kicks at a crate and the hotel staff turn. "She called you here?"

"Yes."

"Are you my wife anymore, Rabbit?" He comes to sit on the step again and looks at her with those watery drunk eyes. He puts his hands on her knees as he had done that night in Cuba.

"I can't be your wife anymore." Now her voice is full of tenderness, because she is the one letting him go.

"But I want you to be. I'm cockeyed lonely without you."

"You have Mary now."

"What is Mary to me? She doesn't even want me. Not for good."

"How do you know that?"

"Let's call it my built-in shit detector."

A woman laughs on the street by the hotel. Then a man says something and the night watchmen laugh too. "What do you want me to be?"

"My wife."

"I'm a correspondent. I don't want to be just a wife."

Ernest stands, holding out his shirt to make breasts. He minces around, his voice falsetto. "*Oooooh! I am Martha Gellhorn and I am the only woman war reporter around!*" At this he lets the breasts go, then grabs at a mop and pail leaning on the garbage cans. He puts the pail on his head and the handle about his chin. He jabs the mop toward her. "Well I am a knight errant and I will win you back!"

He jabs the mop a few times and she laughs. Then he shoves it in her face. It makes her retch and she pushes him away. "Stop it, Ernest." He doesn't and she has to say it more forcefully. "Stop it, for God's sake."

He ditches the helmet and broadsword and sits by her chastised. She barely recognizes him: his skin is pouchy, his stubble roughly shorn. Ernest's head is no longer bandaged but the London wound protrudes like a peach pit. She wishes more than anything that he would take better care; it's as if he can't be bothered anymore. She has called him Pig as a joke, but this is what he seems like now: fat and wobbling, with his small eyes and rough skin, not the dazzling man she had met in a bar on a hot afternoon seven years ago.

"We're tearing each other apart. There'll be nothing on us but bones if we carry on."

"Please can we continue," he says flatly.

"We have to work hard and get things written. That's all we can do."

"I haven't written anything since the *Bell*." He takes her hand. "I'm out of business."

"You're forty-five, Ernest, hardly over the hill. You're a wonderful writer."

"All you wanted was an editor, not a husband."

"That's not fair." This morning she had expected to feel some pleasure in doing this, but there's no triumph now. There'll be no grand party, no drinking, no kissing in the street to mark her liberation. Not when her husband has been rifling through garbage, the dirt still on his hands, his mind half-mad with booze. Martha lights a cigarette.

"I'm scared," he says.

"Of what?"

"I'm deadhouse." He gives her the crooked grin again but it has stopped working on her a long time ago. She remembers when he had nailed her with it at Sloppy Joe's.

"Don't be silly."

"I'm not. I tell you it would kill an ox, this thing. This . . ." He loses the thread of what he wants to say. His eyes turn as hard as pebbles. "It used to be I could write. Now I have to drag the words up and even then they don't hit straight. The *Bell*! The *Bell* was easy; it was about us, and Spain. The longer I don't write, the more it hurts." He pauses. A firework goes off somewhere close. "I have a hole inside me big as a house, Marty. I'm scared."

"Of what?"

"Women or words. Who knows?"

"Dearest Ernest—"

237

"What if I end up like my father?" It's like a gunshot in the dark. "Martha," he says, and it is as if her real name comes out of the deepest place in him; he *always* calls her Marty. It scares her, this place, where Ernest's horrors sit as hard as quartz inside him. What is it that makes him so frightened? She knows he is afraid of being alone. He is scared of the brutish character of his sadness, but there is something more to it, which she cannot name, and neither can he. Down inside Ernest there is something rotten: there is the slag heap of himself, like all this garbage. Were she to delve into this, she would have to commit to him for the long run. And she can't. She simply doesn't have the energy to sort out Ernest Hemingway amidst everything else. "Work," she says. "Work is the cure for us."

"I want to be a good man, a good writer."

"Be one or the other, Ernest, not both."

"I have this longing," he says, and he points to his heart, "to change myself. See it out with me."

Martha looks at him searchingly. She wonders if he has said these words once to Hadley or Fife. "I can't."

"Why?"

"I just can't." He must notice how her voice catches.

"Has Mary put you up to this? I won't see her if I can be with you."

"Mary asked me talk to you about the poem."

"It seems France is where I lose my work. And my wives." He gives a sad smile, rubbing the muck off his hands onto his pants. Quickly he seems quite sober. "I have a terrible feeling I was only of use to you when I had a pen in my hand. Did you love me?"

"Of course." Martha looks at the stitching on her sneakers. "But I think it's time we let each other go."

"Okay, Marty. I'll issue you a divorce. I'll sue you for abandonment. For all those times you left me for your cherished wars. And then—now—for the time you left me for good."

Martha kisses him on the cheek as they stand from the sidewalk. "Darling Ernest, you smell awful."

"So would you if you'd been going through the garbage."

"You were never one for hygiene, old bear."

The hotel staff idle, sensing the scene is over. She hopes they won't tell anyone; she hopes his propaganda will have more traction with Parisians than a sorry story of Ernest Hemingway with his hands in the trash. "Rabbit," he says, pausing for the last time by the door. He lets his lips rest on her wrist then lets it go. "It was good a lot of the time, wasn't it?"

"Yes," she says. "And I will miss you so much." It's the truth. He has been the other half of her for seven years. Martha follows him through the cellar, through the old boxes, flags, and dusty bottles of wine. While they are still in the dark, he says, "I thought I'd left a box of my writing in here before Fife and I sailed home. But that's gone too. Another thing lost."

*

Mary waits for them at the bar, her face tear-stained, her glass empty. Martha will shake her hand and kiss Ernest on the cheek, and then she will walk back to the Hotel Lincoln alone. Then, in the months to come, they will write a few letters and meet again to discuss the details of divorce. And sometimes they will think back to that hot afternoon in Sloppy Joe's, and those weeks spent in Fife's garden, and the mornings together listening to the mazurkas in Madrid, and their serene days of writing in the Finca. She had been his mistress nearly as long as she had been his wife. And despite the vitriol that will come to pass between them, she will remember the old bear with his paws sunk into the garbage, talking to her of fear. But to all others, she will not let his famous name pass her lips. And after that year, she will never see him again.

MARY

31. KETCHUM, IDAHO. SEPTEMBER 1961.

Mary sits in the part of the study that won't get any more sun. Papers surround her: magazines still in wrappers, lottery tickets, charts of the Gulf Stream, drafts of novels, telegrams to mistresses and wives.

Every day she comes into the study as if her work is a kind of vigilance. Over morning coffee the desire to have everything sorted possesses her with violent energy, but within minutes of beginning the desire goes and by the evening she finds herself in Ernest's chair, reading his letters, wrapped in a blanket from which his smell is disappearing with terrifying speed.

Mary has brought back from the Finca boxes of papers and photographs, thousands of dollars' worth of manuscripts in a shrimp boat from Havana. In the boxes there are skeletons of mice and cockroaches, the cockroaches sometimes as big as the mice. Sometimes she dreams of throwing a match into the room, relinquishing it all, every last damn piece of paper.

Ernest's voice feels near when she reads the letters, as if it came in on the winds from the Sawtooths. When her hands get cold at night, she imagines moving them into the warmth of his. Sometimes sitting in his armchair she would put her chin onto his palm and they would read whatever he was reading together. Hands: that's the part of him she misses. Ernest's hands weren't writers' hands: they were hatched with scars and rough from the sea. If she could wish for anything again it would be the confirmation of his touch.

Sometimes she catches Ernest's footfall on the porch. He un-shoes in the vestibule. The snow coat he puts on the hook. Ernest comes into the house with a rifle on his shoulder. Maybe there is a pheasant under his arm ready for the pan: blood clotted in the feathers, its gaze elsewhere. Sometimes she hears her name from an empty room. *Mary.* She continues whatever it is she is doing because she's not crazy; she knows the house is empty. *Look at the garden, Mary. We're early for rabbits.* His voice ghosts.

And then there's the sound of that morning's gunshot. She hears that, too, again and again, even when she's out on the deck, watching as snow comes to the mountains of Idaho.

That's the trouble with reading these letters. They resurrect him.

At night she wonders what it must sound like to hear her crying: it's not gentle, not at all, not a keening sound but rather a bit dog howling at the disturbance of the moon. In the morning the cook gives her a towel she's left in cucumber water in the icebox overnight. Mary holds it to her eyes as she smokes the first of the day's cigarettes. This business of being widowed; it has its scant pleasures.

Outside, beyond the deck, the trees are on the edge of turning. In weeks she'll be able to powder the leaves under her boot. She holds the smoke in her mouth. Many days into September Ernest's office is still a mess; it is a city of paper. She holds on to that thought; only suicides leave their papers neat.

One afternoon she finds a copy of Ernest's tribute to the president.

Ernest had greeted the request from Washington with something close to cold fright. For too long, now, he'd been an unhappy writer. To lose his ability to write was to have lost the ability to clear his mind of itself. To write was to come into a wonderful house: a clean well-lighted place where the light fell in large white blocks on the good wooden floors. To write was to be at home, to be able to see well.

The request was for a few handwritten lines for Mr. Kennedy. That week in February Ernest sat in his study, looking with nervousness over the barrel of his stomach. Misery hovered close. She had often wondered why he couldn't give up on this wretched business. They had enough money from royalties, film options, magazine deals. If he could send off the Paris stories and then put himself to the work of hunting or fishing, he might have a better chance of happiness. But writers and their woes: they couldn't be parted. Not for anything.

Mary went into town to find the right kind of paper and have it cut down to size. When she returned she put it on the desk. "It only needs to be a few sentences." Ernest looked at the paper with grim amazement: as if she were asking him to do something unconscionable, slay a baby. "Could I help, lamb?"

"No. I have to do this."

The sentences amounted to not much more than a telegram.

When Mary returned to the room after lunch, still nothing had been written. Ernest held the card jealously as a boy might an examination paper. He looked at her. "The turnip's been squeezed for its last drop," he said, surveying the blank page.

"Just write one sentence. Just say you wish the president well."

Ernest's eyes were slow, rheumed with liquor. She wondered how much he'd had that morning. "Do you want me to stay?"

Ernest shook his head. "I'll finish it this afternoon." She kissed him but he didn't seem to recognize it.

Mary went out beyond the horse pasture. She walked the quarter mile to Warm Spring Road, remembering the man she'd fallen in love with in the Ritz hotel. What an open vista their life had seemed in the night-time of room thirty-one. How wonderful life with Ernest Hemingway would be! And now? Now he seemed unable to even register the things that had once given him pleasure. Sometimes she snapped at him because she didn't know what she should do with him or herself. His depression sat at the table with them at breakfast and dinner.

She knew she should not but she was tired of making accommodations for his moods. They had grown old together: they knew each other's faults and foibles; when they were scratchy or mean-tempered; at what point forgiveness would be delivered after an argument, and how to avoid the escalation in the first place. But these months—or these years, perhaps, since the plane crashes—had been hard. During his blackest moods he was unreachable. Worse, he could be savage. Fifteen years of marriage wouldn't ever accustom her to the outrages of Ernest's temper. It was her husband who had delivered some of the most colorful insults she had ever had the misfortune to receive.

Mary walked until she reached the snow.

The light had gone from the study when she returned. Ernest was sitting in the stirless dusk, books surrounding him. When she switched on the desk lamp she saw how sore his eyes looked from where he'd rubbed them. "I don't know what to do," he said. He looked at the paper—he could no more write upon it than he could a sheet of ice. Her persuasions made him give up for the night.

But the next day was the repeat of the first. The day after was the same too. "Just a few sentences, lamb," she said later on in the week when he was surrounded by unfinished sentences and discarded drafts.

The president's telegram was finished a week later. Before putting it in the envelope Mary checked the note again. The curls of his handwriting made her think of an instrument of torture: like the braces and loops of medieval stocks, where the hands were fixed and the tongue clamped. Oh, Ernest, she thought, we might be happy if only you'd put down the pen.

Two months on Mary still goes to bed late in the newly empty house. She's fifty-three and yet she lives like a teenager: she wakes late and her bedtime can be three or four in the morning. Her sleep is thick and when she wakes she remembers nothing of her dreams or even whether she's had them. Her friends want her to talk to someone, a professional, about the morning she found her husband. It's not so much what she saw that morning but the sound above all else that still ambushes her in the days: it was like a bureau drawer coming loose from its runners and falling to the floor. Even when it's just the cook throwing the cutlery together, or a back door slamming in a draft, Mary's mind jumps to that morning's gun blast.

This is what the doctor wants her to talk about: the scene itself. He says not talking—not talking about this scene in particular—will make it harder to deal with her grief. The doctor says that the memory is like the shrapnel in Ernest's leg: to talk is to bring it up; not talking will leave it to fester and encyst. But Mary has no inclination to share: not with the quacks or biographers, not with his confederacy of ex-wives. Everyone is chivvying her to speak. *Talk! Talk! Talk!* As if this memory is something to be smoked from a hole.

Mary, anyway, has done her fair share of talking. After the coroner had gone she telephoned his wives and sons. In her address book she found Hadley's number and Martha's in London. For some moments she stared at Fife's entry in the book: a black line through her name. Poor Fife. She had loved Ernest almost as a matter of faith or doctrine. Had she loved him the most? She'd certainly fought the hardest to keep him, Mary thought, remembering how Martha had shrugged him off like a heavy jacket on that too-hot day in Paris.

It was Hadley she told first. "It was an accident with a gun," she said, hearing the stiffness of her voice.

"Where was he going at that time in the morning?"

"To shoot duck," Mary replied. "We had plans."

There was a silence on the other end of the phone. Mary would come to know that pause, over the next few months, that declivity in the conversation, when she said the words: *an accident; Ernest mishandled the gun.* Nobody, aside from the servants, believed her.

"I didn't think it would end like this," Hadley said. "Goodness. I'd never thought about a world without him." Hadley was too old to make the trip but she said Bumby would come—Bumby and his wife who was expecting a child. "I'll tell him to bring red roses. He won't remember why they're important."

She made the calls to Patrick and Gregory telling them what had happened to their father. Then she called Martha, and it had been Martha who'd run screeching from the telephone when Mary had said the words. *Ernest has died. An accident with the gun.* She had not expected that. Not from Martha.

32. LONDON, ENGLAND. MAY 1944.

They were both already married when they met that afternoon at the Charlotte Street restaurant. Mary had thought nothing of it when Mr. Hemingway had asked her to lunch: he was newly arrived in London, and his ignorance of military matters was already famous among the American correspondents who'd been here since the beginning. Mary had assumed lunch was a way for Hemingway to glean information without the embarrassment of facing a gentleman reporter.

She had spent little time getting ready. She found enough lipstick for her cheeks and lips and worked up burnt cork with some water for her lashes. In the mirror her face looked satisfactory. She would never have described herself as handsome, but at thirty-six her face was trusty, usable. Mary knew what men liked was her gumption, her readiness to laugh, her desire to continue singing and drinking when everyone else had turned in for the night. What Mary had, instead of a turn-and-look face, was a grand capacity for a good time.

Dust was still in her hair from last night. She tried to

comb it from the curls but it wouldn't budge. Really, it was impossible in this city to get clean. But Mr. Hemingway would have to make do, she thought, as she gathered up her things, intending to get to the *Time* office later that afternoon to file a story.

Mr. Hemingway was late. Mary sat at one of the outside tables, drawing lines into the gingham tablecloth with her thumbnail. She was too hot in the wool suit and she wished she'd chosen an inside table. That would have been more discreet for him too. In big black letters the sign outside the restaurant read: THIS HOUSE WILL REMAIN OPEN AT ALL LICENSED HOURS, EXCEPT IN THE EVENT OF A DIRECT HIT.

Mary thought of his wife, Martha Gellhorn, who had arrived in London with a kind of royal fanfare. She had struck Mary as a fierce character when she met her at a party. Everyone else in the small Chelsea apartment looked doggish and wan, but Martha was lovely and tanned, with her bright Midwestern vowels and a silver fox stole, their several tails falling just below her shoulder blades. All night she was flanked by not one but two Polish pilots.

Everyone Mary spoke to talked in whispers about famous Martha—newly arrived without her husband—and her exploits in Spain, Finland, and China. "Rumor has it," her friend told her, "that she arrived on a ship packed with dynamite. And that her marriage is on the rocks. Hers and Hemingway's. Imagine. A single man like that in London.

He's going to be ruined by English women before the Huns can find him." Martha Gellhorn stood in the room with great poise: aware of herself as being the attraction in the room, but also choosing to ignore it.

Mary drank the punch. It tasted of rope and garage oil. She was trying to summon the courage to talk to this woman. She had admired Martha's career since she had started at the *Chicago Daily News*—though she worked on the women's pages, not the foreign desk. As Mary reported on trends in color, debutante balls, and whether this summer would be the season for silk or toile, she read Martha's brilliant dispatches from Madrid. She wondered how Martha had managed to get so much further in her career than she had, since they were the same age. As soon as war broke out in Europe, Mary had promised herself she would be there.

And here Martha was, the famed reporter, cowled in foxes, chaperoned by Poles. Mary downed another glass of punch.

Her friend pulled her along to make the introductions. "Martha Gellhorn Hemingway, this is Mary Welsh Monks. Gosh, what a mouthful both of your names are."

Martha offered her a hand and the stole slipped, revealing the lovely apple of her shoulder. "It's just Martha Gellhorn." The color in her face had come up higher. "I can abide it at home but not when I'm working. A pleasure to meet you, Mary. Or should that be Mrs. Welsh Monks?"

Mary was about to tell her that she, too, didn't take her

husband's name; that she, too, was a reporter, and how much she had admired Martha's Spanish pieces for *Collier's*, but Martha had already turned her back to hold a glass of punch up to the tall pilot's mouth. The other one coaxed him in his native tongue until the tall Pole downed the whole thing in one and shuddered. Martha laughed. It was rich and bold. She said something in Polish, and the pilots laughed too.

Mary stepped away from the little group: she was made from tougher stuff than to be spooked by the games of Miss Martha Gellhorn. Or whatever her name was.

Later that night Mary noticed the fur stole had been left on the back of a chair. Typical that an outsider wouldn't know any Londoner would kill for such a warm-looking thing. Mary pulled her hand down one of the foxes—the pelt felt like a dog's. In its mouth the teeth were sharp.

"Oops," she heard someone say behind her. Mary turned, feeling her face warm, as if her express intention had been to steal the cape. "That's mine," Martha said. "Shouldn't leave things lying about I suppose."

Martha picked up the fox, clasped it with an invisible hook just above her breast, and flashed a set of white teeth as she left. "*Ciao*," she said, and made her way out of the Chelsea apartment. The Poles followed, close behind her.

Ernest arrived at lunch ten minutes late, full of apologies but unhurried. Like his wife, he was gloriously tanned. He was bigger than Mary remembered him from their first meeting; just this side of portly. In his face one could see the character of his misuse; it was probably booze— the poison of all correspondents in London.

"That's a fine suit, Mary," he said, seating himself opposite.

"Thank you," she said. "I made it from a suit of my husband's."

Ernest brushed the tablecloth of dust. On the linen were the lines from her thumb while she had sat there waiting. "He's in London?"

"Only rarely. Hence he had no need of the suit."

Ernest smiled. "So you took it to your tailor and attacked it with some scissors? Hardly a way to treat your ex-husband's things."

"It would be an excellent way to treat my ex-husband. However, he's not my ex-husband. Noel Monks is my husband still."

"Noel Monks? Of course," he said, as if it didn't surprise him that she remained married. "I met him in Spain."

Mary already knew this. Noel had written her, when she had told him she was lunching with Hemingway, that he remembered Ernest from Spain as a loudmouth and a bully. But the man sitting across from her didn't seem like either of those things now. In fact, she was amused to see that he was the one who looked a little nervous. He opened the menu upside down and turned it around again with a comic little moue. She wondered what he would make of the food here.

He put down the card. "I have the feeling you like the war, Mary."

"Not at all. You can't like something like this." She gestured over to a building, long ago damaged, where a half a yard of curtain still flapped at the gashed window.

"Female war correspondents. Like taxis. None for miles, then they're everywhere."

"The troops never complain."

"No. I can't imagine they would with you."

"Or your wife."

There was silence for moments as Mary concentrated on the menu. Ernest had a patrician air to him, but a slight hesitancy, too, as if he were unsure of just what he should be doing in this city of mutton broth and bomb damage. The waiter arrived and took their orders. Ernest took a long while to decide and made the man wait, idling on the curb, while the cars pumped their exhausts into the heat.

"Do you know her? My wife?" he said, once the waiter had gone.

"I met her at a party a couple of months ago. She wouldn't remember me—we made only a very brief acquaintance."

"She'd be irked to find other women doing just the same thing as her." Ernest ran his finger along the serrated edge of the knife. "Martha made her crossing over here on a boat stuffed with dynamite. That's how much she loves war. Willing to be blown apart just to see others blown apart. My wife: she has some notions."

"She cut an impressive figure, certainly."

"Whose was the party?"

"A friend from the *Herald Tribune*."

"Was she with anyone?"

Mary shook her head. If Ernest wanted to find out whatever the Polish pilots meant to Martha Gellhorn that night it was up to him. Mary shifted in her seat; her mother had sent her a new garter belt which was a little too loose after her years spent in hungry England. Accidentally she knocked his foot with hers and she felt herself flush. "Sorry."

But Ernest was someplace else. "My wife has a very fixed idea about how she wants her life to look. And it almost always involves people engaged in acts of superlative violence. She's not happy unless somewhere in her proximity some poor bastard loses his life. Well. One man's loss is another woman's profit."

"So why did you come here?"

"Nagged into obedience."

"Ernest Hemingway: nagged into obedience. What a notion."

The food arrived. Ernest looked at the brown broth with its potatoes the size of coins. It came with a slice of toast. "Why didn't I stay at home? That's a good question." He chewed on the bread as if they had turned the flour with sand. Then he broke off a corner and threw the crumbs to a pigeon. Its wings sounded like an eggbeater.

"Careful. I nearly faced an English firing squad because I threw out moldy cheese." Her sandwich, with merely the suggestion of corned beef, tasted wonderful; she hadn't eaten anything decent in weeks. She tried not to devour it too quickly, but when she looked up Ernest seemed pleased, as if he liked to see her appetite. "Your wife has a rather fearless reputation."

"And doesn't she just let you know it." Mary raised her eyebrows and remembered her friend's words: *Their marriage is on the rocks, hers and Hemingway's.* "There's only so much room in a marriage. Even less when the two people are me and Martha Gellhorn. You don't write, do you, Mary?"

"Only journalism."

Ernest looked pleased with her answer. His dark eyes watched hers while the people inside the restaurant watched him: this famous writer who'd come to Europe to work out the score. He ate his soup with little interest and the conversation moved on to the war. She knew, then, that the tenor of their meeting would be work, though she had, as she had left her apartment, felt there was something else afoot in this invitation to lunch with Ernest Hemingway. She told him about fleeing Paris in 1940, her retreat down to Biarritz, the boat back up to England. She told him of the bombing of London: of houses ripped apart, an arm-chair dangling off one building with the Sunday suit still folded on the back of it. The way, in the beginning, when people were still frightened by the sirens, women would run to the shelters with soapsuds in their hair. The fog of grit everywhere. The inability to keep clean. Of the joy of inheriting a jar of peanut butter with a cupful of oil on the top. "*Oil!*" she said. "It meant I could actually fry something!"

Ernest wrote down her suggestions for remedial reading. As she finished her sandwich she wondered if he might sign something for her. She'd be able to sell it afterward to one of the booksellers at Cecil Court. What might she trade it in for? A lemon perhaps. Or even an egg! She kicked herself for not bringing one of his books. She had a copy of *For Whom the Bell Tolls* back at the apartment. The dedication, she'd noticed, was for Martha Gellhorn. She wondered how long ago that had been.

When the plates were cleared Ernest produced a whole lovely orange from his bag. Passers-by looked at him with horror, as if he held a human head. "For you," he said, offering her the fruit. "As a thank-you for all this," he said, gesturing at his notes. "For helping me not look like an ass in front of our esteemed colleagues."

The color of the fruit was almost an outrage. Mary lifted it to her nose. Its smell was heartbreaking. "There'll be a riot if I peel it here," she said, looking at the pedestrians on Charlotte Street. "I'll be court-martialed for public agitation."

"We could take it back to your apartment. Have it there."

So here it was; she should not have doubted herself.

It couldn't have just been about work, not when a man and a woman lunched together. But then she remembered Martha's words from the party that night as Mary had picked up the fox. *That's mine.* Mary looked at Hemingway who was, strictly, still that woman's, whether their marriage was *on the rocks* or not. "I don't think Mrs. Hemingway would like that."

"I don't think Mrs. Hemingway would care."

With great reluctance Mary handed him back the orange. "That may be so. But perhaps my husband might."

Ernest unbuckled the straps of her satchel and slipped the fruit into the bag. "All yours," he said, and then he might have said something like "As am I" but he said it into his napkin, cleaning his beard, and she knew she'd probably misheard him.

"Thank you, Mr. Hemingway," she said, smiling. "I can't tell you how long it's been since I ate an orange."

"You can, if you like, call me Papa. Everyone else does."

Mary laughed. "Sure. Papa it is," she said, and Papa, indeed, looked pleased with her approval.

Back home she washed off the cork and lipstick and sat down at the table, excited. She had put off her deadline so that she could come home to eat the fruit immediately. When she dug her nail into the skin, she dipped her nose into its spray. It smelled of paradise. Wordlessly she thanked whichever god had brought Ernest Hemingway into her life and, in the hot spring day of London, with the war in all probability ending, and ending for all the right people, she sunk her teeth into a world suddenly and inexpressibly sweet.

33. KETCHUM, IDAHO. SEPTEMBER 1961.

Late September and the air has turned chill. In the early mornings the sagebrush in the valley wears the rabbit fur of frost. This past week Mary has given up on sorting Ernest's papers: his letters lie abandoned in the study.

Instead Mary walks in the hills, following gopher tunnels and fox prints. Soon the hills will see snow, but for now they are dark, like the pelt of a great cat they might have shot in the African veldt. The sky is gray, a pool of still water.

Sometimes she walks out to the woods: the leaves of the cedar and birch are just on the turn. Fall has come so quickly and the forest is all mustards, rust and blood. Having loved its beauty so intensely, it amazes her that Ernest is blind to it now.

The press calls continue, despite the fact that in each interview Mary gives the same words without fail: *Ernest was cleaning the gun when it accidentally fired.* Then that pause: the lull of disbelief, before they try to push her in the minutes granted them. *Ernest was an expert marksman,* they say, *what was he doing up so early, at that time in the morning?* Shooting duck, she replies, the words always the same. They were going to shoot duck that morning.

The previous night, Ernest had sung to her with a mouthful of toothpaste. *Tutti mi chiamano bionda . . . Ma bionda io non sono!* He had learned the song from gondoliers in Venice. As Mary folded her clothes she smiled to hear him sing the nonsense lyrics. Increasingly, now, he was in a good mood. The writing seemed a little easier.

Porto i capelli neri! were the warbled words that came from the bathroom.

Mary called to him from her bedroom. "What shall we do tomorrow, lamb?"

"How about a little duck shooting?"

"Excellent idea." That Ernest wanted to be out of the house, moving in the air, getting things done, was a very good sign. Perhaps she might even encourage him to polish off one of these Paris sketches, tell him they should send them off to his publisher. She wanted him to feel again the world's affirmation; it was this that would keep him well. He'd published so little this decade since the *Old Man*; no wonder he felt washed up.

Ernest came into her bedroom to kiss her good night. He'd become tender and affectionate these last few days. She felt his tongue slip briefly into her mouth for a smooch—he still tasted of toothpaste. "Good night, lamb. Sleep well."

From his bedroom she heard him say, "Good night, my kitten!"

And then he carried on singing his song, his voice a big brassy baritone, his Italian still wonderful from the war. *Tutti mi chiamano bionda . . . Ma bionda io non sono!* The words became a hum as he tidied away the things in his room.

Mary closed her eyes, contented. At last, she thought, he's come back. Tomorrow they would have a day of shooting duck and she'd cook him his favorite meal, and she'd tell him caressingly how the world was going to go crazy for the memoir of Ernest Hemingway. She'd nuzzle into his white hair and perhaps in the evening, after a bottle of very nice wine, they would make love. Then the door had shut and cut off the sound of his voice and she had fallen asleep thinking of what the day held for them tomorrow.

And the next sound she heard was the gun blast.

Mary doesn't care that the journalists don't believe her. They don't need to. She couldn't give a fig for the opinion of a *Times* staffer. Why on earth would Ernest be in such high spirits the night before? Why would he have so carefully cellophaned the leftovers? Or bought the lottery ticket for the next week's draw? Or left plans for vacations they were going to take, or left his letters in such a state, if not because he would be there, in the weeks to come, to sort it all out? He hated the sloppy way his father had taken his exit; he wouldn't have done the same. He wouldn't have chosen to leave her so alone.

Shooting duck, she says, to whoever it is, and the conversation is killed there. Mary remembers her own journalist's training from the war: push the subject off his prepared script and you'll get the true story. And so she says the same words again and again. She will not veer.

At the lake Mary watches the ducks and heron on the water. She breathes in the scent of the forest floor as water-birds approach; they like to push it as far as they can with her. She lets a partridge, all fat-bodied and russet, peck around her walking boots. If her husband were here he would shoot it and have it for lunch. But she has no appetite for hunting now; all of their guns are locked away.

She has come to sit by the water often this summer, and has continued, into fall. Whenever she sits here a vivid memory from her childhood surfaces. It is a memory of skating out on the lake in Minnesota. She figures she must have been seven, because the date she carved onto the sawmill door was 1915.

The freeze had arrived early that year, on a night of no wind, so that the surface of the lake was as smooth as a plate. Mary glided around the lake feeling the slip of her blades until she had built her own dark path into the rink. Near the long grass the ice had frozen thinner and she stayed away from these parts although she liked to see the trout dart under the ice.

A sawmill stood at one corner of the lake. It was the color of dried blood in the white landscape. On the door there were the scratched names and dates of the kids brave enough to test their weight on the corner's thinner ice. Mary had just managed to carve the figure 5 onto the door when she heard the same dry sound as when her father's axe bit into timber. Under one of her boots the ice had begun to tear.

Mary tried to take little steps sideways, just as her mother had told her, but when she moved, the ice began to crack under the other boot. Black water began to come up over the shelf. Without warning, all of the ice under her began to split. Water filled her boot.

Mary grabbed at the door handle but it only turned when she twisted it, and nothing else on the sawmill could hold her weight. Shouts came from the shore. Now there was no ice under her and she could hold on to the handle no longer. She felt herself go into the open hole of dark water and down into the terrific cold.

The lake now is calm as the ducks swim and the light slanting in through the silver birch is beginning to go. Ernest always described his loneliness as *cockeyed*—as if it made him squint, as if he couldn't see straight; but her loneliness today is an ache, a song.

In her mind Mary has grafted the two accidents together, since Ernest had no more wanted to be dead than she had wanted to find herself under the ice. Perhaps he had tripped, just as she had as a child. Perhaps he had tried to grab the vestibule handle, just as she had placed her tiny hand on the sawmill door, but the doorknob had turned just as it had for her. And maybe, Ernest's finger, which had been resting gently on the gun, may have been forced to the trigger. And then she wondered if the moment had been the same for the both of them, as the bullet had been discharged and she had gone down into the ice. It was a moment not of outrage but curiosity. *What's happening to me?* he might have thought. *What am I doing down here in the black?*

34. PARIS, FRANCE. SEPTEMBER 1944.

"Papa," the private said, "there's a dame here to see you."

The private stood between the door and the frame. As he half-listened to the room the young man wore a knowing look as he watched her. "I didn't know they handed those out so easily," he said, nodding to the badge—"C" for correspondent—on her arm. His eyes swept her breasts flattened by the military jacket.

"When you've been doing it as long as me they practically give them away."

Something was said behind him and the private said, no, not her. It had been like this all week: one had to get through all the lackeys first before one could get to Ernest himself. "Tell him it's Mary Welsh."

When her name was repeated Ernest appeared and the young private quickly moved aside. "Hello, pickle," he said.

She kissed him on the cheek, removing his hand from her ass. Her happiness this week had felt close to delinquency. Most sensible people—certainly all of her friends—had warned her against any kind of alliance. Short attention span, they warned.

"My pocket Venus," he whispered to her as he planted her near the window while his "irregulars" filed from the room. Inside there was still the alarmingly strong smell of the horse shank they'd cooked on his gas stove a few nights ago. "Champagne? We haven't exhausted the supply yet." A bowl of oranges sat on the side table.

Ernest's suite was as well stocked as a general's mess. Wherever he went he came equipped with booze the rest of the correspondents hadn't seen in years. To parties he'd bring jars of marmalade, peanut butter, tinned ham, boiled peaches. If he'd written not a single book he still would have been a celebrity in no time with his famous wardrobe stuffed with delights at the Dorchester. In London, they had gone out for a few more lunches and dinners together: both of them mindful of their absent spouses. Mostly she filled him in on troop movements, lines of attack, the battles of the past five years. After his car crash she had brought him yellow tulips to St. George's Hospital. When she kissed him near the bandage he smelled of soap and camphor. "What happened?" she had said in the dusty room of the clinic.

"We rammed into a steel water tank. Couldn't see a damn thing."

"It's called a blackout, you silly fool." She arranged the tulips in a vase. "Here. These flowers will be good for you."

"You're good for me." She smiled. Ernest wore a delirious look on his face—he nursed his concussion with a bottle of champagne. Mary chucked the rest of the bottle down the sink while he protested but he did it with a smile, as if he liked her mothering. He said that Martha was coming to visit him later that afternoon, the grand dame herself. He put up his fists and made a few jabs. "Care to stick around? See who'd win in an Irish Waltz?"

Mary just laughed and declined. After the Chelsea party, the Polish pilots, and that very particular snub in the fox cape, she had no desire to see Miss Gellhorn again.

Ernest opened a fresh bottle of fizz and they watched the cork fall to the cobbles below. Under the mansard roofs opposite, the patisserie owner in her big smock swept the dust from her shop. Men lined up to buy their evening newspapers at a street kiosk. There was still a wine-colored stain on the street from the dead horse a week back, and the flags hung from windows were beginning to look tatty and dusty. Paris had begun to grow used to its freedom.

The champagne bottle clinked against the nickel bucket. "*Vive la Libération, et vive ma Mary.*" Ernest toasted her glass, his head still bandaged. He wore his uniform barefoot, but he looked a world away from the man who had his elbows deep in garbage cans the other night. Mary wondered about these deep swings in mood: how sure and in possession of his senses he was now. She wondered about apologizing for the lost poem but thought better of it. She remembered Martha's warning words.

Ernest sat in the armchair by the window, his face caught in the last of the light.

The champagne was delicious, butter on toast.

"No socks," she said, pointing her cigarette at his feet, and then tapping the ash out of the window.

"Perfect for the sockless jive," he said, scratching his ankles with the toes of the other foot. "My first wife and I lived in Paris, you know. An apartment over a mill. On the worst days sawdust came out of your eyes in chunks."

"What happened?"

"With Hadley?"

Ernest shrugged and stood. He placed a record on the phonograph and applied the needle. He did everything with a delicacy that belied his big hands. A scratchy sound, then a piano began. Chopin: a mazurka. For some time he stood watching the disc spin. Then he looked back at her, his face ashen. "Sometimes there's this feeling of things being repeated. I put the needle on the same place in the same track and I expect a different tune."

He had drunk nothing while she was sipping at her champagne; now he picked up his glass and sunk the whole thing. "What do you think Freud would have me down as?"

"A neurotic?"

Ernest gave her a sad smile. He tipped back his glass again but realized there was nothing in it. "I remember seeing her at a party in Chicago where we first met. She was wearing a blue dress to the knees. She looked as if she'd never been to a party before. When we spoke she wasn't shy but full of candor; very poised. Instantly I felt I could say anything to her. And I thought surely this is it: surely this is the woman I should marry. I was twenty-one." He watched the bubbles as he poured himself a second glass and then topped up hers. "There was an extraordinary quality to Hadley. Some insane capacity for gentleness. That's what I fell in love with. Now tell me why I got bored of a woman like that."

"Familiarity?"

"The old bitch familiarity. I was a fool."

It felt odd, listening to Ernest unburden himself. In London they had only ever talked about the war or, with a kind of ironic intimacy, Ernest might joke about Mary becoming his wife. But it was all in jest: after all, what could they do while the both of them were already husbanded and wived? Poor Noel. He'd taken the reporting job in North Africa and left her behind in a London crazed with bombing. Noel was sweet and lovely—but she'd never had quite the amount of fun with him that she'd had with Ernest these past few months.

"You don't need to feel guilty," Mary said. "Paul and Hadley always struck me as very happy with each other."

"You know Paul?"

"Only as Mr. Mowrer. He was my boss in Chicago. At the *Daily News*."

"My wives," he said. "They have a way of finding each other without me being involved a jot."

"And Pauline?" The words came out in her smoke. She wafted it away out of the window, knowing that he disliked the smell.

"Fife?"

"Yes. Has she remarried?"

He shook his head. "I feel badly for how it went with her."

"She's still in Key West?"

He nodded. "Hash says she still carries a torch. That's her expression. Fife . . ." He looks around the room. "What to say about Fife? She was the bravest woman I've ever met. We were unbelievably happy at times. But for a lot of the time we were useless. All we did was fight." Ernest tipped the last of the champagne into the glasses and upended the bottle into the bucket. "This is a funny line of questioning."

"I've met Martha. I figured I should like to meet the others."

"Sometimes I look back and I can't work out how it's done. How they all fell apart. Each and every one." Ernest looked rather blindsided by it all, sitting in the Ritz armchair, looking back at his decades of lost women. "You think who was to blame, but we were all to blame. I understand that. But me more than the others."

He took the needle from the vinyl. The room was silent. Looking at him sitting there in his armchair, with no shoes

and no socks, and with his head still turbaned from the
car accident, Mary remembers a boy she saw on the drive
to Paris, his head bandaged, dead in a Normandy ditch.
The boy's blue eyes were ancient: wrinkled and red. His
belly was swollen, as if he were six months gone with
child. It was so sad to see him there, lying alone in his
American uniform in the French earth. Mary came away
from the window and held Ernest's wounded head in her
hands. "Do be careful," she said. "Do be careful with your
poor head."

"You forgive me, don't you?"

"You're here now, Ernest. Culpable for nothing."

"What I'm saying is that I'll stay the course with you."

"Remember the old bitch, familiarity?"

"No. I feel differently this time."

"How is anything different?"

"I'm an old man."

"Old man! You're not more than forty-five, surely."

"Exactly. That's old enough for me."

Ernest took her glass and put it to one side. "Too old,
too tired, too in love, pickle, to do this all again. You'll have
me in my autumn years, and then the wintering time too.
Let's put both our lonelinesses out of business." He kissed
her, nuzzling her face with his nose. "You won't be able to
get rid of me. I'll be as faithful as a dog. This is the last
time, I promise. You're my last go."

"I'll tell you what, I'll consider your proposal if I can get
the dedication to your next book."

"That means you'll be my wife?"
"No. That means I'll think about it."
"Done."
She laughed.

That night Mary passed some sleepless hours. The room was hot though they had left the window open for the draft. Late in the night, but not yet early in the morning, Mary heard singing from the street and went over to the window. A group of men were passing a bottle between themselves.

> *Après la guerre finie,*
> *Tous les soldats partis!*
> *Mademoiselle a un souvenir,*
> *Après la guerre finie!*

The men swung their bottles to and fro like salted mariners. When they saw her up at the window, one of them gestured with a bottle. "*Venez!*" he said, then they all joined in. "*Venez!*" Mary smiled and put her finger to her lips, miming the gesture for quiet.

She finished her cigarette and came back to the bed. She wondered what it was, this sensation: if it might be called happiness, or whether it would more rightly be called fear. *I'll stay the course with you*, Ernest had said, but she had no means to test those words.

Caught in the evening light, her awake, him asleep, she felt some surge of power. With a feeling of extravagance she pulled back the sheet. This was the part of him that no one else got to see. She looked at him as if trying to memorize him, as if for an article, as if trying to put down in words the quality of Ernest's erotic body. What struck her instead was how much of him was scars. Opened by shrapnel decades ago, his right leg was hatched all over his calf and knee. Bits of the bomb, he said, were still inside him. His knees were discolored from the force of the automobile accident in London, and the tips of his fingers were dark as if they were frostbitten. There was an oval scar on his other leg—it looked like a gunshot wound. The wonder was that he had managed to stay whole at all.

Ernest looked vulnerable like this: naked and asleep. The damage he'd done to himself, the scars, merely served as a proof of his nudity. She felt an enormous inrush of happiness, a maharaja's pleasure. All this, she thought, with sure possessiveness: all this is mine.

Mary kneeled between the V of his legs and she slipped her mouth over him. She felt Ernest wake above her and he stroked behind her ears. A gunshot rang out in the streets below and the men swapped their song for chanting. *Ré-sis-tez! Ré-sis-tez!*

Ernest brought her up to him with a kiss. He put his hands into her soft blonde curls and guided himself into her. "I love you," he said. "I'd do anything to make you happy." All this he said looking up at her entranced, intoxicated, as if she were a kind of saint or savior; as if she had come to deliver him from all the world's ills.

More gunfire sounded along the roofs of Paris. *Ré-sis-tez!* they shouted. *Ré-sis-tez!*

The next few weeks they spent jaunting along Paris streets, getting what good food they could, eating lunch with Picasso and his girlfriend in the Marais, buying books recommended by Sylvia at Shakespeare's, making love in the evenings with the rattle of guns still outside the window. They lived at the Ritz and their objective, he said, was to deplete its stocks—they'd leave only once they had drunk the place dry.

Then one night, over a silly fight about some tiny thing, Ernest hit her. It was hard, right on the jaw. She held her cheek: stunned. How could he have done this, she wondered, after these marvelous few weeks? She went into her room to think over what she was doing with a man like this. "Certain things are being said about me and Ernest Hemingway," she wrote to her parents. "These are only rumors. Nothing has been confirmed."

35. KETCHUM, IDAHO. SEPTEMBER 1961.

Ernest's study is a palace of paper. There are books everywhere: his own, in many different languages, as well as books from friends and publishers, asking for quotes. Hundreds of condolence telegrams and letters which she has not yet responded to, but must, at some point, when she has the energy. *Across the River* sits on the bureau. She doesn't know why Ernest had pulled it from the shelves the night before his death. The dedication reads: *To Mary with love.* Boxes of his things are on the floor: French weeklies and issues of the London *Economist* and red-wax-sealed manuscripts and other people's letters: all waiting for her to put them into some kind of decent order. But Mary wants to be his wife, not his executrix.

She puts on the mazurkas and wraps herself in his blanket, tenting herself in the last of his smell. From Ernest's armchair she listens to the piano endeavor at the difficult rhythms and the needle stick in the same place as it always has. It's their music from Paris. It brings her back to their room at the Ritz, cordite blowing in at the window, making love to this man who wanted to make himself her husband. Mary had once read an interview with Martha, and she said how they would listen to Chopin while planes bombed Madrid. It didn't matter that the music was shared between them. Ernest had, by default, to be shared. There weren't two women in her marriage; there were always four— Hadley, Fife, Martha, and Mary. The thing was not to be heartbroken about it.

Mary tries to sort his letters chronologically. She finds some from Harry Cuzzemano, ever the milksop come to beg off him what he could. At the back of her mind she wonders if she will find any from an unknown woman. Perhaps this is why she has been putting off this task. She has no appetite to find Ernest has lied to her. There are a few from Adriana, a young woman whom Ernest had longed for, she knew, with much desire for many years. But she had never felt threatened by Adriana: she hadn't been much more than a teenager when Ernest discovered her as his new obsession. And Mary could tell that though Adriana wanted him for a friend, she had not wanted anything more. Then she had disappeared from his life. Just like all of the others.

Mary looks to the strongbox at the top of the glass cabinet. Ernest always kept the key in his locked bureau. She has, so far, resisted opening it. She is scared of what's inside: he always told her not to ask him about it. Its contents baffle her. What if there are letters from an unknown woman in there? An unknown woman, struggling out of the dark, like a blind grub in the night.

The sound of the telephone pulls her away from the study, and she's out of breath by the time she reaches it in the kitchen.

"Oh, Mary, I didn't think I'd catch you. What have you been up to?"

"Sorting Ernest's things," she says to Hadley. "It's taking a long time."

Mary sits at the kitchen counter where July's obituaries are piled on the countertop. The *New York* and *Los Angeles Times*, the *Herald*, the local rag. Ernest's photograph is on all of the front pages. Every morning she looks at his face while making coffee or grilling toast and feels a sudden fury that he's not here to have breakfast with her. "There's so much of it," she says to the papers.

"He kept so much trash, didn't he? Candy wrappers. Grocery lists. Radio schedules."

"Some of it has to go, I'm just not sure what." Mary catches her name in the articles on the countertop. "Mr. Hemingway accidentally killed himself while cleaning a gun this morning at 7:30." The next morning all of the obits used the same quote.

"Have you thought about going back to work?"

Mary laughs. "I haven't done any reporting for sixteen years, Hadley. You'd have to scrape the dust off my notepad."

"I just worry about you needing more of a purpose."

Mary wraps the telephone cord around her thumb, watching it go plum. When she unwraps the cord, the blood sinks. There is a clicking on the line. Perhaps Ernest was right and the phone is bugged. But why should they still be listening in, months after his death, to his first wife and inconsequential widow? "I have purpose."

"How's the Paris book coming?"

Hadley means the sketches Ernest had been working on these past few years. Ernest began writing them after discovering, in 1956, some trunks he had left at the Ritz, when he was fleeing his first marriage to set up his second. Mary shouldn't have asked why Ernest never threw out a scrap of paper; he'd had such bad luck losing things in the past. And this discovery had seemed like deliverance: finding all those notebooks made him want to write again. "The lawyers are going to have a field day. There'll have to be a libel read."

"He could get frightfully honest, couldn't he?"

"There's a brilliant one about Fitzgerald's manhood. Ernest is full of grave reassurances that it's all a normal size, et cetera, but you can hear his laughter in the background. It's all rather wonderful. Walks down the Seine, madcap motoring tours with other Americans, that kind of thing. Tons of food: what white wine to drink with oysters, when to mash the egg into a steak tartar. There's a story in there about you."

"Not about the suitcase?" Hadley's voice has gone quite anxious.

"No, no," she says, quick to reassure her friend. "It's all very sweet. *I wish I had died before I ever loved anyone but her*, that kind of thing. In fact it all makes me feel rather a spare part. As if our life together was just the appendix to a greater life he had once before."

"Those Paris days—take no notice. Ernest fell headlong in love with them, but only after the fact. They were splendid, and they were damned difficult at the same time." Hadley pauses. "Is there anything about me and Fife?"

Mary is delicate in how she phrases this. "There's lots of talk of her . . . *infiltration*. You and Ernest come off very well from the whole thing, while Fife, well, he's made her into a kind of devil in Dior. I'm glad she's not here to read it. It's not the version I know from either of you. He began to think some strange things, in the end. He felt quite strongly about certain matters he'd never mentioned before."

"He was quite different these past few years."

Mary lets this lie. She knows where Hadley is trying to go with this. "I was thinking we could call it *A Moveable Feast*. It's from one of his letters."

"Do you think he would have liked it? I do. You'll let me read it beforehand?"

"Of course," Mary says. "Hash?"

"Yes?"

"I want him to come home." Mary looks down at Ernest's face in the paper's obituary. "I miss him so much."

"I know."

"It's not fair."

"Mary . . ." Hadley sighs.

"What?"

"These wild swings in mood . . . The paranoia you told me about. The alcohol. Don't you see? Cloaking it as some kind of accident, it can't—"

"It *was* an accident."

"I think he was very depressed."

"He was feeling better, Hash, you should have seen him the night before. He was his old self again."

"Apparently that—"

"It was a mistake. That's all." A door out back slams and Mary's heart races. She sees again scraps of plaid dressing gown. Blood and teeth on the vestibule walls. His gun held crossways against his body. But the housemaid comes into the kitchen and her heart stills.

"The gun misfired. That's all. That's just what makes it so sad."

That night, Mary dreams of him. They were back on *Pilar* motoring toward the shore. As they approached, the seawater went from dark to light and gulfweed surrounded the boat. Nothing more than thin-blown clouds in the sky and a light breeze that encouraged them toward the shine of the beach.

Ernest buried her in sand, giving her colossal breasts, going all the way up to her neck then studding her in cowrie shells and stones. When he gave her a long wet lick across her cheek she laughed so much the sandy belly jiggled. "What a delicious salt lick your face is! I could be here for hours!" He tongued the wets of her eyes and the wells of her nostrils and the holes of her ears until she was helpless with laughter. And she asked him to unpack her from the sand so that she could hold him close to her heart.

When she wakes it's with a sob, gasping, as if she's spent too long underwater. Her pillow is wet with tears. They had gone shelling like this on a beach in Bimini. She wishes he could have seen more of it. The joy of it all; of being alive.

Outside the weather is fretful and the trees are moving with the wind. Mary tries to shake the afterimage of the dream. She hates these dreams where Ernest is alive, and yet in her waking hours she wishes so dearly for him to live again. Out on the decking Mary drinks a glass of water and smokes a cigarette. Widow's privilege.

She thinks: what if it wasn't an accident? The question surfaces like a bubble escaping a shipwreck. Gregory had asked her this at the funeral and she had pretended not to hear the question. Ernest's three sons had stood next to each other at the graveside, and she had thought how dearly she would have liked to have given him a daughter. But after the first miscarriage, only months after their marriage, he'd told her he couldn't ask her to do this. "I wouldn't ask a man to jump from a building without a parachute," Ernest had said. "You mean more to me than any daughter." But standing there watching his casket lowered into the earth, she had wondered if a daughter might have somehow saved him from himself.

Mary finishes up the cigarette. She's about to go back inside when she sees a big stag tread through the garden, caught in the last of the quarter moon. The animal is nothing less than majestic. Its antlers are huge and its legs have such a drifting, dignified walk, it's as if they don't even really touch the soil. Lonesome creature, with such a heaviness on its head, she wonders how he bears the load.

36. HAVANA, CUBA. 1946.

On the night of their wedding Mary locked the door of her bedroom so that he could not get in. "Mary, let me in!"

The handle moved up and down and the door, already weak from the termites, shook in its casings. "You brute! Go away!"

Mary held the handle fast until she heard Ernest's steps retreat to the living room. At once she began to pack her things: the wool suit made from Noel's civvies, her cotton frocks, her few books; remembering the day she had arrived and unpacked all of her things. How exciting—how glamorous—the Finca Vigía had seemed to her then after the Paris winter!

Now, she couldn't wait for colder climes. She wanted to go back to Chicago where the air was flat and sensible. *How long did your marriage to Ernest Hemingway last?* her friends on the women's pages would ask her at the *Daily News*, maybe even for a few inches in their gossip columns. About twenty-four hours, she'd have to respond. She could just see the headline now: FOURTH HEMINGWAY MARRIAGE LASTS UNDER A DAY.

Now the only question was whether she should leave still in her wedding dress. It could be passed off as traveling clothes she supposed—both of them were old hands at marriage; neither of them had wanted much fuss. Mary unpinned the flower corsage and dropped it in the waste-paper basket.

With her suitcase packed she prepared for the confrontation. Ernest would be sitting in the lamplight of the living room, watched over by kudu, nursing a Scotch, ready to make his emollient apologies. Mary would, without drama, walk past him and drive away. She would not listen to Ernest's protests; he was becoming too skilled at his apologies.

When Ernest had driven up to the Finca, the morning of her arrival in Cuba, she had immediately smelled hibiscus and lime. Before her was the most enormous white mansion, bright as a pebble in the Caribbean sunshine. Scarlet flowers splashed down the steps. Ernest stood outside the car, scanning her face for a reaction.

"Oh, Ernest," she said, taking his hand. "It's *glorious*."

The trees sounded with enough noise to make an aviary. He led her up the broad stone steps, pointing out the pool and the ancient ceiba tree, then bringing her into the living room with the animal heads studding the walls. "It's as if I'm Elizabeth Bennet," she said.

"How's that?"

"This might just be your Pemberley, Hemingway."

"Remind me, do Darcy and Miss Bennet marry?"

"She's very suspicious of him. Then she sees his house and is persuaded otherwise."

"You like the house?" She nodded. "A good sign, then."

Cats wrapped themselves around her ankles.

Ernest left her to unpack in her room. Mary opened up the furniture to see the insides of things. The bureau drawers came out nicely on their rollers; everything smelled of wood and was empty and clean. Fresh roses were on the bedside table and the vines outside the windows were as heavy as drapes. This room, she knew, had probably been Martha's.

Mary lay on the bed in her underclothes. As she watched the ceiling fan turn she wondered if she might just be crazy. She had given up her job at *Time*, given up her apartment in London, given up on her gentle husband, to be in this paradise of lemon light and hot sweet air. When Ernest was good he was entrancing, but when he was on the sauce he could be vile. She wondered, too, what might be her purpose here. Manage the staff? Go fishing and shooting with Ernest? No longer would she be a correspondent with her own stories and salary. A bird of some exotic description cawed outside. Would she have enough to do?

Knocking came at the door. Mary raised herself, looking for a gown or robe. She felt a little nervous of him. After six months of close but independent living in Paris, here they were in Cuba, as if they were man and wife. "Would you like a swim, Mary?" he said behind the door.

"Just a minute." She changed into her bathing suit and checked herself over in the mirror. She was as white as paper; her skin hadn't seen real sunshine since the Liberation. She held the robe at her chest and opened the door.

Ernest stood holding a bowl in his hands. "Peaches in champagne," he said, offering them to her. "Soaked overnight. A real humdinger."

The spoon he held clattered to the floor. He picked it up, gave it a lick clean, replaced it back in the bowl, and whispered in her ear. "I'm too excited to see you."

At the pool, when she disrobed, he gave her the most enormous smile—a grin, she would later learn, that was reserved for when he'd hooked a fish and it turned out to be a real monster. As she started to do laps, smelling the frangipani and eucalyptus wafting over, and seeing the palms over a mile away in Havana, she let out a sigh. This might be Pemberley, indeed.

An hour after the wedding Mary slammed shut the door of the convertible. "I wanted to stay, Ernest." It was a half-hour trip back from Vedado to the Finca, and Ernest screeched out of the Spanish mansion.

"Not with those clowns."

"Clowns! They're our friends!"

"Marjorie was drunk. Didn't you hear her slurring?"

"*You're* drunk, Ernest."

The wedding toasts had gone well, back at the house of one of their friends, until Marjorie had made some dumb joke about Mary taking Ernest for all he was worth: royalties, options, books, and more, and Ernest had savaged the poor woman and pulled Mary out of the apartment by her wrist.

As he drove toward the sea a herd of goats moved in front of the car, their hapless shepherd following and uttering expletives in Spanish. "Biblical times we are living in!" Ernest shouted, to whom she didn't know, but the shepherd evidently thought the invective was aimed at him, and he started shouting back in Cuban Spanish so thick— something about Ernest being the mother of something, or was it his mother was something else?—that even Ernest couldn't understand him.

Around them came people on bicycles and motorbikes, able to weave in and out of the goats; all the while the Lincoln stayed by the Malecón. The sequins of her wedding dress bit into her skin, and the orchid corsage gave off an alarmingly sweet smell.

By her side Ernest was getting hotter and angrier. No wind upset the palms. He'd be a fool if he thought he could manhandle her like this in front of their friends. He was a sauced brute; what a fool she had been to marry him. "Drive me back. At least let me enjoy my wedding day even if my husband won't accompany me in it."

Ernest didn't answer but sped off from the last of the goats, nearly decapitating one as he went. He drove far too quickly; she'd be dead before she could file for divorce. "Slow down, for God's sake!"

He sped up and the royal palms in the valley flew past faster.

"Slow down, you maniac!"

Minutes from home the heavens opened. There was no

time—and precious little desire for cooperation—in order to roll up the cover. Cuba became one solid raindrop. She held her jacket over her head.

The car screeched to a stop outside the Finca. Ernest's wedding suit stuck to him; Mary was drenched. In the traditional Spanish manner their servants were lined up in uniform outside the villa, each of them holding a small gift. A couple stood with umbrellas, ready to greet the newlyweds. What they did not expect to find was Mr. and Mrs. Hemingway, drenched to the bone, and shooting each other murderous looks.

Mary slammed the door and shouted, "Go drink another glass of hemlock, you bastard! Since this marriage has gone about as well as the last one!"

She stormed into the house only to hear in her trail the popping of a champagne cork and the rather lost voice of the gardener saying *Felicidades, Señor y Señora Hemingway* . . .

Now the suitcase stood by her shoes, ready for New York.

Knocking came again from behind the door, but gentler this time. "Pickle?"

"I'm leaving."

"Please open the door."

"I don't want to speak to you."

"Mary, I'm sorry for acting like an ass this afternoon. I only wanted to spend the last of our day just with you."

When she opened the door he wore his kicked-dog

expression and held a glass of Scotch. He offered it to her. Only reluctantly did she take a sip and feel the drink's warmth.

"Let's never get married again, kitten."

"Certainly not to each other."

With the light behind him he looked older than his years: his hair was going white around his temples. He wore the glasses that his vanity wouldn't let him wear outdoors, though he needed them, she knew, more than he admitted.

Ernest tugged at her dress but she remained still. His eye caught her case. "Pickle, you wouldn't leave me, not so soon? At least stay long enough to get changed out of your dress. You're still dripping onto the tiles."

Ernest directed her toward the bed and they sat down. "Convince me I haven't left a perfectly good marriage to the shambles of another."

"My temper, sometimes . . . I'm sorry."

He smiled at her. He wasn't forgiven, not yet. "Ernest?"

"Yes?"

"Please promise you'll be nice to me."

"I promise, kitten. I'm so sorry. I'll be better. You'll see."

"And I want something else."

"Anything," he said expansively.

"Take down Martha's damn war map from that room. I can't stand the sight of all those little pins everywhere."

He laughed and said, "It would be my pleasure."

*

Mary gave up on her old life with the ease of sinking into a hot bath. Cold Europe seemed a lifetime away. It made her laugh to think of how madly she had wanted her career to catch up with Martha's. She hadn't even got close— but she had, however, inherited the woman's house. She remembered her haughty words at the party in London: *That's mine*, Martha had said, reaching for the fox tails, holding herself in high regard. Well, Mary thought, looking around at the hibiscus villa, not anymore.

Life in the Finca was a life undreamed of. Mary went about in the hot afternoons exterminating termites, supervising the carpentry, renovating the house. They took long trips fishing off *Pilar*, to Bimini, to Cojímar, bringing back dinners of marlin and dorado. Each morning she took a naked half-mile swim before lunch; in the afternoons were the promises of frozen daiquiris. Vacations in Italy, New York, France, the fiesta at San Fermin, plans for East African safaris. For Ernest's fiftieth they ate lunch in the garden with all of their friends: winter-melon soup, slippery chicken, ice cream in coconut halves.

Afterward, everyone blind, they erected a coconut shy and it was a smooch on the lips from Ernest—men of the party included—who managed to knock down a coconut. Mary used Martha's old Winchester to bag her catch and earned herself three of the longest kisses that afternoon. "Happy half a hundred, lamb," she said, as she watched Patrick and Gregory, young men now, go at the coconuts.

"You're my guy," he said, with his arm around her.

What a life of plenty this was! And when he published *The Old Man and the Sea*, after a long time when no one much had liked his stuff, the world once again went mad for Ernest Hemingway. Accolades, sales, and a Nobel Prize; nothing, it seemed, could be improved upon.

37. KETCHUM, IDAHO. SEPTEMBER 1961.

From the woods she can see a car traveling up her driveway. Its hood points to her house; its only objective could be her home. The sky this morning is so high and wide; the car looks a tiny thing in the expanse of air. Mary's heart drops. Visitors.

Closer up she sees it's an old Ford though there's no driver to be seen now that it's come to a stop outside her house. The car's paintwork is so dented it looks as if it's been stoned by Idaho natives. A man is looking in through one of the living room windows, pressing his hands against the glass. He takes a few steps back to look at the concrete walls and square planes of the house, as if he's scoping out an opponent's bulk. Not much can be seen, at first, between his collar and hat. But when he walks back to the car she sees who it is.

Ernest would be rolling in his grave to see Harry Cuzzemano on his drive.

"Mrs. Hemingway," he says. He smiles at her as if this

is all perfectly normal. He's grown better with age: his weight has softened his face. The scar that was so livid at the Ritz ("Friendly fire," she remembers him saying in the lobby) has faded, though it still runs down the better part of his cheek. "How good it is to see you." The press of his hand is soft in hers.

"Mr. Cuzzemano. This is a surprise." She feels herself observed by him—she supposed she would be much changed since they met in Paris so many years ago.

His face becomes grave. "Mrs. Hemingway. I'm sorry for your loss."

Mary nods her acceptance.

She's always had an affectionate spot for Harry Cuzzemano, believing him to be the unfortunate target of some of her husband's more wrathful moods. Still, he always seemed to know how to stir Ernest's displeasure. Sometimes he even seemed to court it, like an animal holding out its neck for the catch rope: letters, late-night telephone calls, copies of advertisements in French newspapers detailing the lost suitcase. It seems he would do anything for Ernest's attention; even goad him.

"What are you doing here?"

"I thought Ernest would have a bead on me before I could even get up the drive. I figured I was safe now." He says this as if it were an answer to her question.

"Are you on your way somewhere?"

Harry Cuzzemano nods but does not elaborate.

"Where have you come from?"

"The South."

His blue eyes are so intense Mary finds it difficult to hold his gaze. "Do you want to come in?" she says, because she doesn't know what else to say. Cuzzemano nods and with his long step he walks over to the vestibule door.

"That one's locked." Mary hasn't yet moved. "We'll go round the back."

Cuzzemano's expression changes as soon as he steps into the house. It would be uncharitable to think he wasn't moved by being here. It's as if the entire room emits grace.

"The man himself," he says, immediately taken by the portrait that hangs in the recess of the wall. Ernest stares out into the room: his eyes are like the twin holes of a rifle. The white beard almost reaches the frame; his grin is nearly as wide. She called him Santa Claus when she thought the beard needed a trim.

"It was taken at his sixtieth."

"You should have seen him as a boy. He had the look of a god." Cuzzemano is close to the picture. "It has his likeness. Very much."

Mary wonders what this means, given Cuzzemano hasn't seen Ernest in over a decade. The book collector moves from the portrait to the sofa, padding his lower back with a cushion. His eyes travel the room, taking in the skulls and pelts and books. She'll have to frisk him for paper and silverware before he leaves.

She seats herself on the sofa opposite and is about to

ask what she can do for him when Cuzzemano begins speaking. "You know, Ernest took such an instant dislike to me." His tone is offhand, as if he is returning to the subject of a previous conversation. "Even when he was a nobody in Antibes. He never understood I was trying to do things for him. Find suitcases. Lost novels, poems. Zelda and Scott: they never despised me like Ernest did."

"Perhaps because you weren't shy on loans for liquor."

"The Hemingways, the Fitzgeralds, the Murphys. God, how I wanted to be part of it: the golden set, the Riviera gang. Mary, these people . . ." he exhales, "they were part of the elect."

"What does it matter now, Mr. Cuzzemano? Everyone's gone."

Cuzzemano's eyes fix on the corner of the table. "When Zelda died in the fire, I couldn't stop thinking about that night in Antibes: Ernest holding her in a fireman's lift and Scott releasing his volley of figs. That night at the Villa America. It was *magical*."

Mary has never heard this story about figs or Zelda and she wonders whether it is true. Their friends said Cuzzemano could be a great dissembler when he wanted to be.

"Poor Zelda," he says. "She hated Ernest. She was the only one. Everyone else fell in love with him, men as well as women. People were obsessed with trying to please him; I saw that obsession in Fife. She was one of my camp. Too much a fan." He raises his eyebrows.

"I always thought," he says it slowly, as if this will be his last chance to best represent his intentions, "that I would find Ernest's suitcase. I put ads in Paris papers. I interviewed bellhops and train guards and the shop woman who'd sold Hadley the cigarettes. Of course, it never came to anything. But I always thought I would find it. Then I would give it back to him and he'd forgive me and want to be my friend. How foolish I was. How mistaken."

Mary watches Cuzzemano. He must be in his late fifties now, just a shade off Ernest's years, but his face is somehow ageless, as if he is not affected by time. "Coffee?"

He nods and looks back again to the portrait of Ernest.

When she comes back into the living room, Cuzzemano is on the sofa unchanged. His hands overlap neatly on his knees and he gives her his best smile.

"Cookies!" He says the word with childish exclamation.

Mary places the plate on the coffee table. She wonders if he has raided the room's treasures in the time it has taken her to make a French press.

Outside, the day has turned. Now rain strings down the windows. Mary switches on a light. "What can I do for you, Mr. Cuzzemano? What's the nature of your trip? A pilgrimage perhaps, or an auction? Or is it a journey for absolution?"

"I'd like my letters back."

He says it without any reserve or reluctance.

She pours him a coffee while she waits to find her response. "Cream?" He shakes his head. "Sugar?" He answers no again. Mary sits down with her cup and says, "What do you want with them?"

"I want . . ." Cuzzemano wets his lips, ready for a cookie which he then returns to the plate uneaten. He seems nervous. "I want to erase myself from the records."

The windows behind him are only water, and steam curls from the top of his cup.

Mary thinks about the five or six letters she had found in the study signed with his extravagant handwriting: *H. Cuzzemano*. It was an innocent enough signature for a man who'd been living off them for decades, a flea on the coat of a big dog, trading on their manuscripts, their letters, their papers. "Why should I say yes? The rest of us have no choice in the matter."

"They're letters from a madman, Mary. How I badgered and bullied him. I was," he says, taking a sip of coffee, "obsessive. I see that now. Let me erase myself from the story. I've burned the ones he sent me. Give me the letters, Mary, and I'll consign them to the fire. And I won't even be a footnote in history."

Cuzzemano's eyes are persuasive. He picks up the same cookie and takes a bite.

The study bolt slides noiselessly. Mary opens the window to let the wind blast the room's staleness. By the glass is

Ernest's tall desk where he would write standing up. His typewriter had been cleaned and given a new ribbon only weeks before his death. It was as if he were ready to come back to the page.

In the study is everything she has brought back from the Finca: all the paper she could salvage. She's brought back drawers of doctors' notes, letters from lawyers, publishers, foreign editors, bank managers. Paper has been attacked by jungle rot. In Cuba she had suggested—not jokingly either—that a servant should take *Pilar* out and sink her. What would she do with a boat that size? A boat had to be cared for, painted, dry-docked, loved. And so she said in all seriousness they should go out and sink her, let the sea wash reach its gunwales. *Relinquishment*, that was the right word, she thinks, as she surveys the study. The abandonment of cherished things. Sometimes Mary dreams of relinquishing it all, every last damn piece of paper.

Mary finds the book collector's letters and searches another file for more. She piles together whatever evidence of Harry Cuzzemano she can find. There will be more; of that she is sure. Just before she slides the study bolt Mary sees, behind the cabinet glass, that box again. She thinks about finding the key and unlocking it. Instead she locks the office door.

38. HAVANA, CUBA. 1947.

Years passed before Mary realized another woman had a place in their marriage.

This year, with Ernest, had been wonderful: it was the marriage she had hoped for in her most optimistic of moods. Duck shooting out west, playing tennis at the Finca, seeing the orchids come into their own, the bougainvillea climbing the walls, the mariposa nodding their white bonnets. Iced coconut water and gin. Drinking and dancing in Havana Vieja. Parties with writers and artists. She had never spent so much time unhooked from obligation and she marveled that she felt no nostalgia for her old life as a hack. Here was light and warmth and good Ernest by her pillow in the morning. It was as if, only after they had married, that she had let herself fall in love with him.

And then another woman showed up: a woman of neat outfits, an eye for renovations, and the proper way of doing things. A woman who already knew the contours of Ernest's heart, who knew what he wanted and what he didn't want, only as Mary was gradually beginning to learn all of these things for herself.

Fife had arrived.

Eighteen-year-old Patrick had had a terrible car accident that spring. Fife had written insisting that only her presence would speed up his convalescence. "She hardly cared in Key West," Ernest said to her. "Now she won't rest until she's with him. Well, I suppose the boy will want his mother. You don't mind, do you?"

They lived like this for months at the Finca: Ernest, Mary, and Fife, with Patrick in the guesthouse, recovering. Ernest looked happy during this time: like a dog scratched behind the ears. And, after the initial jealousy of having his ex-wife in their home, Mary had to admit she liked Fife: her sassy honesty, her black charisma. Though she was more than a decade older than Mary, her hair was still as black as macadam. And she still had some irrepressible glamour to her, as if she would forever be a child of the Roaring Twenties.

It turned out that Fife was immensely knowledgeable: she knew how to plan an intricate meal, what wines would match it, how to dress the table, and above all, what to do with the garden's acres: she and Mary could talk about plants for hours. They loved to drink together and sometimes they'd hide from Ernest when the writing was hard and he was doing his best turn as a majordomo around the house. Then they would go down to the rose garden and get sloshed before supper. Mary liked having a girlfriend around—even if it had to be Ernest's ex-wife.

Fife became a fixture at the Finca until it became natural that, of an evening, they would dine just the three of them out on the veranda under a creeping vine that Fife had helped train against the Finca wall. The way she looked at him over dinner: it wasn't jealousy, Mary realized; it was love. Fife was still so much in love with him. Mary remembered Ernest's words that day in the Ritz: *She is the bravest woman I know*. Yes, she certainly is, Mary often thought as she watched the former Mrs. Hemingway laugh at one of Ernest's silly jokes over a dessert of drowned peaches. But Fife, to Ernest, was a woman confined to history.

"Have you always been this color?" Fife asked, touching the curls of Mary's hair late one night when Ernest was still out on the boat. Both of them were a little liquored as they sat by the Finca pool; Fife made a wonderful martini.

"I changed it once," Mary said, "with bleach. Ernest went wild for it, but I never minded it being mouse."

"I dyed it once even blonder than you." Fife scratched the scalp underneath her short black spikes. The green light from off the pool made her cheeks into shadowy holes. "Because I knew how much he liked blondes. But Martha," she said. "Martha was the real deal."

"He'd be happy in a field of lady dandelions."

"You've got that right."

They lay on the new loungers. Fife had encouraged Mary to replace the old ones which had been too rickety. "I remember when I first met her, this Martha Gellhorn. She had an odd accent: sort of Anglo-Midwest. Proust, she said, was a real *dagsbady*. She talked about the *foocha* of literature." Fife laughed. "The night we met I thought Sara Murphy was going to throw her soup at her. Somehow, you don't think your husband will be stolen from you in your own parlor."

Fife stared at the buckling light on the pool, her mouth a straight line. "I don't even think Martha really wanted to marry him. I wish she had. Then it would somehow have been forgivable, that I didn't lose the most important person in my life to a woman who treated him as a play-thing. A person of no consequence." And then she said, with agonizing slowness: "He was everything to me."

"I think he meant something to her, Fife."

"She got rid of him after four years. Four years, Mary, and I gave him twelve! *What am I meant to do now?*" Fife blinked back the tears as if the pain were still very raw.

"Ernest once described you as one of the bravest people he ever met."

"Brave? Well: ha, ha. Hardly sexy, is it?" she said. She took a deep breath and sighed. "I'm glad he's with you, Mary. More than anything I want Ernest to be happy."

She gestured with the glass. "A welcome physic." She drained the last of the martini and smacked her lips. She sucked on the olive then spat it back into the glass. "Lord! I've been keeping you up with my babbling. I shall leave you in peace." Fife planted a kiss on her forehead. Mary noticed it was her eyes that were beautiful, as clear as gin. Her breath suggested she might have had more than two martinis tonight.

When Mary returned to the house she caught Fife in his bathroom, staring at the pharmaceutical graffiti on the walls. Inked notes covered the plasterwork: blood pressure counts and Ernest's weight measured against dates. Cabinets were stuffed full of medical equipment: amber bottles and blister packs, medication for his heart, his eyes. Fife looked sorrowful, as if she longed to protect him. "Make sure he takes care of himself," she said to Mary, squeezing her hand—longing, perhaps, to touch him again. Though Ernest was wary of the relationship, she was not. She counted Fife very much as her friend.

Jinny cabled the news of Fife's death from California on the second day of October in 1951. A heart attack at three in the morning; nothing could be done. The night before, she and Ernest had had a searing row about Gregory. In no uncertain terms, Jinny told Ernest over the telephone how he had killed her sister, and how he had ruined her life pretty much from the moment he'd met her over a chinchilla skin at a party in Paris. "You bastard," Mary heard through the earpiece, "she gave you everything!"

Ernest fought back a little, but he let her sister quarry her grief.

The year of Fife's death they returned to Key West to sort out her friend's things. They spent two weeks in Fife's house, surrounded by the brick wall and the dying poinsettia, feeling as if they should not be here without her. One night, from up at Ernest's study, Mary watched her husband swimming alone in the saltwater pool. His body looked as busted as an old car. When he stopped at the deep end, a tear rolled down his face. Mary knew he had loved Fife more than he had let on: for giving him that time in his thirties, for letting him write, and write so much; for being the best friend she could be after his father's death. Mary remembered Fife's words by the Finca poolside: *He was everything to me.* As a tribute to her friend she did not go down and console him. Instead she let Ernest swim alone, lost in the memories of this fine house, in the tropics of Fife's splendid garden.

It felt wrong to lose one of them. Wrong for her to die so young. Wrong that Fife couldn't see she would overcome the loss of him. It felt that they all should live as long as Ernest, that they were all needed, somehow, to bear witness. In the narratives of their lives, which Mary had imagined more than once, they would all outlive Ernest— and Ernest himself would live a good long time. And in the end they would all be reconciled, and each would stand as herself: Hadley Richardson, Pauline Pfeiffer, Martha Gellhorn and, finally, herself, Mary Welsh.

A strange family indeed; such unlikely sisters.

39. KETCHUM, IDAHO. SEPTEMBER 1961.

When Mary comes back from the study, Cuzzemano is not in the living room, nor is he in the kitchen. Perhaps he has driven off in the midst of screeching tires and churned gravel. What should she do? Put in a call to the police? Call Hadley? Or even Martha? She'd be deemed a patsy for even letting him into the house. He could be well on the road to a New York auction house by now.

But Ernest's things are still where they should be: his fishing rod, typewriter, first editions, wire-rimmed spectacles. Nothing is gone. The house is quiet.

Mary is just about to make the call when she catches a shadow through the frosted glass of the inner door. A gap in the frame shows Cuzzemano's well-oiled curls and the gully of the scar. He sits on the pine ledge where Ernest sat countless time to un-shoe. Around him are woollies, parkas, snow boots. He's as still as a saint.

"We don't use this entranceway, Mr. Cuzzemano. I told you that."

His eyes open and they're that shock of tender blue. "Mary." His tongue gives a sweep of his lips.

The vestibule isn't even really a room but rather a passage between inside and out where they put coats and scarves, muddy boots and guns. In her life she's spent no more than a few minutes in here at a time. This room meant nothing to her until she heard that gunshot, watched her slippers take the stairs two by two, shouting "Ernest! Ernest!" to find her husband alone in the vestibule, blood on the door handle where he'd tried to catch himself while falling.

She says again: "We don't use this room."

"Was it in here?"

She concentrates on the sleeve of one of Ernest's hunting jackets. "Yes."

"Oh, Mary, how did you stand it?"

"It was an accident," she says. "It just happened."

But Cuzzemano brings out one of the newspapers from the kitchen. He reads aloud the quote they have used from her. He looks at her not as if she is a fool, but as if she is somehow a woman orphaned.

"And you've come to persuade me otherwise, have you?"

"Not at all, Mrs. Hemingway. You are the only one, the only one, who might know what happened."

The leaves of the nearby cedar are still now. Patches of light show where the sky is darkest. Rain threatens again. Hesitantly, she walks into the vestibule for the first time since that day. *Vestibule*: she thinks how the word belongs to the architecture of a church, and it feels like that in here—very calm and still, as if this room were the sanctuary of the house.

At the window Mary sees a covey of black birds break from the nearest tree. Without thinking she says, "I planted those trees while Ernest was at the clinic. Flowering plum. Mountain ash."

"The clinic?"

Mary doesn't turn from the window because she doesn't want to see his face. Only their closest friends know about the clinic.

"What was it for?" Harry asks. "His stay there?"

"Blood pressure," she says, and though she believes it is the truth, she also knows it is a lie.

Those birds are high, now, and not one of them has broken rank. Close together, they bank on the air and turn in the afternoon sky. The way they move is like wind in a cornfield. They fly east until they have all but disappeared completely.

"It was electroshock therapy. For depression." She wonders why it is to Cuzzemano she is unburdening herself. "He called it *frying the bacon*. It took me a long time to persuade him to go."

"Yes."

"He didn't stay long. He managed to convince the doctors he was well again; I don't know how. When I came to pick him up again he was sitting in the doctor's office with his suitcase neatly packed and a grin like the Cheshire Cat's. I should have protested. I should have made him stay." She holds her hands together. "But I didn't."

"And then?"

"A week later." She tears up. "He wasn't himself."

Mary goes over to the bench to sit by Cuzzemano. They sit for a while in the vestibule where Ernest died and watch as the mauve clouds gather and the room darkens. The rain, spots at first, begins again, then pours. It's not unwelcome. It drums on the vestibule's roof. The plum trees shake in the storm.

They sit close together. She takes some comfort from

him being here. "It amazes me Ernest can't see color. That he no longer has words. I'm perplexed—no—I *marvel*—that he doesn't have that pleasure anymore. When you read his words it seems an outrage he's not here anymore to put down what's going on." Mary smiles. "You should read these Paris sketches, Harry. They're going to make people *laugh*."

For minutes they watch the thrown shadows of the branches against the inner wall. It's the kind of light which comes after a storm: deep and massive, able to fill valleys. This alchemy of water and light, this beauty of fall in Idaho.

"You know Ernest liked to hunt big game. Leopard, lion, buffalo—anything enormous. When we came back from an African trip one of the cats was in a bad way at the Finca, its back hip sticking from the fur. He said that there was nothing we could do. I asked him why it had to be so quick and Ernest said that the cat would begin to feel it soon. Someone fetched his gun. He held the cat, snuggling into its neck, telling him what a beautiful kitty he was. Then he shot it right there, on the terrace, in full view of everyone, blew its head off clean.

"I never heard him howl as he did that day. He wasn't a man insensitive to others' suffering. I'm sorry you always saw a crueler side to him. And I'm impressed you loved him anyway."

Cuzzemano offers her a half smile and she takes his hand

in hers. "Don't worry," she says. "Ernest always attracted obsessives. You were only one of many. And secretly, sometimes, I think he was flattered. Nobody ever stalked Fitzgerald."

Mary then asks him about the scar. It has always felt as if there is a longer story behind this pink line that joins his eye to his chin. "Friendly fire," Cuzzemano says, but again he won't elaborate.

When the storm has passed Mary fetches his letters from the living room. "If I find any more," she says, "I'll consign them to the fire. Here you are." She hands them over. Cuzzemano has his hands already open as if he is asking for benediction. "History's pardon."

Outside on the drive he kisses her cheek with his good side and then walks over to the wheel and starts the engine. Ernest had told her about their chance meeting on the Riviera in 1926: how he had, at first, encouraged the book collector to look for that suitcase, thinking how lucky he was to have a free private investigator on his case. Ernest told her he'd regretted it ever since—what a leech Cuzzemano had become. But Mary, at least, has made her peace with him. She wishes she could extend this forgiveness from Ernest, but it is not hers to give.

Before setting off, Cuzzemano takes a sip from a hip flask, as if coming here to his hero's house has depleted him. Something about his soft mouth, the way it waits for the hit of the liquid; it reminds her of Ernest. Before leaving he takes one last look at the house and sighs. He's a fan; of that he's incurable.

"Take care," she says.

After he's gone she follows the car's contrail of dust down to the Big Wood River. Mary sits at the felled cottonwood tree with her thoughts, pleased to be alone again.

They used to sit on this trunk, looking out across the valley, until Ernest became too frightened. So much space, he said, they might be got at from any angle. "Ernest," she would say, "Ernest," as if his name might coax him back to himself. She wondered what devil had chased away his sanity and left him as this man afraid of his own shadow.

In the woods he was a wild creature. "Mary," he said, with new vigor in his eyes. "The FBI. They're listening in." He went over to the river: bulrush and reeds slanted in its current. He scanned the valley for a sweet spot where the enemy might be hiding, then hurried back up to the log. "They're trying to set me up. They're going to drag me to jail. They'll say I haven't been paying my taxes. The IRS, they're in on it too. Listen, I'll write you a note. I'll say you had no knowledge of our finances, that you only had the sketchiest idea of the accounts. I'll say you didn't know what was kept in our bags when we traveled. You don't realize, do you?"

Mary looked at his eyes, trying to connect with the old version of him she knew and loved and who understood the world for what it really was. "I don't understand what you mean, lamb."

He threw up his arms as if it were to the trees that he formally surrendered his sanity. "Come and get me, you BASTARDS!"

In the woods the trees held their silence.

Ernest walked into the grasses as if thrashing for snipe. "The day is ruined!" he shouted. "The day is *ruined!*" And in the minutes that his back was turned Mary allowed herself one great wrenching sob, before she went into the marshes to try and reclaim him. It was that afternoon she had telephoned the clinic.

40. KETCHUM, IDAHO. SEPTEMBER 1961.

A daytime fire has always struck Mary as odd. It feels instinctive to have a bonfire at night, but she wants to do this before the light goes. The garden smells of pines and blown earth and musk, as if the stag she saw the other night has left behind his smell.

She makes a woodpile from the branches come down in the winds. Then she brings out newspapers from the kitchen in a crate which used to hold oranges. Ernest's face stares up from the front page, and Mary remembers how much delight Ernest had taken in reading his own obituaries back in '54, when their plane had come down over Murchison Falls. When their second rescue plane had burst into flames on the runway, Ernest had used his head as a battering ram to get out of the exploding airplane. It was a farce, Mary thought, but a bloody awful one.

Not one editor had waited for any bodies to be pulled from the wreckage. "Well," Ernest said, reading one of the death notices from India in the hotel the next morning, "looks like no one enjoyed *Across the River* but everyone has me down for perpetuity with *The Old Man*. I was a charming gent with enough charisma to woo famous women into bed with me. My four wives were all sucked into my designs by my winning smile"—he was grinning now, as if really tasting all the different flavors of the world's loss—"and I set up the louche life in bohemian Paris that all writers have since tried to emulate—though all, since, have failed. I was a champion boxer, hunter, deep-sea fisherman. Oh, and I also created a whole new school of writing. What do you think of that, Miss Mary? Not bad for a fifty-four-year-old."

But when Ernest woke the next morning, his pillow was soaked with cerebral fluid. As a tonic he took cold champagne "to clear my thoughts," he said. But this wasn't like the hospital in London, where he had been trying to impress her, and he wouldn't give up the bottle. Instead he swatted her away, quite forcefully, with his burned and still bloodied hands.

After the crashes, she sensed something change in Ernest. His moods, which had always been erratic, grew worse; the liquor became harder; and the right words, in the right order, became more difficult for him to put down. No longer could he snap from himself the flat terse sentence. He told her alcohol helped, but if he drank every time he felt pain in his kidney or spine or spleen, he'd be drunk all the time, and then he wouldn't be able to write. And writing, he said, was the only thing worth sticking around for.

There were still, after the crashes, the wild parties at the Finca and the marvelous trips on *Pilar* to eat wahoo with lime and go shelling on island beaches. They had a wonderful life—but in private, and alone, he started to believe the bad things he thought about himself.

Always, now, when she found him at his desk, it was with a baleful look, a look that was almost aggrieved, as if he were being denied the pleasure that, since he'd been a twenty-five-year-old putting together his first collection of stories with a print run that numbered a couple of hundred, he had come to think of as his right. Writing. It was beating the pith from him.

Now he drank vodka or gin rather than wine, and if there wasn't any liquor in the house he'd drink mouthwash. One day, he wanted to get his ears pierced, like the Wakamba tribe he'd met on safari, then in the middle of the night he accused her of treating him as cruelly as his mother had his father. He upbraided her about not taking the danger seriously, about the amount of taxes they owed, how broke they would be if she didn't pay attention to their bank account.

Mary was baffled as to what she was meant to do with him. He asked her to keep him from cracking up, but she didn't know how she was meant to do that. Perhaps she should have removed all alcohol from him, insisted he stayed on at the clinic, had more electroshock therapy, seen a psychiatrist, but it's hard enough to help anyone like this—least of all when the patient is Ernest Hemingway. All she could do was bank on him returning to the type of man he had been at the Finca, their dreamed years of honeyed light and happiness, of the times when he'd put his arm around her and said, "You're my guy."

Mary feeds the obituaries to the woodpile. Into the garden she carts wheelbarrows of magazines, weeklies, newspapers, paper already turning to mulch. None of it's of any interest. Some of the magazines are still in their wrappers; they'll be in the public archives if the scholars want to surmise all manner of his mother's mistreatment from his particular reading of an *Economist*. There'll be complaints; of course there will. She could write the headline for this afternoon's fire herself: HEMINGWAY'S WIDOW TORCHES HIS TREASURES. But she can't find it in herself to care.

All over the papers is the word *accident*, but a year ago Mary had watched Ernest walk toward the moving propellers of a stationary plane. She had screamed across the runway but her voice wouldn't carry over the sound of engines and trucks. He was stopped only yards from the plane by one of their friends, his eyes entranced by the circling blades.

After take-off he watched a herd of does in the snow-fields from his window seat. The plane came up over the shelf of cloud. "Lamb, everyone has their own sack of darkness. Right there deep inside them," she said, hoping to console him.

"I'm just a desperate old man."

"You're not old. I wish I could help you."

Months later she found him early one morning in the vestibule. He was wearing his plaid bathrobe, the shotgun lying crossways on his legs like a sick dog. She told him how much she loved him. She talked about his wonderful Paris sketches, and how much people couldn't wait to read them. She talked about the dinner she was going to make him that night, and the new books that were arriving next week, how wonderful it would be to read them. Two shells were readied on the windowsill. Slowly, Ernest gave up the gun to her. It might have been the last time she was in the vestibule again until that morning.

July's newspapers catch first. Colored flames leap from the paper, then the branches smoke. The fire builds, bright and hot in the garden. Skeletons of transported mice and cockroaches pop in the flames. A very moveable feast, Mary thinks, with a smile.

But maybe Ernest had had more than every man's

sackful of darkness. Maybe his darkness filled his throat and his mind like the darkest of all his inks. No man should be asked to live with so much sadness, and with so little promise of relief. Ernest chose to go, she finally thinks, watching the fire turn the papers black. He loved her but he could not live anymore.

With the fire going strongly now Mary steps back from the flames. It gives such a pleasing amount of heat that she'd like to roast chestnuts or marshmallows. Make a festival of it; give it the feel of a fiesta. Ernest would enjoy that. He always knew how to throw an excellent party.

She thinks of Harry Cuzzemano and his letters. Those, too, will probably be thrown to a fire somewhere, wherever he lives. How slavishly he had tried to find that lost suitcase for his hero. Mary remembers his words from this afternoon—*suitcases. Lost novels. Poems.*

It strikes her then that Harry Cuzzemano shouldn't know about the lost poem. The only people with any knowledge of that poem were herself and Martha. She remembers the chambermaid's words: "Don't worry, Madame, it will not reach the Sûreté." Perhaps the maid had been on Cuzzemano's payroll, just as Ernest had said, and the length of lavatory tissue is now boxed up in his private collection. Well, if he has the poem, let him keep it. Mary has no energy left for grudges. The past— she thinks, as the newspapers fold into soft gray ash—the past is over now.

*

Branches, magazines, and newspapers are now all embers at the bottom of the garden, and the night is dark. The smell of wood smoke follows Mary into the house. The kitchen is empty. The living room still has a plate of cookies and crumbs from where Harry sat hours before.

Mary heads for the study.

The door's bolt slides. Mary takes the key for Ernest's strongbox from the bureau. She opens the glass door of the cabinet and brings the box to the desk. The box gleams like a tooth. She wonders what could be inside. Wouldn't it be a leap of faith, she thinks, to take the box downstairs and throw it to the fire, never to learn of its contents? But she cannot do it. The lid gives easily as the key turns the lock.

Inside, it is not at all what she has expected.

At the top is one of Martha's books: *The Trouble I've Seen*, with a bookmark from Shakespeare and Company. Inside, there's a photograph of Martha pinned to the back cover: on the reverse is a dedication. Though the ink has blurred, the words are still legible: *Nesto! Be mine forever*. The date is May 1938, when Ernest would have still been married to Fife. Underneath Martha's book is a letter from Fife sent to his Madrid hotel. *Come back darling, the studio is ready and there's an abundance of food.*

Deeper inside the box are letters between Hadley and Fife. She wonders how he has come to acquire them. How odd it is to see these old letters from ex-wives to dead women. *Wouldn't it be fun if we vacationed down in Juan this summer; all of us—un, deux, trois?* Letters go back and forth between them—though most of them are from Fife—until the correspondence abruptly stops. As it probably would do, Mary thinks, when a husband jumps from the wife's to the best friend's bed.

An album follows, a book of wives. In each picture of each couple a ghost wife hovers behind them. Each decade has its triptych.

Mary is about to lock the box when she realizes there's nothing from her in there. In her bedroom she takes a handkerchief and spritzes it with her perfume. Cuts a lock of her blonde hair, ashier now than when they first met, and binds it with a ribbon. She picks out her best report from her *Time* days when they had begun their flirtation in wartime London, when he had offered her an orange in a Charlotte Street restaurant and set the rest of their life in motion. These will be the things she leaves him; this is Ernest's inheritance.

In the study, almost as an afterthought, she finds a photograph of Ernest fishing. He looks happy, with his broad grin and shoulders. He is out on calm waters, perhaps waiting for the silver twitching of a marlin's tail. Perhaps this is what he always craved—stillness, stillness as a prelude to sleep. She places this photograph on top of all the others. How unusual it is, to see Ernest alone.

To close the box Mary must press all the things down firmly so that the lid will shut. Oh, Ernest, she thinks, you were a man of too many wives. It almost makes her laugh.

*

Out on the deck Mary has a glass of wine and smokes a cigarette. She waits, hoping the stag will come back to the garden with its gentle step. Occasionally, from the hills, she can hear the call of a coyote. Down in the garden, the trees have nearly lost their leaves—winter will be here soon and the snow will come to cover the earth. *And best of all he'd loved the fall.* That's what she'd written on his headstone, in the grove of willow and aspen.

The cigarette buzzes on the wet grass as it hits the garden below.

Mary remembers again her fall into the Minnesota lake. She remembers the thought as she had gone down into the open hole of water: *This is it.* And she wonders if this thought might have been similar to Ernest's, months ago, as he had made the decision to step into the vestibule, early that morning in July. *This is it,* he might have thought. *And the world is done.*

AFTERWORD

This is a work of imagination. To find out about the real lives of Hemingway's wives (and the other women more briefly mentioned in this novel) the best place to start is Bernice Kert's group biography, *The Hemingway Women*.

Hadley Richardson's life, from self-avowed spinster to the first Mrs. Hemingway, is amply shown in Gioia Diliberto's biography *Paris Without End*, which follows from Alice H. Sokoloff's *Hadley: The First Mrs. Hemingway*. Sokoloff based much of her biography on interviews with Hadley Hemingway Mowrer: these audio tapes can be heard at www.thehemingwayproject.com. Paula McLain's novel *The Paris Wife* also gives a fictional representation of Hemingway's first marriage.

As biographer Ruth A. Hawkins has noted, Pauline Pfeiffer was unlucky enough not to outlast her husband nor was she able to give her own version of events. A new, generous, and much-needed biography of Pauline Pfeiffer, which details her editorial influence on Hemingway and the importance of her family's monetary support to Ernest's career, is given in Hawkins's *Unbelievable Happiness and Final Sorrow: The Hemingway-Pfeiffer Marriage*. Many will know Pauline Pfeiffer from her role in *A Moveable Feast* as one of the "rich" come to "infiltrate" the Hemingway marriage. However, the restored edition of *A Moveable Feast*, published in 2011, includes previously excised material—some of which casts a much more favorable light on Fife. Many photographs of Fife and Ernest's shared home in Key West, Florida, can be found at www.hemingwayhome.com.

Martha Gellhorn's novels and short stories are still in print; her reportage is collected in *The Face of War*. Her letters (many to Hemingway) are collected in *The Selected Letters of Martha Gellhorn* (ed. Caroline Moorehead). Gellhorn is the subject of two biographies: Caroline Moorehead's *Martha Gellhorn: A Life*, as well as Carl Rollyson's *Beautiful Exile: The Life of Martha Gellhorn*. Shots of La Finca Vigía can be found at www.hemingwaycuba.com.

Finally, Mary Welsh Hemingway penned her own thoughts about marriage to Hemingway in the only memoir written by one of the Hemingway wives, entitled *How It Was*.

For photographs of the wives and for a longer list of recommended books on Mr.—and Mrs.—Hemingway, go to www.naomiwood.com.

ACKNOWLEDGMENTS

I am extremely grateful to my editor at Picador, Francesca Main, who has lent her insight, hard work, and passion throughout the writing, and rewriting, of *Mrs. Hemingway*. If Ernest was lucky to have Max Perkins, I am very lucky to have you. My thanks to all at Picador; in particular Paul Baggaley, Kris Doyle, and Sandra Taylor.

I am grateful for the energy and passion of my agent, Cathryn Summerhayes, who, typical of her dedication, read this manuscript with her baby Ernest in one arm and Ernest on the page in the other hand. I am grateful for her consistent support since our first meeting, with many a daiquiri along the way. I would also like to thank from WME: Annemarie Blumenhagen, Becky Thomas, and Claudia Ballard.

My thanks as well to Tara Singh for her work on early drafts, and Patrick Nolan and Emily Baker at Viking for their passion for *Mrs. H*.

I have been very fortunate to receive funding that has greatly contributed to the research stage of writing *Mrs. Hemingway*. I would like to offer my hearty gratitude to the Eccles Centre at the British Library for its support during my tenure as its Writer in Residence in 2012. I would not have been able to write this book without the Centre's help. In particular Philip Davies for being so kind and generous, and Matthew Shaw and Carole Holden for providing a compass around the archives of the British Library.

Acknowledgments

My thanks to the Arts and Humanities Research Council, which funded this project at an early stage for a three-year doctoral grant. Special thanks to Professors Giles Foden, Rebecca Stott, and Andrew Cowan at the University of East Anglia for their wise words and encouragement. Carolyn Brown and Mary Lou Reker also offered wonderful support at the Library of Congress, Washington DC, during my Kluge Fellowship in 2010.

Writing *Mrs. Hemingway* has offered an exotic travel itinerary. My thanks are due to the staff at the Hemingway archives at the JFK Library in Boston and the Beinecke Library at Yale University, and to the staff at the Hemingway heritage homes in Oak Park, Chicago; Key West, Florida; and San Francisco de Paula in Cuba.

Last but not least I would like to offer my thanks to the following people who offered kind words when times were rough, and for sharing the celebrations when times were swell. My family—Pamela, Michael, and Katherine Wood. Friends, early readers, and colleagues: Alaina Wong, Alastair Pamphilon, Alison Claxton, Ben Jackson, Bridget Dalton, Charlotte Faircloth, Edward Harkness, Eleni Lawrence, Eve Williams, Hannah Nixon, Jonathan Beckman, Jude Law, Julie Eisenstein, Lucy Organ, Maggie Hammond, Matthias Ruhlmann, Natalie Butlin, Nick Hayes, Nicky Blewett, Nicola Richmond, Rebecka Mustajarvi, and Tori Flower. Thank you!

MRS. HEMINGWAY

Naomi Wood

Introduction

Naomi Wood's fictionalized account of Ernest Hemingway's extraordinary marriages begins in southeastern France in the 1920s, where the young writer vacationed with his first wife, Hadley Richardson, and their son, Bumby. Hemingway's legendary writing career had already won him a name in Paris, and his and Hadley's storied days there included hobnobbing with artists, writers, expats, and bohemian cognoscenti. They were poor, but full of ambition and love, and the brightest days seemed ahead of them.

But then a third party entered the scene, the glamorous *Vogue* writer Pauline Pfeiffer (aka "Fife"). Back in Paris, Hadley had befriended Fife and her sister, but soon Hadley found Fife joining her and Ernest in their apartment during cozy evenings, ingratiating herself to Ernest and helping him with his manuscripts. That summer, Hadley was forced to grapple with the truth: Ernest and Fife were having a passionate affair. More painfully, Hadley suspected that Fife was a better match for her dashing husband.

After Hadley granted Ernest a divorce, he and Fife set up a home in Key West, where they had two sons and Hemingway wrote notable works including *A Farewell to Arms*. As the years wore on, the increasingly negative critical reception of Ernest's work and his ever-growing taste for alcohol soured the marriage. Enter Martha Gellhorn, a beautiful young reporter Hemingway met in a bar, with whom he quickly became infatuated. As Fife desperately tried to hold on to her husband, he drifted closer to his bright young protégée.

Ernest and Martha fell in love amid the mayhem of the Spanish Civil War. After the war, they moved to Cuba. Domesticity would prove as much a battlefield as war, however, as Hemingway suffered from writer's block and Martha wanted to pursue her career. Her work during World War II separated the couple often, and by 1944 Martha's rejection was certain, leaving Hemingway to find a new paramour, Mary Welsh—yet another expatriate writer. And unlike Martha, Mary wanted to be Mrs. Hemingway.

As Hemingway's fourth and final wife, Mary stood by her husband during his worst dry spell of all, as well as major health problems resulting from alcoholism, high blood pressure, and the injuries sustained from two plane crashes. Ever the loyal devotee, Mary tried her best to protect his legacy after he died from a gunshot wound to the head in 1961, denying that it was suicide.

Told in four parts, *Mrs. Hemingway* gives each fascinating

woman her due. Wood's exquisitely written, emotionally gripping novel investigates the contrasts that distinguished Hadley, Fife, Martha, and Mary while laying bare the inevitable parallels of their common love for a brilliant, impossible man.

ABOUT THE AUTHOR

Born in England, Naomi Wood was raised in Hong Kong and studied at the University of Cambridge. Her first book, *The Godless Boys*, was published in 2011. While working toward her doctorate, she started her second novel, *Mrs. Hemingway*. She lives in London and teaches creative writing at Goldsmiths, University of London.

A CONVERSATION WITH NAOMI WOOD

Hemingway and Paris in the 1920s continues to be a source of fascination for readers. What drew you personally to this subject matter and what made you decide to go beyond it to the darker periods of Hemingway's life?

I wanted to write this book as soon as I had read Hemingway's love letters. Compared to his prose, his letters are positively squelchy with baby talk and sweet nothings. In his letters he calls his wives "Kitty Kat," "Small Friend," and "Pickle," while Ernest himself answered to the nickname "Little Wax Puppy." These billets-doux were a revelation to me: I had only really known of Hemingway from the hypermasculinized myth: the boxer, the bullfighter, the big-game hunter. These letters showed Hemingway as husband, and I was puzzled as to how this role fit into all of the others. Then, as I began to research, I wondered what his wives were like: what kind of man it was who made four exacting, clever, independent women turn a blind eye to his many faults and infidelities.

The title of this novel is ironic, as there is no single Mrs. Hemingway, and yet each of these women hoped they might be the last. What was it, do you think, that kept them (either individually or collectively) hanging on to this fantasy, despite the growing evidence of his inability to be faithful?

Talent is seductive, and Hemingway had talent in spades, of course. It must have felt incredibly exotic to be the muse of a man who everyone said was a great genius. And then there was the major problem of their being in love with him. Leaving someone you love, even when you know he is acting despicably, must have been hard—monumentally hard. I think many of them felt, if that indiscretion could go away, or if that love affair could be ignored out of existence, their marriage might just be able to survive. And sometimes that meant accepting a marriage à trois. Mary Welsh said being loved by Hemingway was like being in a beam of light—and I imagine when that beam was turned off, it must have been a very heavy darkness indeed.

How does history, real or imagined, inspire your storytelling? Did this book change your writing process?

Writing within history's parameters was challenging and rewarding. I knew that certain events had to happen in a certain order, but I was free to imagine the small scenarios that went into these characters' falling into—and out of—love, while letting the rest of the dramatic plot be dictated by history. Getting to know the characters felt like a journey—a friendship; my shelves now groan with Hemingway books, memorabilia, and photographs. On the second part of that question, I think every book you write changes your writing process. With this one, I tried to keep a few of Hemingway's lessons in my mind when I wrote: stopping in the middle of a scene, for example, so that you never have to start the next day "raw" in a new chapter. I also think my writing style has come on since the first book: it's a cleaner prose—probably inspired by the maestro himself!

While writing Mrs. Hemingway, *did you feel that your prose was influenced by Hemingway's writing style?*

I decided straight off that this book was not going to be an exercise in ventriloquism. I am a huge fan of his work, but it would have been deathly if it had ended up as cod-Hemingway! I decided to stay faithful to my own style of writing (probably flowerier than the lean stylist would have liked) but I also tried to bear in mind Hemingway's aesthetics. I tried to make each word count. I cut out what didn't need to be there. I doffed my cap to the master by using certain words he loved: words like *good*, *cool*, and *fresh*. But it was the work, interviews, and memoirs of Hadley, Fife, Martha, and Mary that probably formed a bigger influence on *Mrs. Hemingway*, since it was their voices that I was trying to bring to the page.

There are four separate points of view in Mrs. Hemingway. *How did you find your way through the individual perspectives while tying together a single narrative?*

I did this by giving myself an enormous headache! At some points, I did wonder whether it was an exercise in insanity to write one book in four voices. Perhaps the first thing I did was to create a distinct voice for each of them. Then I tried to look at the sweet spots: when wife three overlapped with mistress two . . . or wife four then became friends with ex-wife two . . . In the archives, I looked at letters sent between "the graduates of Hemingway University" (Mary Welsh's term). In the biographies, I looked at any moments, however small, where they came face to face with one another. In my story, these moments were amplified, so that we have memories viewed from different angles—Mary and Martha's first meeting in London, for example. Sharing all of these memories made all of the women inextricably bound to each other—whether they liked that or not.

On a personal level, Hemingway was certainly a flawed character— some might say abusive. How did you feel about him over the course of writing this book, and where did you stand by the time you finished it?

I started off thinking he was pretty detestable to his wives. That hasn't changed. I think in some situations, he acted appallingly. However, I don't think these women would have stuck around if he had been simply monstrous all of the time. Why would they have? What I wanted to show was a balance, because that's what life with mercurial Hemingway must have been like: exquisite when he was nice, vile when he was nasty.

But over the course of writing this novel, my opinion of Ernest—the man, not the writer—has changed. I don't think there has to be "team Ernest" or "team Mrs. Hemingway";

over the course of writing about three divorces and a death, I developed a lot of sympathy for Ernest himself. By the midfifties, he was so busted up, so unhappy. He could be exceptionally horrid to others, but most intensely to himself. Norman Mailer wrote that Hemingway "carried a weight of anxiety within him . . . which would have suffocated any man smaller than him." Reading about the depression and paranoia that accompanied his suicide moved me, and I think a good deal of human compassion makes you understand his behavior while refusing to excuse it.

Though the documentation of Hemingway's life is fairly thorough, you had to take certain liberties in bringing these people to the page. How, as an author, do you decide where to diverge from the "official" story?

Early on, I decided that what I wanted to give in this account was an experiential—if not always empirical—account of each Mrs. Hemingway. The needs of four narratives did distort the empirical truth, but I always believed I was giving a just idea of the experience. The first section, for example, is set within a day. In reality, the decision for Hadley and Ernest to break up took months over that dangerous summer. If it was a full-length book just about Ernest and Hadley, I might have shown it slower, in gradations, but I had to fit their story into the quartet. If I'd truly followed every locale Mr. and Mrs. Hemingway ever summered in, the reader would have gotten travel sick and the tale would have been everywhere.

What mattered, in the end, was to get the right balance between the facts and the fiction. Readers hungry for the historical account behind this novel should definitely read Bernice

Kert's addictive *The Hemingway Women*—there's so much in there that I couldn't fit into the novel, and much more time spent with his mother, his sisters, his mistresses, and near mistresses.

Toward the end of the book, we come to see Hemingway in his darker years, and the romantic notions we might have had about him are stripped away. What makes Mary so well equipped to deal with him in this stage? Could you imagine one of his earlier wives in her place?

I think Mary was very patient but also very thankful for the life Hemingway gave her. She also celebrated, rather than resented, giving up her career. And I think she loved him very deeply. In the archives I found a little Post-it note in a box of papers that says "1974: I will never cease missing him." That long-lasting love she felt for him must have made the difficult times in some small part endurable. She was strong; she stood up to him, but picked her battles. I think that's why her marriage was perhaps the longest; she was, perhaps, the canniest.

Martha, I suppose, would be the one I could not imagine looking after Ernest in his "wintering years." Wouldn't she have hated his neediness and weakness? In her own advanced years, she hated that about herself. Hadley and Fife? I'm not sure. Perhaps. They were much better at putting him first and making him comfortable. But it's almost impossible for me to imagine that the carousel of wives and mistresses didn't turn each decade. . . .

Of Hadley, Fife, Martha, and Mary, which perspective was most compelling for you to assume and why?

This is a difficult question! Writing Fife's perspective felt important: because I wanted to claw her back from her role as predatory "husband-snatcher" in *A Moveable Feast*. She was badly behaved—but she also got the most rotten deal. She fell in love with someone she really shouldn't have, married him, got dumped, never remarried, and then died young. She also never got to tell her side of the story. I felt compelled to show her as a real person who had her own sorrows, joys, and regrets—who ended up much worse off than Hadley. I also enjoyed writing Mary's perspective, because it's through Mary's love and grief that our sympathy returns to Ernest. But I found them all truly compelling. Writing about each woman was a pleasure and a privilege.

What are you working on now?

After feeling like the fifth mistress of Ernest Hemingway, I'm taking a short break and working on short stories. They're fun little projects: not based on facts, not based on real people; I feel as if I'm luxuriating in my imagination again. I'm gearing up to write the next novel—probably historical. Now I'm just picking between ideas!

QUESTIONS FOR DISCUSSION

1. In fictionalizing real-life events, Naomi Wood had to make some guesses about Hemingway's private life. Which parts of the story seemed to be more factual, and which seemed to be the imaginings of the author?

2. In Antibes, Hadley gives Ernest an ultimatum. What is the ultimatum and why does she decide to set up this arrangement?

3. Hemingway's wives shared some unmistakable similarities. What did they have in common, and what made them distinct as individuals?

4. In what ways did Fife's influence change Ernest? What made their marriage successful and what made it untenable?

5. Ernest's third wife, Martha Gellhorn, was more skeptical of the institution of marriage and more independent during their time together. What effect did this have on their relationship?

6. Understandably, Hadley, Fife, Martha, and Mary each have their own opinions about one another. How would you describe the way they regard Ernest's other wives and mistresses?

7. War and its aftereffects is a thread that is woven through this book. How has it changed Ernest over time, and how has it influenced his decisions with regard to his romantic partners?

8. Ernest Hemingway is a larger-than-life figure. What lesser-known aspects of his personality did this book reveal and what surprised you? Have you read any of Hemingway's writing? If so, which of his works have stuck with you and how, if at all, has reading *Mrs. Hemingway* influenced your view?

9. What was it that drew women to Hemingway, and why did they stay with him over time?

10. Which (if any) of the Mrs. Hemingways do you consider to be the "true" one and why? Which (if any) of these women was the best match for him?